MEAT LADDER TO MARS

A novel

by

Eugenio Negro

Copyright 2016 by Eugenio Negro. All rights reserved. This text may only be reproduced, in part or in whole, with express consent by the author except for educational purposes.

Published by Editorial Éxitos Gnosis, San Francisco Bay Area, catalogue number EXGB-001

Inquiries: exitosgnosisexg@gmail.com

ISBN: 978-0-692-65904-5

Printed in Santa Clara, California, by Minuteman Press

This text is a work of fiction.

To AJD, my biggest fan, my editor,
with gratitude and friendship.

1

Loading specialist shift leader

Odors of Earth rose up in threads of vapor to nimbostratus' orifices. The rain approached a day earlier than expected, rose up as a shadow from within every color, and its low tides soaked into buildings' skins, polished train tracks, oiled the trashstrewn streets, and drained down from the surface through the crossed bars of the launch silo's lid.

So the shadows stained the silo's interior darker as they dripped down toward its black bottom, the casing from which the shuttle would be fired like a bullet. Among those shadows swung a weird tropical glare on the huge orange fuel tank filling silently with liquid hydrogen and oxygen, and on the white rockets like pontoons upon which the old scaly shuttle would ride. Zosime had her head down, pulled with her back at a knotted chain, and she didn't see the clouds gathering.

When she got the chain loose she felt her phone vibrating in her pocket and dug it out. She checked the laptop on her cart and saw that the enormous missile was fueling up according to code, then looked at her phone. From her mother she expected some important odd-hours message, but it was only a news story.

She tried to read past the telling headline that mentioned Ecuador, but the news on the phone's screen grew more difficult to read with each stroke from her greasy blue latex thumb. She tried to rub the grease off, which only curved a straight smear into a circular one, in which more hairs of fine daylight could rise, blotting out the words. She decided thereupon to rub the phone's screen against her short left sleeve, risking the whole story.

It was still there. Her eyes flew up as the space shuttle's payload bay doors cracked crankily open, then she found her place again. She called out to Clayton to listen.

—What's so important about your news? Clayton's muted voice called from around the bulkhead. —Your cousin's tryin to convince the world how much she loves her husband?

—Ha ha. She didn't feel like laughing. Two days in, his refusal to speak punctuated by his cute shucking goshing was exhausting. She called back, —No, listen. The native American protesters in Peru have broken up the road to the mountain where they want to build that new mine. They needed that metal, so the sky ladder might not be fixed for years now.

—Good, Clayton's broad Midwestern voice and body to match waddled through the high massive doorframe.

—More work for us. I wanna stay on here long as I can, and save up. She watched him waddle his hips forward, so confident that he'd last long enough to save up. He poured the rest of his canteen out over his head and shook his stringy brown hair out like a dog, sputtering a body-temperature mist into the humid air before jamming his ballcap back down. In the bowels of the earth the Olususun landfill's chemical stink extinguished, but Lagos' weather kept cooking the sooty sky and everything under it. Now she was stuck fifteen stories down here in it with him, with the radiofiltered voice of doctor Chesky and the unlearnable long litany of temporary workers' names.

—Not good if you want to work on the sky ladder.

—That yer career goal? Clayton's heavylidded eyes smiled halfmoonish at her.

—I worked there before I came here.

—Oh. His Midwestern oh was deeper than the wide silo, and its echo languidly waddled all around it before it dispersed amongst the catwalks, ladders and cranes that caged in the shuttle in its nose-up repose. —What happened?

—You didn't hear?

—I don't listen to the news! Clayton chuckled, —I mean, Rush Limbaugh, but …

—The sky ladder was attacked, Zosime explained. She let him see how much she was working, gathering loose chain, hoping he'd take the hint. —We're lucky the sky is only about a hundred kilometers high. Now she had his attention. —That's how much of the cable fell east into the Andes after the weight burnt up. There were six people on the weight.

—What happened to the cable?

She was tired from describing so much in English.

—It fell on something.

—That's too bad, someone's always gotta ruin it. Yer accent's cute, Zoseemy!

—Go get something to clean up the water. It fell all over the floor from you.

She heard the growling of the forklift's tires coming down the hall toward the silo and put her phone away. The rules stipulated not to use cellular devices in the silo, except for the work interfaces that she couldn't access, but never said why.

With a rumble and skid of rubber on cement the forklift came in the monumental doorway whence Clayton had come. Rodríguez the foreman was riding with and he hopped off in front of the two before it let down the final shipping box. The sensors under the yellow square upon which it squarely sat sent a signal to the launch center, and one of the heads up in the window ordered the robotic bridge crane far overhead to let down its four cables. Zosime circled the box that was like a railroad car but a third as long, batted the sooty cables down from its roof with an alloy rake, and shackled them knee-high at the box's four corners.

After weeks of hauling up shuttle supplies and replacement parts, now there was only the payload itself to load. As soon as her hand took up the fifth cable, a safety tether, she smelled the earthy stink emanating from the box. She couldn't hear inside it, but sensed that its contents were alive. The strangeness of such a cargo amplified its small smell.

—Should I tie it up?

—No. What're you two gettin into? Rodríguez demanded.

—Just passin the time, said Clayton with his homey innocent voice. Rodríguez waved at the thick black tar on all the silo's surfaces. —You could pass a rag over these walls. Look, this exhaust from last month's gotta be half an inch thick. He rubbed along the handrail of a catwalk leading out to the shuttle's huge bellshaped engine nozzles, turned to them and presented a black fingertip.

—You know the rules and routines by now, Zosime. You two don't at least try to clean, we're all gonna end up with lung cancer. Or worse, someone slips and breaks somethin. There's no workman's comp in Nigeria.

Zosime half ignored him, circled back around, rapped her knuckles curiously on the rust-red box and sniffed.

—What's in this thing? she asked.

—Just check the number, Rodríguez replied tersely.

—No, I know it's the right one, Zosime retorted, —I mean I want to know what's in it.

Indulgently, efficiently, Rodríguez inspected his list.

—Pigs.

—Pigs?

—Yeah. He looked up at her like are you happy now.

—Eight couples of pigs. Surprised?

—Is there life support for them in this box? Zosime demanded now. —Are they prepared for liftoff?

—I don't know, Rodríguez automatically responded to her demand with a male defensive tone, —but they have to keepem alive if they're gonna breedem once they get there. His tone turned to teasing. —You wanna go up into the shuttle and trainem?

—There's a county fair out there? guffawed Clayton.

—Let go before it drags yer arm off.

Zosime let the chain slide up over her wrist and through her hand until it climbed overhead. The bridge crane lifted the box up, took the smell of animals and earth with it, and positioned it precisely, corner by corner like a marionette, to stow it under the retired space shuttle's open carapace. She followed its path with her eyes until repelled by the huge lamps in the sooty walls. In the glare hung the launch command center's window, in which her superiors' heads surfaced and sunk.

They were all men here, except her, almost all Americans. Most of them were under thirty, most had nothing to spend their pay on but drinks. They came from Alabama or Nevada, or in the case of Clayton, from the deserted, permanently-poisoned fracking fields of the Dakotan Missouri. They came to Nigeria on cheap plane tickets for the steady unskilled work, for the English that the natives spoke, for the allure of exotic women, some of whom at this moment desperately picked through Olususun's bottomless, imported trash above her head.

Many of them had grown up without the presence of women or girls and only had the radio or television and older men just like them for education. They probably hadn't even learned in school that the first Taliban, Islamic State, Ku Klux Klan, all boogieman groups, began by seducing youth practically the same as them. The cool subterranean air blew up the belly of Zosime's baggy company polo shirt and reached her sweatringed neck.

—Beautiful, the foreman nodded at the shuttle, then at her. —Zosime, take a break.

—I don't need one. I can go up to the shuttle and detach the chains.

—Leave that to me and take a break. And remember to clock out a break. Clayton, whatta you need? Chop chop.

She went out through the armored blast door's gaping bulkhead, down the overlit hallway past the elevators, the locker room and the freight elevator, and through a second bulkhead into the huge tomblike cafeteria whose capacity would probably never be used. She sat down near the heavy yawning doorway without getting anything to eat, unnoticed by the single cook lady, also American or English, who strode the length of her overload of duties behind the monumental lunch counter. Zosime was tired of side salads, potatoes and the local cassava. The space between them was a somber forest of concrete columns and greasy shadows.

She grabbed a bottle of water from an unnecessary and blinding refrigerator. Having to haul the containers to a recycler in the city gave her something to do besides drink with dull coworkers who disappeared every four days. She looked up, up, up at the skylight, up a tunnel that reached the surface. It'd likely been clear when this place was slapped together, but now daylight only seeped wetly through a thick layer of plastic and paper trash. Zosime couldn't stop looking at it, steadying herself each day for when she'd look up to find the wide-open black eyes and chocolate face of one of the locals pressed suffocated against the muddy plate glass.

It took that instant for the flat televisions to sense her presence and glow to life, all of them, lighting up the cafeteria's every murky corner. Their single video, en lieu of muzak, began to play out its half-hour loop, beginning with the parade of corporate logos followed by the word LAGOS! in festive umbrella-capped type. Then the screens' color dimmed, evoking an earlier, wiser age. Walter Cronkite, a talking head on American television, and his two guests, novelists Robert Heinlein and Arthur C. Clarke, began to exult the Apollo 11 moon landing. They spoke eager to agree with each other, sharing an exclusive power that only men like them had.

—We will be sending more men up to move out in their spacecraft, further than these men dare go, said Cronkite portentiously. Zosime had concluded weeks ago that this was supposed to motivate the staff, but she only found it incomprehensible and irritating.

Thoughts cropped up in her head like tufts of spinach. Why send live pigs to Mars only to be butchered and eaten? How did they know the animals would survive escape velocity? Obviously Rodríguez, loading foreman, knew nothing. Perhaps the heads up in that yellowed window knew. Some did her same job, but one step after, once the shuttle was in space. The payload engineer, as he was called, and with he one is to always mean he, sat and reassured the shuttle's payload commander as he floated helpless in space. She was only shift leader of a shift comprising Clayton and the four different young men who'd come and gone in the last five days.

She took her illegible phone back out, cleaned it with drops from her water bottle, and reviewed the latest messages between herself and her mother. With no real responsibility at work, waiting out these breaks and lunch hours just drove her crazier. Was her mother happy right now, comfortable, or stalking around the apartment with a hand pressed against some pain, or sitting in some clinic? Was this separation really the only way to make themselves a living? Or was the wayward daughter caught grasping for the first opportunity in an attenuated wave of duty?

She chose not to worry, for now, knowing that the bosses approved of her industry, her model-minority focus, that'd carried her this far.

She went back to work and found the same shipping box, same number, still trapped like a large fly in the crane's silky cables. The payload engineer in the launch center gingerly lifted it out of the shuttle's yawning payload bay. Then the computer took over and the bridge crane moved the box on its precise track until precisely above the yellow square thirty meters below, letting it carefully down on the deck in front of her, back where it started. Clayton was scratching his dark whiskered jowls and waiting for a cue.

—What happened? she enquired impatiently.

—I don't know, his don't know drummed on the Doppler, —they said on my radio that an alarm went off in the box.

Zosime went to the laptop and checked her email, where an automatically-delivered message now sat unread. —A carbon dioxide alarm. Life support.

She dragged a fat two-twenty cable that unspooled from a recess in the wall, like a firehose, and plugged it into the shipping box. She punched her low-level code into the box's door and the bolts fell back mercifully to let her open it.

—Stay out here, she said, —in case the door malfunctions. She said into her radio: —Launch center, don't anyone touch the crane controls! She stepped into thick earthy sewer air. The box had just enough open floor in the pale inspilling light to pivot the sixteen cages, as advertised, in and out through the door. She found the flimsy cord and pulled the cheap diode lamp on and forgot about the smell.

In sixteen common wire chicken cages, two rows of four stacked on four, were trapped the bulging bodies of sixteen unwashed common yearling hogs. She approached the front eight cages. The pigs laid shoulder-tight in the metal wire, their skin swelling through the wire squares, irritated, lacerated, bleeding in places, feet invisible. Each cage had an aluminum floor and back wall where collected the slimy shit that some pigs had already excreted. The box had power, and was insulated for pressurization, but there were no umbilicals for air whatsoever.

Zosime saw the clock counting down on the wall and didn't even notice the carbon dioxide alarm flashing red next to it. The pigs were utterly still, snorting and sniffing pitifully as if far away, their doughy pointy mandibles quavering. That clock must've been counting down the duration of the sedation drugs they were under.

Twenty more hours remained on the clock, before this box was to blast off, with only the wire of cages to restrain the animals against the gravity force, until the shuttle shoved its way free of Earth into shit-drifting freefall and the freeze of space, until it presumably docked with the space station just in time to either take care of the animals or drug them again. The hogs drooled and dreamt of mud, of digging, of newborn shoats, of the sky. The sky imprinted in their corneas, their true blue proof of earthly citizenship, that was now revoked and only a dream.

She reached up, the alarm was mounted high enough where only a tall American could easily reach, and reset it.

—Tell them the alarm is clear! she called. Stepping back out into the springtime heat of Lagos she found Rodríguez and one of the heads from upstairs standing with their legs apart and their arms crossed. Rodríguez looked scared and the other was all business.

—Leave the door open, said the blond head with the subtle acne scars. —I know, answered Zosime.

—How's the livestock? Do we need to call doctor Chesky?

—Not necessary. They're breathing, but it's very low. They're drugged.

—We know, the head said. —This is the shift leader?

—Yeah.

Now he thumbed at Clayton. —How long you had this guy?

—Two days, offered Clayton.

—I was talkin to Rodríguez, two days. Where you from, shift leader?

—Quito of Ecuador.

—Hispanic?

—Persian and Greek.

—In Ecuador?

—I'm stateless. She exaggerated on her mother's behalf, who had fled so much.

—Ah, the young blond head nodded his regulation four-day beard-upholstered chin, —easier to get work out here, right?

—Right, Zosime tossed the small talk down the silo.

—I'm Gopman. What's your name?

—Zosime Sorush.

—Good work, miss Mesorush. You ready to see your first shuttle launch tomorrow?

—Yes, she affirmed as if there were any other response.

—Great, great. Keep your eyes open, uh? We gotta take good care of this shuttle ... she's the only shuttle left of her kind. Only way to get this much weight up there at a time. They were sposed to be scrapped. He winked and grinned at her, nodded to Rodríguez and stepped away back toward the elevators. The foreman immediately turned to Clayton. —I need you to show more initiative, Clayton. Why didn't you do anything? Why'd you call him down here?

—I can't get into the box like she can, the new guy protested.

—Why didn't you call her, then?

—You told her to take a break!

The foreman turned his glare to her. —How long was your break?

—Ten minutes. Rodríguez looked down at the grease-tracked ground and smoothed thumb and forefinger over his thinly-buzzed mustache. —Okay. How'd you get in the box?

—With my inventory code.

—Good. Clayton, I'll see about getting you an inventory code soon. But I need you to look alive. I don't need the guys from upstairs down here watchin over my people for me. Please clean up a little, yeah? There should be something in the closet over there on the other side of the shuttle.

The foreman stamped off back to his desk, in a corner of the locker room beyond the bulkhead, without another word. One more unlisted duty for her, another unwritten rule, was now clear: don't involve upstairs. Clayton looked without answers at Zosime. —What's the rules for a carbon dioxide alarm?

—Not every box has them, Clayton. That's a pressurized cargo container with living animals in it! Clayton flinched at her voice and looked upset. She turned and strode over to the clipboard hanging on the wall, gave it a glance. —In eighteen minutes there's the last box coming with supplies. You can tie it to the crane, like I did. Did you see how to do it?

—Yah.

—Meanwhile I want you to go into that closet and bring what you can to clean the railings and mop the floor. He's right that we could slip and kill ourselves. Ask me if you don't know what to do.

—Okay, okay. I'll ask. Talk, talk, talk …

—One more mistake like today and you'll be on your way to home in North Dakota. Now she felt like laughing. She loosened her hold on an unlisted duty of her own, the portrayal of an efficient goal-oriented minority woman, and laughed once. Her tone was foreign to him, so he couldn't measure her humor.

2

Orbital systems analyst

She'd been scouted and interviewed to be up in that window with Gopman, doctor Chesky and the other heads. But she didn't learn that the life support systems analyst position had already been relocated to Florida, the United States, and filled up from under her, until she arrived in Lagos. She found the launch silo dug into the ground and surrounded by a razor-wire perimeter in the middle of one of the planet's largest landfills, interred away from the winds and the moon.

The only job handy was loading specialist, which means one who schlepps cargo containers when the radio commands. The two-week mark she'd reached must've been some kind of employment record for this company, for thereupon she was promoted to loading specialist shift leader, which means one who tells other loading specialists what to schlepp while in charge of a stack of redundant lists.

On top of that she was responsible for all these surprise unpublished duties, like cleaning and reporting on time clocks and safety, evidently because Rodríguez somehow couldn't do it himself with his overload of duties. She'd hooked and unhooked chains that puppeteered the shuttle, its two booster rockets, the external tank, and all the shuttle's supplies.

Throughout those two prior years in Quito, though, she'd been an orbital systems analyst, monitoring weather systems, seismic reports, the lunar cycle, the sensors at the base of the sky ladder, and everything having to do with maintaining the great, almost invisible cable's tension and centering its weight. It required an unyielding, constant focus, but it wasn't so different from growing up amongst the vineyards of Corfu. In both cases Zosime got to spend her days absorbed in the elements, the wind, the sky, the invisible actions of the universe against the surface, her body and senses enveloped and gently lifted by nature's mathematically perfect currents.

Sometimes her colleagues would talk about going up into space herself, but Zosime couldn't stand the idea. In space there was no wind, no moisture, no temperature to guide her, no cool oceans in which to lose and find herself.

She didn't think about much else during that job. She enjoyed exciting new experiences like the constant contact with her English counterpart doctor Wood aboard the orbiting counterweight. He was a witty, kind man who presided over a collegial, international operation, able to make a joke about any scientific or mundane detail of the job. No one like Gopman or Rodríguez would've been allowed near a workplace like his. Together with his five colleagues on the counterweight and eight on the ground they made a tight team, and their sky ladder never wobbled once, not even when Typhoon Ahe blew up the mountains over it.

When he'd come down to Quito for his short relief periods, doctor Wood always stumbled out of the climber, seasick, weak-kneed, an inch taller, and popped open a real bottle of champagne he'd stashed in the counterweight all those months. In orbit he'd drink champagne from a foil packet with them to toast the safe return of each climb. Climb number twelve was beginning its descent from the counterweight down the ethereal cable when Zosime heard the distant but loud pops, one, two, threefourfivesix, then boom, a salty jet of smoke and flinty flames a kilometer outside their big window, and the immense gossamer thread began to fall over the gentle giant Andean foothills and the cradle of Quito.

The counterweight and the climber were too small to even strike a matchlight in the sky. Their signals went dead, the ground crew's screens went black, and that was it. The group who called themselves Pichincha had practically used firecrackers, and until today still hadn't been found. There was no money to retain the whole staff with no plan to rebuild the sky ladder, and Zosime was out of a job.

The smell of the pigs' heat and shit lingered in her hair, on the edge of her chin. In those two years there was no free time for reflection, away from her mother and her work, from the beauty of the city and of Ecuador, no reason she should wonder what was going up those climbers, on whose behalf, on whose dime, for what purpose. Now she had nothing but time to wonder. If only she could see the records of what went up that sky ladder! Maybe they were preparing to send livestock into outer space as well. Now she had time for the nagging question of whether she really believed in this company's facile dream of space travel by the cheapest and most expedient means.

The laptop emitted a happy twitter and Zosime leapt upon it to see what was happening. On the shuttle monitor's software there had popped up a flashing dialogue box: the orange fuel tank was full and ready to go. Just then her ear tuned back to the familiar rumbling of the enormous refrigeration system connected to the fifteen-story tank, just in time to hear it shift down to maintain temperature. Now the insulated tank would do its part to keep the fuel cold. Zosime felt the cool wind of Quito on her shoulders for a moment as she looked back down at her cart. That shuttle was no dynamic interaction with nature, just an old bullet.

—See ya at the bar tonight? Clayton asked as he shucked the work polo off his abundant abdomen.

—Maybe, Zosime did the same and put her windbreaker on. —Have you been before?

—No, I haven't ventured outta my hotel room yet. He was in a hotel across the district from her. Small miracles.

—It's called Bushmeat. It's on the outside of Ikeja.

—Where's that?

—It's where we live. You take the bus to Agege station, then you walk east into the Ogba road, like you're going to the stadium. It's easy to find,

—What's the station?

—Agege,

—I'll use my phone.

—Use your phone, then. Be careful. The radio squawked that the four fifteen van was leaving the launch site. She left him there and took the elevator to the surface.

The air was soot yellow, without a trace of the nearby ocean in it, thick and sticky. They drove through the launch site's perimeter fence into the rolling trashscape of Olusosun, where trucks and tractors built fresh mountains of waste for the citizens to mine. In the corner of her eye Zosime saw a child throw her hands up and sink into the trash. Her heart jumped. One of the women nearby saw it, and dove down to catch her up.

The trash was like an enormous mycelium that lived under Lagos, mushrooming above the ground here and there. In Iwaya and Makoko districts people built endless slums out of and on top of the trash, and over in Ajegunle it rose up during heavy rains to flood and bury the streets.

Midday heat was still thick and heavy against the chest when she found the van full of temporary workers, and she ended up seated next to one striking, dressed-up local kid with a briefcase in his hands. He was probably the only local he'd seen on this job. Maybe he was one of the heads up in the launch center.

—Do you work at the silo? Zosime asked him.

—I worked there, until today. I was an intern. His voice was forceful but polite, as if he were trained to speak in public.

—An intern? You're a student?

—Finished with my degree. I was working in the launch center, trying to get a job.

—They weren't paying you?

—Of course not! Interns don't get paid. Now they say they don't need me.

Undeterred, the kid snapped open his little snappy attaché case and showed her and the temp worker to his left his entire résumé. His name was English, Godsend. He narrated that he'd studied physics and mathematics at Unilag, had held two jobs for over three years, was never late, never reprimanded, a word he pronounced with a force and rhythm unknown to Zosime. It was a force projected from a native speaker of English, but an English fundamentally different from the British academic input and American cultural input whence the rest of the world draws its English.

After he finished his presentation no one spoke until the American driver asked the kid if he'd given that same speech to the management at the launch silo. The question had that mean American condescension that did not really understand comic timing or even sarcasm. The kid didn't answer the driver, but smiled his penetrating smile at Zosime and the temp guy. He knew that these were Americanized employees, that their own chances at success forbade them to put in a good word for him, to break rank to make suggestions, to try to help people. But he couldn't waste the chance to make an impression upon them.

—I wish you luck getting another job with the company, Zosime offered.

—We'll see, Godsend smiled at her. —They seem to need a lot of new people. Remember me!

She rode in the van through the landfill's perimeter fence, and between the landfill and her district at least the Ikorodu Express Road offered relief from the megacity's absurd permanent traffic. In a few minutes she was back in the Ikeja Government Reserved Area with its police college, its golf club, its teaching hospital, its airport and malls, its stamped and approved western History with a capital H, where beneath lay the land's forgotten history. She said good luck to Godsend, the nice young Nigerian, and bade him farewell. From the van she walked, and her walk to and from the van rendezvous point was part of the disorienting effect Lagos had on her: to wit, in this zone the crush of rainbow umbrellas, rainbow people, dingy vehicles and scattered stuff up and stopped, as if the whole district were a model, a museum.

She arrived at the Protea hotel and ascended to her room, showered, and sat on the palmfrond-patterned bedspread to read through her phone. Part of her hoped that this job would be over soon, if she couldn't get a better position, for after a month into this job she still wasn't accustomed to her mother's absence. Her mother was a woman that had to be contained in order to know her, and Zosime knew she couldn't contain her from half a world away. But part of her wanted to stay on with the Mars mission. She'd earned it. Beyond her lay NASA, the ESA, respectable work, research, and no more commercial space exploitation. Maybe one day she and her mother, her father, even her brother, could all end up in Greece together, and if they haven't died, they're still living happily to this very day.

It would have to happen while her mother's nerves were in halfway decent shape, when she'd cooperate in leaving Quito and not flee ahead of some foreseen displacement. As a relieving high-altitude breeze blew through her gauzy curtains, through her coalsmoldering hair blew intrusive thoughts: her mother in Lagos, working night shifts selling greasy boli and moyi-moyi at a lean-to snack counter. Yelling at the locals in the one or two Yoruba phrases she'd have learned. Or up to her waist in trash, prying the gold from computer hardware above her daughter's head in Olususon, drifting too close to the launch silo's perimeter on a launch day when it would vomit flame and smoke.

Impossible, unnecessary, but invigorating. These images sprang from the fear of failure, the yawning hunger of instability, pulling at Zosime from her earliest memories. From before Greece. Those weren't even her memories, but her mother's. There was no reason to worry for now. Tonight she'd get paid, tomorrow the shuttle would launch, and that'd hold their spread-out world together another month.

Evening brought a breeze off the ocean and the brilliant red sunset permeated the smog until, saturated, it dispersed in purple and crimson scraps on a great yellow atmospheric puddle. Zosime didn't have the humor to go out to Bushmeat, but she had to get something to eat. And if Gopman or Chesky were there, she could maybe set down the pigshaped stone lodged in her right ventricle, which thudded against her soft heart tissues and restricted her lungs. Time and routine had weakened her show of propriety, and Gopman seemed approachable. Just as before she'd let go and laughed at Clayton, she now felt ready to talk to her superiors if the situation should arise.

She took the bus to Agege, where a train from the north ended and didn't connect at all to the central Lagos station, and waited in the street, feeling charitable toward the surely lost North Dakotan. Beside her a leathery rope of elder woman, wrapped in her most attractive striped kaba, drew across the road with a big basket in her arms.

—Chicken and rice! she called out, —made at home! Zosime's nose was hungry, but her stomach wasn't.

She peered carefully for Clayton into the flux of people streaming past, the carts and taxis and bicycle rickshaws or scrimshaws or what the word was in English, in case she saw him wandering around. But she didn't peer too long. She joined the throng of bodies, the muddy, spicy odor of moving night, and walked or waded toward the stadium, around a rain-cracked stucco façade and into the roofless confines of the bar.

Launch systems analyst Gopman set his bottle of Star down and whispered hey to launch chief doctor Chesky.

—That's the intern. The ex-intern.

—Ah god, where?

They hunched over their beers at the bar, surrounded by anonymous foreign workers but still trying to form a private space. Here the two men tended to let go of their pretense of professionalism, a custom they clung to here in Nigeria in case anyone back at home looked.

—So you had any dates yet? Chesky teased his colleague, who scratched his gel-stretched blond waves and rolled his eyes. —I don't know dude … I just keep thinkin, yknow, in Africa, that they're just gonna think my dick's too small. His chief stuttered out a loud laugh.

—Serious shit! Haven't you thought of that?

—I don't know … Chesky's eyes looked up from his beer, turned left and collided with those of the bright young former intern.

—Doctor Chesky! Godsend said in Chinua Achebe's stately English, —so it's true you have dinner here!

—We're launching our space shuttle tomorrow full of cargo going to Mars, Chesky boasted to his beer, to the barkeep, —tonight we're drinking.

The chief didn't stop the kid from sitting down, who ordered a plate of chicken in half English and half Yoruba. Despite spring's increasing heat the former intern's shirtsleeves, chest and back were still fresh as morning. He had the focus of a student about him; wide, attentive eyes.

—Ah, to Shango himself! he said, —some real men must be preparing to travel to him. But as far as who sends them up, have you consulted with the boss about finding me a new position?

—Look, Iyiola, it's like I told ya. We already got a launch systems analyst, he gestured with upturned palm at Gopman's beer, —your role, as well as his, have been reevaluated according to what we need for this mission, and that job's gonna come out in the shape it comes out in, once we know what we need. We don't know just now. We've got a launch tomorrow, and then maybe a launch as early as next month. And think about it, there's no time to learn all the systems.

—Yes, Iyiola persisted, —but the last launch was only your first, correct? And you learned. The two Americans regarded him uneasily, unable to lie. They were definitely the new ones here.

—The only jobs we have are in loading.

—Ha ha! Iyiola laughed an obscure laugh, genuine, scornful or both. —Who would take an unskilled job with training like mine?

Chesky's close-set brown eyes crept up his long nose as he watched Zosime sit down at the bar to Iyiola's left. She nodded at the young man, who stood coolly and said nothing to her. But it wasn't all him. She recognized him at the last moment, and would've said something to him any other time, or sat with him rather than with her bosses, if not for this gravitational field her bosses had. The vibe suggested that she had an unlisted duty not to talk to former employees. He'd said to remember him.

—I'll be at the university library when you need me. I can quit there any day! He took the plate of chicken just as the barkeep handed it to him. He found a seat next to three older black men at the long yellow bench under the outstretched limbs of the bar's plump Ivory Coast almond.

Behind them a boisterous, musical voice shouted boli. For an instant Chesky thought it must be Iyiola cursing him in his native African. He spun around to find Iyiola standing next to a stout shaven-headed man wheeling a cart into the patio, and he was the one shouting.

—Hot boli! Who's hungry?

Unnoticed by the other men at the benches, he approached Gopman and Chesky and repeated his solicitation. No thanks, they said without looking at him, no cash.

—Not here, the lithe barkeep reproved him with a surprisingly sonorous basso voice, —my kitchen's cooking here. The barbecue man threw a sneer out, but nodded respectfully at the barkeep, and went on his way. Doctor Chesky didn't hear Iyiola ask the barbecue man if he knew who those two princes were at the bar.

—Anyway, Gopman continued right where he'd left off, —it can't be that hard. I'm just being a pussy. There's whores here, right?

—There has to be.

—Plus people don't shower here as much, so I don't think they'll criticize anything about me. Hey. You ever pull down yer pants and confuse the smell of come with the smell of yer regular dick? Serious shit! He looked at his phone. —Where's the fuckin food, already?

Just then doctor Chesky perceived who the woman was two stools away. —Shut up! he told Gopman,

—Shush! He turned to Zosime. —Hey ... you're our loading shift leader, right?

Zosime was trying to swallow her shot, and even though it was expected that he should await her response until she finished, she was annoyed that he said something to her midswallow. —I am, she addressed the empty shotglass with its miniature stem and foot, —unless you have something better. She nodded after Iyiola.

—Hah, yeah really. Whatcha drinking? Pernod? Sounds good. You tried the local beer?

Zosime shook her head. —Yep, Gopman observed with relish, —Star dappa doo dar. That's why we're in Lagos, Nigeria. Not cause of the equator, but cause the beer matches the company.

—I wish it wasn't so far, Chesky talked through his swallowing, —the boss'll probably never come out from California to see us.

—Why don't you think? Zosime asked.

—He's lived in airplanes all day for ten years! Chesky explained. —He's reinventing the world all day, by the time he gets to Silicon Valley to check on his money, he's gotta go back down to So-cal to check on the Mars mission!

—He's a genius, Gopman added.

—He's the innovator of innovators, Chesky gushed,

—you'd wanna work for him no matter what, to be part of the future! To really make your mark on the future of the human race.

—Or clean the mark with a mop, Zosime mused.

The chief paused to remember. —I remember when his biography came out, I was just an undergrad, I tried to get a copy so, yknow, it'd be a conversation starter. I couldn't even afford to buy it, my rent was so high for my studio. There was … I remember it, seven holds on each of all their copies, in town and down in Oakland.

—Swear!

—I tried Frisco. A hold on thirty-nine copies. I even tried to get it from San José. Multiple holds on all nine copies. So, I mean, yeah, I got it on my phone. But the boss … he's like, bigger than Steve Jobs!

—Serious shit! I mean Steve Jobs … he's just like, digital! The boss is like, voluminous, yknow, like he says, physical. He knows the drag coefficients for everything he builds.

—He's like, the definition of innovation. I mean, the sheer achievement.

Zosime was beginning to perceive another unlisted duty: adulate the boss. —I don't really know anything about him. I haven't had time to look. Before I was hired I thought I was working for New Sky Lines, I didn't know it was Star-X. The two young men looked dumb at her, then carried on.

—So, we're gonna make a lotta money off this job, Gopman suggested to her across his boss's chest, —my advice to you is work hard in the silo, and get into real estate now, while there's nothin holdin our money down.

Zosime's curiosity about fraternizing or sororizing with the chief began to wane. She wished she'd just followed the charming Godsend. He probably knew as much about the silo's management as the chief.

Chesky sneered at his analyst. —You're really gonna jump in and buy houses here?

—Cmon, chief! Remember the famous Airbnb class at Berkeley? I was in that fuckin class! I already got people findin me property all over, right here in Africa. Fix some places up, flippem. It's the same everywhere.

That caught Zosime's attention. She found his idea absurd, but he seemed to know what he was talking about.

—Where is the good real estate?

—It's wherever they're redeveloping. One neighborhood at a time, they're redoingem, makin the houses more upscale. I mean, this whole city is, like, a fixer-upper.

—Are the neighborhoods abandoned? Zosime asked rhetorically.

—I dunno! Gopman threw his free hand in the air, not rhetorically, —But the poor people'll go somewhere. If you lived there before the redevelopment yaren't gonna wanna pay higher housing prices. There's plenty space. There's a new economy now. Innovators like us need room! We need space to innovate. It's a process.

—They'll move until there's nowhere to go. The distinct young woman earned a goggling from Gopman. —The slums in Lagos have to, how do you say, take in the people who lose their homes. But they can't all go to the slums if you send them out, and they have a right to,

—That's ridiculous! Gopman chugged his beer,

—you're not even re-tarded. That's pre-tarded. They're not addin an iota of value just sitting around bein poor! They could've innovated before we got here!

Doctor Chesky nodded, then turned his head left to his loading lady, trying to shield her from Gopman.

—Anymore of your staff coming tonight?

Zosime eyed the chief warily. He was young, like she was, like everyone on this job. Chesky saw the whole continent's blackness glimmer in her left pupil, or maybe it was just the night's blackness, or any other dark color.

—My staff? Clayton said he'd come. He may be lost.

—Why? He's new? Zosime nodded coolly. —He's from North Dakota, in America.

—What's that mean? Gopman ventured, leaning across his superior's shoulder.

—He doesn't really know what's going on yet. He was working for the hydraulic fracturing. He's not educated.

—Oh god, Gopman groaned, —does he work hard? Zosime regarded him a moment. —I don't want to get him in trouble.

—So he doesn't?

—Forget it, forget it, we're celebrating. Tomorrow's a big day. Chesky ordered them another beer. Two rotund stars, their glass sides lensing evermore distant suns, fell from the barkeep's heavens and landed with a soaking tsunami of dew on their paper coasters, violently ending the era of the tyrant dustmites.

—So, more about you. How do you say your name again? She knew that he was using the non-Englishness of her name to his advantage, covering the fact that he'd forgotten it. He was clever after an honestly ignorant American fashion, like a person hard of hearing.

—Zosime.

—What's it mean?

—Hold on, Gopman interrupted, —let's look it up, hold on. It's Greek. You're Greek, right? It means … why isn't there fuckin wi-fi here …

—Look up free wi-fi wiki,
—It means likely to survive. Whoa …
—Yes, Zosime confirmed quietly after nodding affirmative to another Pernod, —it means I'll live.
—Are you excited for the launch tomorrow?
—I hope it goes well.
—I got it all ready, boasted Gopman, —I've written the tightest program, the simplest ever for all the systems. Wait'll I fuckin sell it to Star-X. Not gonna need a fuckin IPO. I got feedback on all systems, one to the other, all of it done in Python. This is me makin space travel cheap, disrupting, guys! I'm the company's vision!

He laughed a moment, stretching the acne scars peppered above his Ben Franklin Generation beard, then asked Zosime across his chief's chin: —Yknow what Python stands for?
—Python?
—Like the snake, Chesky suggested.
—Púthon? Python?

Gopman hastily waved them away. —I have no idea what that means. No, listen, when I first tried it and I was livin in Frisco, I was like, it means punch yer tiny hot oriental nannee hee hee! Right?

A little kid on a bicycle, not yet near sixteen, came tearing into the garden and skidded to a stop in the damp dust, his right knee locked to brake with the drive chain. He called out mister Biggs, mister Biggs.

—Right here! Gopman's right index finger flew up. The kid squeezed between Gopman and the Chinese guy, held out his hand and named the price. Suspicious, Gopman checked the price on his phone, reached into his pocket and presented a twenty-dollar bill to the kid.

—You don't have change? I don't have change for this much!

—No, just take it, Gopman insisted impatiently.

—I take this back to the store? The manager takes all of it from me, no tip at all. You're not helping me with this.

—Just take it!

The kid looked toward the barkeep, who had his back turned pouring a martini for an Arab, and didn't say anything about his own kitchen cooking. The kid helplessly looked around once more for backup before trading the bill for his cargo and heading off on his bike.

—Fuckin mister Biggs app, Gopman grinned as he tore the paper bag open, —I love it.

—So, Chesky leaned back and gave his loading shift leader an easy smile, —do you like Nigeria?

—I like the work and the new things to see, Zosime lied, —I haven't made any friends yet.

—Yeah, you pretty much hafta be married to someone or … it's sure cheap here, that's for sure. Man, it makes me see how out of control Palo Alto had got. Two black men, perhaps locals, sat down at the bar, leaving only the empty one between Chesky and Zosime. —You were working on the sky ladder in Quito, right?

—Yeah, cut in Gopman, who'd already dropped his food and got out his kendama toy. He was trying to catch the ball on the string in all of the lathed wooden cross's three concave dishes and then land its hole on the toy's point.

—That was terrible, Chesky mused at his beer before hungrily drinking once more from the big dipper in Zosime's left eye, —I can't believe the counterweight just burned up.

—I know, Zosime sighed, —I don't know why he didn't fire the jets and go into orbit. I guess there was no time.

—I'm sorry. We don't have to talk about it.

—There's like, watch … Gopman was on his phone again, licking his greasy fingertips so the phone's screen would respond. He added something up on the device's bright, smooth calculator screen. —It's a hunnerd and forty million miles to Mars. There's like twunny million people in Lagos. They're all like six feet tall. So eight hunnerd eighty people makes a mile, you could stand everyone in Lagos on the other guy's head and make a sky ladder to Mars.

—What?

—Watch … hold on … eight eighty into twenty million … oh hold on, I fucked up. That's only a hunnerd thirty-six thousand miles. Fuck. Well, we shoulda left the fuckin sky ladder to the Mars mission and not even built one here! Gopman threw back his Star, —Mars has thirty-eight percent of our gravity. The sky ladder woulda been basic there.

—But it was a beautiful piece of engineering, Zosime mused to the launch chief, —it was almost invisible, almost weightless when you think of its size. It was a piece of art.

—That's why it fell apart, Gopman said to the kendama that now replaced his phone, bouncing it between his fingers, —a piece of art doesn't mean shit but some gay meaning! In this world, STEM rules!

Gopman rediscovered his fried food and dug in with both hands. Its greasy odor was annoying Zosime from the other side of her launch chief.

—Stem?

—Science, technology, engineering and mathematics, Chesky held his tongue desperately at the tiller of the conversation, port to starboard and jerking to port again. —Do you wanna go back to Quito?

—Of course. Zosime felt she could lower her guard a little despite how wrong she'd felt about Gopman, —Do you know anything about it?

—I know it's in Ecuador, the launch chief sheepishly shmiled, —Are there Indian structures there?

—No, that's in Peru. In Quito they're all gone.

—Fuck Ecuador, Gopman called out with his face wide open in excited anticipation, —it's all about Colombia. Watch this trick! With the force of his elbow he bounced the ball on the string three times, catching it each time in one of the three catchers, spinning it on his finger like a gunfighter in a western spins his pistol.

—Fuck yeah!

—When the sky ladder is fixed I'll go back, Zosime went on, —but this could take forever.

—Well, the launch chief said pleasantly, —we're happy to have such a qualified person in charge of our cargo. Is everything ready for tomorrow?

—Yes, she took her chance, —including your live pigs.

—Ha ha! Yeah, the pigs. That'll be a real innovation!

Her eye followed his attention and his scabby fingertip toward his phone's screen.

—What's in your phone?

—Oh, it's just … I'm just clearin out my email. I get so much crap, stuff I don't need to know to get the shuttle off the ground.

—When is the Mars mission taking off?

—Um, Chesky squinted and danced his head from side to side, —it's not certain yet. The … well, what I can tell you … what anyone can tell you … is that Star-X wants to build the Mars craft in space, and we're waiting on the tools and funding to come through. See, your sky ladder was bringing materials up to build that spacecraft,

—Is the spacecraft finished?

—I don't really know, Zosime. You can see for yourself. The company doesn't wanna say anything until they feel like progress has been made. And we're gonna lose this mine down in South America,

—I know about it. The newspapers say that the people who're blocking the mine are the same who attacked the sky ladder.

She gave into the seduction of her little glass of Pernod, took it up and swallowed it. —If the mission isn't ready to leave, why are there live pigs going up now?

—It's kinda crazy, huh? They could wait. Maybe they're just gonna see how these ones do in space. She noticed that he nibbled at his cuticles, and he pressed the swollen knuckle of one middle finger against his cold bottle.

—They've sent everything to space already, Zosime protested, —fruit flies, monkeys, sheep, ducks,

—Yes, dogs, frogs, mice,

—Why spend your investors' money on that?

Chesky wanted to say something, but he prevented himself. —Like I said, I don't really concern myself with the cargo. I've got too much on my plate already. I know they wanna have real food ... Earth food ... on the Mars colony. But I don't know any more than you. Want another drink? I like talking to you.

Zosime ordered herself another Pernod. He persisted:

—this is the first grownup conversation I've had since I've been here!

—There's room for one more box on the shuttle.

—Just beer for me, thanks. Well, no, yeah, and a vodka ... yeah, and unfortunately you're not gonna get it until first thing tomorrow. It's late arriving in the port. He seemed nervous, like his grasp on the launch had a weak knuckle.

—It's a refrigerated box, Zosime noted, her head full of the stink and bloody swollen flesh of her captive hogs,

—and the serial number on it shows that it's going to Mars.

—Is it? Well, it means it's intended for Mars, right? That could … what would they send up frozen?

—More meat?

—That's it, it's for sure, Gopman said loudly, but for himself, —there's never chicks here.

—So go find some, Chesky growled at him, —it's a big city.

—I'm gonna. Peace out, bro.

—Be careful, and don't stay out too late! And Gopman left, and Chesky was visibly relieved, though Zosime couldn't tell whether he wanted to be alone with her or just away from his subordinate. A third Chinese wanted to get in, so Chesky slid over to the barstool directly adjacent to Zosime, leaving a spot open between him and the new man at his left.

—Way to stand up to Craig.

—I was only saying the sense of what he said.

The chief exhaled warm air into the night. —Well, It's early, and we're celebrating. Still no sign of your loading guy?

—I thought he would be here, Zosime glanced around the patio. The former intern was gone now, his finished plate abandoned like campfire ashes on the peeling yellow bench where he'd been. —Maybe he's found something he likes better. Like the American bars by the water.

—There's a lotta them down there. There's a Johnny Rocket! Oh … that's an American burger joint.

—I'm sure he found it.

—Can I order you something? Some fried chicken and rice?

—Thank you. I don't eat chicken. I ate earlier. She looked around at the men eating their chicken, drinking, chatting under the strings of yellow stars. —Why do you come here and not there, where the rest of the Americans are?

Chesky nodded while he patiently formulated his response. His lips made a contemplative click when he opened them again. —It has to do with the job. They don't really want us talkin about the Mars mission to people. They don't want us startin a conversation with hey, I work in the Olusosun, but I launch spacecraft out of it. It'd be hard to keep quiet around all those go-getters. Plus we don't want the locals talkin.

—It's supposed to be a surprise when the rocket bursts up into the sky? She smiled at the idea, a genuine smile. He shared the absurdity with her and smiled too.

—Anyway, I like it here in the evenings. I can just watch here, just be normal, eat a piece of pie but not be working for a piece of the pie, like the guys down on the island. Yknow, they never stop working. They eat, it's a meeting or a competition, they drink, it's a pitch. I mean, the boss is like that, but … I'm not at his level yet.

—That's everywhere now.

—It's better to be here, where you can see people relaxing, he gestured at the men eating their chicken and rice, drinking, the Chinese engrossed in contemplation of their plates with leveled pupils, remembering the time they ordered a huge sausage plate at the Bembel in Frankfurt-Main and couldn't touch it. —I'd rather relax, with how much we have to deal with on the job. All the security.

The loading shift leader observed that her chief had a soft spot, that he could be opened like a bottle of wine if worked in the right direction. The launch chief found a calm place, or thought he found a calm place, in the swirl of noise and heat in the quartz night of her left pupil, in the burning night of her straight hair. Was there really any information that it'd hurt to tell her?

—Tell me, where are you from? she asked, and ordered a Star out of curiosity. But in a glass.

—Orange county? Chesky spoke the name with a query mark, —in southern California. I went to college at Stanford, by San Francisco. Zosime didn't bother imagining the places, just found them on the pallid tattered map in her mind. —How did you come here?

—Basically I got in at the ground floor. From Stanford I started as an intern at Tesla. I worked all through my undergrad and half of my doctorate, I was helping with problems for the batteries. After I finished, I asked around about their connections to the space projects and they kinda just made a position for me. From there I got to come here. He shrugged as if to confess. —I've always been interested in exploring for life out there beyond Earth.

She hid her sudden but not unexpected rage. A position they just kinda made for him. She swallowed, washed her bile down with Star, kept searching. —Were you here for the last launch?

—No.

—Did you see the burnt-up ground around the silo when you arrived?

—Yeah! It's pretty dangerous. But I guess the rockets're helping dispose of some of their trash. I guess that's part of the sell.

—Where does the shuttle land?

37

—Right up there at Ibadan.
—You're joking.
—No!
—I guess I should be happy I'm not working there.

Chesky slurped a fleck of foam off his virginal upper lip and shook his head. —There's no work there. New Sky Lines hires a private security contractor when it lands. They drive it back here, and that's where we come in, to clean it, prep and launch it again. He thought hard for a moment, then smiled again at her. —This stays between us, I hope.

Of course, as if no one noticed when a space shuttle was towed down the Nigerian A1, as if no one were discussing it casually on the internet somewhere in the Northern Hemisphere. Somewhere where it mattered to people, where it wasn't just the latest foreign enterprise taking place above the heads of the common people on the highway. —Of course, she purred into the faint red shining on them from the strings of chili lights. He didn't share the absurdity with her that time.

—Your turn! He persevered, as if they were playing a game, —What's your story? You're from Greece, and …?

She gave in. —My mother's Persian. She's a refugee from Iran because our religion is Zoroastrian. My father's Greek. My older brother is still in Iran.

—It must be really hard for them.

—So I grew up there, on … how do you say it in English? Corfú? That is a very famous island with beautiful beaches. My father teaches at the university. But you remember when Greece defaulted on its debt. When the Golden Dawn told people to stop giving jobs to foreigners, my mother thinks she's back in Iran again, and without a second thought she took me from Greece. That was seven years ago, already. She stayed in the Netherlands long enough for me to study and have my first job, then I took her to Quito when I started working on the sky ladder.

She stopped, threw back the rest of her Star and switched back to Pernod. The barkeep smiled at her now and called her madame.

—I always wish I could know more about people, she said to Chesky candidly, —like this man's life who's working at the bar. There's no time when you're always working to know anything about the place.

Chesky nodded with a pensive, slightly bewildered smile, at his phone. —Yeah, it's called Corfu. Um … do you ever think you'll go back to Greece?

Zosime sighed, suddenly tired. —It would be a long … how do you say it … a long journey to a job.

—A long commute!

—Yes, a long commute.

—In Orange County, there's some serious long commutes. That's normal in America.

—The rest of the world knows this. Do you want to go back there?

—To the States?

—To Orange County.

—Well … he showed her a deep American truth, some gamble or conflict over expressing an opinion about a region. But then, this was in every country, in all people.

—Of course Berkeley and Stanford are the best places,

—Are those schools or cities?

—They're both. By San Francisco.

—Right. She suddenly was out of things to say. She was drunk and exhausted, tired from pushing out so much English on a variety of topics, tired of negotiating with this man.

—No boyfriend or husband back in Quito?

Zosime laughed up some air, almost snorted. Did he feel he was probing further? Had she held him back with her snort? —I'm around men too much at work already. There aren't any I want to be with.

He smiled a loose, drunk smile, but leveled his eyes with her. Her face had heavyish muscles, heartshaped but harder, seen by some as mature too soon in youth, but stunning in maturity and age. But he knew nothing about how to see any of that. His aimless mind was asking the mundane questions of home, whether she shaved her pubic hair, whether she required lots of gifts and meals.

—I know you must think that men have a lot of negative qualities. With how much you've had to work and struggle for jobs, I mean. It's really stressful. I know we're not supposed to be able to listen. Men, yknow. But I do know how to listen, he spoke gently, leaned down toward the bar, —and what I hear is that this is the first time, yknow? The first chance in your life, after all you've done, to be interested in men. And that's why you're seeing so many of the negative things. Maybe your eyes are just opening more.

He opened his forwardleaning shoulders, presenting himself as just the right man to open up more for.

—Maybe. But to have my family together, I miss this much more. Look. It's getting late, and you have to launch a clay pot into space tomorrow. Goodnight.

Just like that, from his perspective, and with nothing more, from her perspective, she paid her bill in the exact naira and left Bushmeat. Only on her way out was her guard down, did she perceive the eyes watching her. But what they saw, what they wanted, what they were drawing on her from within their lives, it was too much to bother thinking about. The fingertip-sized leaves of the almond glittered as she passed. She hailed a taxi in the street that was mostly vacated for the night.

The clock read almost one in the morning already by the time she sat down on her bed. She was drunk, dehydrated. She had to throw the window wide open since room service had closed it, and then threw herself back down on the palmfrond-patterned bedspread. She looked out through the hotels and bank highrises on the main island in the southeast, like bars in a tiny window, over the smoldering nocturnal rubble of Lagos, toward the muddy shore where darkness and sheet metal shacks crouched. Out her window there was no mountain arching up invisible into the night, no chain of red lights stretching up into the nada, nothing to warn airplanes of the sky ladder's taut presence. It raised the senses of an orbital systems analyst. Why was she comparing here to Quito? When did the past become familiar? When did she stop hurrying from one place to the next?

Her choice to explain her family life to another person had changed something. Perhaps it was the liquor chasing the hurry from her swelling, torpid nerves, but she felt deepest that feeling of no longer hurrying, no longer running, as it inflated inside her and made her hipbones, buttocks, shoulders, calves and head heavy yet buoyant on the bed. The slowness made her realize how long her family had been apart, how spread out they were by distance and by all the things with which they busied themselves in order to ignore the distance. Over the balloon of slowness within her rained a rapid shower of nostalgia, a wet line zigzagging over landscape.

She rose to drink a glass of water and refocused her thinking. Doctor Chesky was pliable in the right situation. She was confident that she could convince him to find a better position for her, if her timing was right. Perhaps during the launch there'd even be a chance to show her worth. But she had to be honest with herself: it'd be hard to respect herself when working for his attention. Why did these American youth bother her so much? They were clueless. Besides her anger at her own lousy job outcome she felt bad for the intern Godsend, felt a tingle of inanity for being tied up in this knot of jobs that management pulled every which way.

3

Commander, pilot and payload commander

Daylight brought payday and the completion of her first launch after so many weeks of anticipation. She'd really been paid at midnight, while she was still metabolizing Pernod with doctor Chesky. As soon as her phone's alarm woke her up, she logged into her bank's website, found her salary, and wired two thirds of it to her mother's account, enough dollars for her vivienda in Quito, and doubtlessly to be passed on from Quito to her big brother Behrouz in Tabriz, city of withering dignity, starved by sanctions. She knew he'd hate to find out that money came from his little sister, whom he only knew through letters, but it was all that her mother, and thereby all that she, could do.

She didn't need the other third of her pay, either, but it was good in case she needed an escape plane ticket. It was barely too late to call her mother in Quito, at one in the morning there, without disturbing her earliest, deepest sleep of the night. At least her mother'd live well another month or two, where the sky ladder once buzzed with work, where the men on the job had to be educated professionals.

She was bloated from the beer, with a ring of rotten alcoholic vegetable essence stained upon her hypopharynx, needing to pee and already soaking in the humidity at sunrise. In Quito it was breezy alpine spring; here it was monsoon season. She'd just said that word to herself, monsoon season, when the bassy monsoon of the wind and sibilant season of the rain began to pour down outside like flakes of snare drums. She shut her window and turned on the air conditioning. It was too early for a swim and it'd be too late by the time she ate breakfast, so she took one of the otherwise opulent Protea's famous lukewarm showers.

A minute into her shower she was overcome once more by the dread, the compassion, she got from the pigs on the space shuttle. How much more had they contaminated themselves during the night in their sedation? How long had it been since they ate? Was their skin getting infected, or were they shellacked with antibiotics? Were they each in a shoulder-tight cage so they don't knock around during launch? She couldn't do anything about it now. What did she want for them, anyway? Was a pig ever safe? Was any living thing launched up in a spaceship as important as the launch of the spaceship itself?

She stood in front of the mirror, naked in the humidity, and brushed her hair. She ran inventory on her body, swept doctor Chesky's eyes off it. He had a lot of nerve trying to gain her good graces at the end of last night. He probably liked her because her body didn't belong to the American race of ox women, horned blond opera singers. Like many American men, as she imagined, he probably thought that relatively short, dark women were exotic, when in truth it was those bloated pink ice giants who were exotic on the earth.

She was her mother's child, not long and lithe as an Attic sunbather might be, but toned and supple, rooted to the ground by her Aryan calves, wanderer of rivers and qanats, climber of mountains. Nothing he'd know to appreciate. But she was glad she'd woke up hungover, as it prevented her from waking up aroused with only him to think of.

She was also glad to have left for work a little early, alone in the van while the express road was still expressive. The rules strictly stipulated no tolerance for tardiness, and she'd had ten coworkers in the past month to show for it. The rule was enforced even in uncontrollable circumstances, such as this morning's line of three garbage trucks that blocked the way into the silo's perimeter fence. The one in front had caught fire from a chemical reaction in its trash load, and a single policeman walked the line of traffic, shouting instructions through his muffled gas mask to protect one's face from the smoke.

Nevertheless the acrid soot intruded into the van, and Zosime's hangover almost overcame her as the caffeine and eggy food made their own chemical reaction high on her stomach. She squinted over her sleeve, through the rain-rutted glass, and watched the barefoot children circling the van, running and calling out in spite of the smoke, oblivious to the drizzle, demanding money or anything, rapping the palms of their hands on the van's side panels. The van driver, nameless as ever, casually tapped the horn to disperse them.

She made it on time, and the hour of launch drew nearer. The elevator trundled down into the earth, and beneath the soggy coastal surface it was oddly dry and cool. The silo's doors must've been left shut in hopes of waiting out the rain before launch time. She couldn't take two steps into the deep, wide silo before Clayton accosted her, his glowing cellphone screen held high like a mirror.

—Didja get paid last night?

—Yes, she passed him without a glance and put on her baggy company polo.

—How much did you make?

—I thought we all made the same, she booted up the laptop computer on its rolling cart to print out her daily checklists. The printer spit out two sets from yesterday inexplicably before printing the current ones.

—Look. Look! Finally she took his phone from him, out from under her own nose, and shot him a scowl.

—What'm I looking for?

—See my pay stub?

—Yes. She waited for him to get on with his point, but he wouldn't, just stood there sulking over his gut. She realized what he wanted; he was like a jealous child.

—Fine, look. Here's mine. You happy?

She held up her phone and showed him hers. Clayton perused the screen. He didn't look pleased. —See? You got paid by New Sky Lines. And my stub … look at it … mine says General Atomics. We're not even doin nothin with atomic power.

She caught his full name. Clayton Hieb. Dickinson, North Dakota. —So what?

—So what the fuck? Doesn't Star-X pay more?

—Who knows? I've been paid by four different firms already.

—They didn't say that'd happen.

—They don't say anything but the procedures.

—I don't think they're playin fair here! They just move people's jobs and salaries around however it suitsem!

He'd seen it, too. She repressed a grin. —So quit.

—Oh no, he put on his homey chuckle, goshed away his paystub problem, —I'm gonna be the first North Dakotan in space! Ya know, it's funny I ended up workin down in a launch silo. Cause North Dakota's the third most heavily-armed state in the world!

—What? She frowned down at her checklist, observed a timestamp for a delivery.

—Yah. Russia, the US and North Dakota.

—Is that where they keep the nuclear missiles underground?

—You betcha.

She leaned over and looked at the clipboard, then up at the shuttle. —Did Rodríguez get you an inventory code?

—No.

Good, she thought. If he opened any package, he wouldn't know what to do with its contents. And she wasn't going to encourage any more wild swapping of duties and job titles. She dug the radio out from a crowded wire shelf on the cart.

—Enjoy your first paycheck, then. Rodríguez. She waited. —Rodríguez. What's this delivery eleven minutes from now, over?

The radio was silent. She looked over the list again. Just a handwritten serial number and time, no description.

—Am I sposeta get a inventory code today?

—No. Here, she pointed at the binoculars hanging from a wire rack above her laptop, —take those glasses and scan the top of the fuel tank for condensation. Look for sweat and water streams. Go inch by inch and write down where you see it! He went to it while she read the work order again. What was coming so late?

Suddenly a brittle banging echoed through the silo from above and all their heads followed it. It was the obnoxious analyst Gopman shaking one of the launch center's xanthous windowpanes. Clayton could see almost clearly through the binoculars. When Gopman had their attention he pointed at one eye as he mouthed eye saw. Then he held his open palms out this wide and his lips boomed in and his teeth boomed out as he mouthed a big dick, again the same way with lips and teeth, a big dick.

—What's he doin? Clayton's doin was as rotund as his waist. They exchanged a look that held words like unprofessional. When they looked back up, Gopman held a long black Mag Lite in one hand and pointed at it with the other, his face a wide-open shocked O.

A set of footsteps that didn't belong to Clayton tapped lightly into the silo. Zosime turned around to find doctor Chesky in starched white lab coat and freshly-pressed slacks, smiling serenely.

—Morning everyone! He looked both ways. —No foreman yet?

Clayton's oh mouth and eyes revolved away from the binoculars toward Zosime and he rubbed his brown scrub of beard. —Anyway, the chief continued, —I just thought I'd go ahead and come down for a change and wish you a happy launch! It says upstairs that everything's ready to go, so you've all done a good job, the way it looks. The shuttle's crew should be here any minute!

He focused his attention now, which had spread upon them both, upon Zosime.

—Did you figure out the question you said to Rodríguez on the radio?

—No, Zosime responded, —I want to know what's coming right now. I can't prepare loading equipment if I don't know what it is.

—Look on your clipboard.

—There's nothing but a number. Chesky's eyes and brows dropped. —That's odd.

—Can we launch without it? Clayton volunteered.

—All cargo is essential, the chief eyeballed him.

—Well, I meant yknow, like, can it go up next time.

—Each launch costs the company millions of dollars, each delay, tens of millions. We don't alter the schedule, failing a hurricane.

—Okay, just an idea.

Overhead a plume of smoke from the burning garbage truck smudged the daylight coming through the bars from the surface. The radio squawked. —Chief, pick up, over.

Chesky accepted Zosime's radio. —I'm listening, Gopman, over.

—The foreman's on the phone. He's stuck behind a fire. Over.

—Send the call down here.

Zosime went around the bulkhead into the mouth of the hallway and picked up the buzzing phone mounted on the wall. —Yes, Rodríguez,

—Zosime?

—What is it?

—I'm stuck behind a fuckin burning truck! And there's a supply truck behind me headed for you! Zosime and Chesky exchanged looks. —Why can't you go around the truck?

—There's too many other trucks and shit! Look, I don't know when it's gettin over there. Tell Gopman to open the silo hatch and get the crane up, it's the only way to get the payload down in there and loaded up in time to launch!

—You hear that, Gopman? Chesky spoke into the radio. —Ten four, came the reply. Over the unnoticed hum of the refrigeration system now broke out the crack and clanking of tractor chains. The steel, glass and concrete of the silo's hatch clove in two and began to slide apart, letting rain fall steadily down into the silo.

—Why was I lookin for sweat? It's gonna get soppin wet in here! Clayton protested, his binoculars blinded by two lucky drops. —That's what you're for, Chesky said curtly, —it won't hurt. Back the electronics out into the hall if you need to.

Zosime dropped her head and blinked away a few heavy stray drops, set her weight against her cart and leaned into it until its casters groaned away. Just as its momentum hit its swing, she leaned to the left, got it turned sidelong to the door, then right, and it glided left under the bulkhead. Clayton watched from beneath the bill of his ballcap. Overhead the big robotic bridge crane slid off to one side and another crane, red with a familiar lattice boom, began to swing up toward the rainy surface. The odd cool and dryness was gone, and Lagos' muggy heat rained down in advance of the deluge.

—Is this the right thing to do? Zosime demanded of Chesky, her eyes following the crane.

—You're gonna have to get up there, the chief replied,

—to the tenth floor, to get up on that platform. You'll have to manually attach the container to the loader crane. Here, he took a slip of paper from his breast pocket and wrote four numbers on it, tucked it suddenly into Zosime's hand with his soft, bitten fingertips. —Call that into the elevator, then throw it away. What's his name?

—Clayton.

—Clayton! You're goin up to the surface to hook that thing up to the top crane. Go on. Bring gloves! The chief and the loading specialist trotted down the yawning hall and waited for the elevator. Chesky didn't get in the one that came for Zosime, but waited for its twin. —Hey, we can do this. He smiled a fatalistic American smile, which told her that he was probably very nervous on the inside, and that this cockup of a launch was likely to be his first ever, and went on: —I'm goin back upstairs, I'll watch you from there. The shuttle crew'll be here any minute. Be careful!

In the launch center doctor Chesky strode in a hurry to his desk and reviewed the shuttle's vital signs, found a passably re-grown pinkynail and chewed it. The rain wasn't hurting anything so far, and the payload commander would see to any water intrusion in the payload bay. He watched through the spitting of rain for Zosime to appear up on the top level beneath the open silo hatch. He glanced over at Gopman, who stepped away from the crane controls.

—Everything alright up here?

Gopman ignored the question as he turned to the interface on his computer. —Ready to see me launch this thing?

Behind him on the back wall of the launch center there had hung a large panel-mounted print of the mission control room for Apollo 11, full of at least eighty white-shirt thin-tie men. The boss'd hastily had it replaced with a print of Star-X's mission control center, populated by twenty-five people or so, in order to modernize the launch center, as he put it, and as not to make the center's crew of four feel understaffed.

—No hands, baby. Just me, my program, and this space ship. This is what fuckin disruption is all about. He shot his open hand out toward his chief. —Gimme my kendama.

—Your what?

—Fuckin kendama! I wanna do a trick. Toss it to me! Gopman gesticulated at the cruciform wooden toy two meters away on the edge of Chesky's desktop. —Craig, we're kinda busy. I needa get on the chat with mission control.

—No, watch! It's gonna be hands-free! That's part of the disruption!

Chesky grabbed the toy and opened a drawer to toss it in. Gopman leapt over and tried to reach into the drawer, met Chesky's hand that grasped his wrist, and pulled at his chief's hand to free himself.

—Givittome! I wanna do a trick!

—Get over it, Chesky soberly spoke over him.

—Givittome! his voice rose, —Givittome! Givittome, you jew!

Chesky stomped against him, and he backed off. The kendama stayed in the drawer.

—You'd better get yourself together and mind the shuttle, the chief told his shorter analyst under the shocked glares of the two other technicians. He was halfheartedly using the affected tone of a stern schoolteacher, for he didn't know how else to sound like he had authority. — The shuttle crew's gonna come right now! You want them to see you acting like this? What's the weather say?

—Light rain, that's all. Half an inch.

Chesky turned a sixth monitor on and called up the camera system on the surface. It appeared that Rodríguez now ran toward the elevator door on the west side of the silo's mouth, called the elevator, went in. Another camera angle flashed onscreen and Clayton was standing at the edge of the silo watching the crane's boom rise up like a rapidly-unfolding orange fern. Behind Clayton stood a line of trucks in the distance, the first in line still smoldering as a fire crew tried to put it out. He switched cameras again and saw a pixelly phantasm of Zosime.

—Zosime, you okay?

—It's wet up here.

—Any problems reaching the bridge crane?

—No. In the black mind within the digital video of her head, Zosime told herself that this probably wasn't legal. Another unpublished duty. —I'm not sure how I can get the chains from here to where the top crane is.

The camera's view on the entrance cone flashed back onscreen again. A semi truck had now appeared and was maneuvering itself into the arc of the crane's boom. A minute crept by as the crane's hook came down and Clayton climbed upon the truckbed to catch up the chains.

Now Chesky could see that the container was small, round and wrapped in insulation that hung off it in buxom tufts, the size of a normal cargo drum bound for the International Space Station. He sighed; this would be easier than shoe-horning in a seagoing box, as they'd done yesterday. As soon as the final payload was in the air, the semi truck folded itself up again twice to make three-point turns, and was gone in a digital blot of diesel exhaust. In his small chat window on his main computer screen winked a new message. Mission control had the affirmative from the space station commander, ready to reccive.

When the round container came dripping down from the surface above her, Zosime fitfully figured out the manual controls on the bridge crane and waved her outstretched arm so the launch center would stop the top crane. She had the payload barely a half-meter below the bridge crane's girders. She squatted on the crane's massive, four-cable trolley and rode it out over the abyss to meet the dangling container, not looking down the fifty meters to her contractual workplace.

She looked behind her shoulder. There were no harnesses, ropes, ladders or anything to secure herself with. This whole silo was setup for automatic operation except actually fastening the cargo to the cables. There was a single hook eye on each side of the puffy cylinder. How would she get back, even if she did get it attached? The trolley was getting slick under the raindrops. She had to move fast, or else she'd end up dead in a wet-polo contest.

Without warning the trolley moved, as if possessed by a radioactive duende from the French nuclear test site in Algeria three thousand kilometers to the north. She rolled on her hip, stemmed her left palm down on the wet trolley and fell to her knees. She waved her arms desperately and screamed at a glass window that couldn't hear her. —Stop!

After a moment the trolley stopped. She duckwalked to the manual controls, ears ringing, heart pounding, pieces of the distant floor swelling up into the rounded corners of her eyes, and moved herself back into position.

She let out one cable long enough to where she could still heave it up, gathered it until she had its hook in her hands and shackled it to the ring on the payload's near side. Under Lagos' monsoon heat, bitter words steamed up from her stomach. Stupid! Why was she killing herself? So pigs could go to space? She tugged on the tuft of insulation gathered at the cylinder's side and found it heavy enough to hang on. She let out a second winch's cable, gathered it and tied it loosely round her waist. It would keep her hands free, but wouldn't help her in a fall. She climbed onto the container and crawled only about twice as far as she was long, squinting against terror, until she reached its other side. Her hair started to fall in her face, gathering drops.

She found the far grommet, took the cable from around her waist, and shackled it blind. She crawled backward, fell off the cylinder onto the crane's trolley, and rode back to the catwalk. This could be a new job title: suicidal loading tightrope walker. Three meters below her, the square canvas roof sections of the astronauts' gangway lit up a cheerful yellow path to the space shuttle's door.

Doctor Chesky and his crew cheered their employee's courage, though she couldn't hear them. The bald payload engineer worked both cranes at once, let down the payload cylinder from the boom crane and let out enough chain to follow it to the shuttle, and then with the loader crane waltzed the cylinder into the lap of the shuttle. It landed snug at the bottom of the payload bay, its glistening steel tether swaying from the top crane's boom. Now the shuttle's payload bay was full.

The chief met Zosime down in the tunnel as she stepped out of the elevator. —You did it! He offered her a fresh lab coat and a dry work polo. —Are you okay?

—I need a raise. There's no safety equipment up there. There's still smoke from that garbage fire in the air.

—Okay, okay, he silenced her, smiling, —go change so you don't get sick. She went down the tunnel to change. He wished she could get into the shuttle; now he'd have to make Rodríguez do the same balancing act.

The second elevator now humdinged as it alighted, and out strode Rodríguez and Clayton, their shirts slick and veined with retained rain, stuck to their guts. —Well done, gentlemen, the chief shook their hands, —Clayton, do you have a change of clothes?

—No,

—Go see if there's anything extra in the locker room. Rodríguez, walk with me. They went out into the silo and Chesky pointed up at the scaly old shuttle. —You got a code for the shuttle gangway?

—Yeah, the loading foreman yeahed grimly, blinking raindrops from his eyebrows.

—I need you to gahead and go up into the shuttle. Don't touch anything. The payload bay hatch is already open. I just need you to go ahead and unhook that chain from the top crane. Wait for my tech's signal, cause he's gonna start pulling it in, and I want you to let it go right before it gets taut, cause it's gonna swing when you let go.

—I got it. The foreman retraced his own shiny slick bootprints back down the tunnel to the elevator. —Wait! One more thing. Is the freight elevator still working, after all?

—Why shouldn't it be? The foreman's voice, turned away into the tunnel, echoed off its blank concrete walls.

Safe and dry in the launch center once more, Chesky found Gopman indicating a monitor.

—We made it look good just in time.

Onscreen a limousine from the airport now heaved itself around the firetruck and the burning wrecked garbage truck. Out into the waning drizzle and its steam heat stepped three tall, crewcut white men in sharp slim suits. The digital video didn't resolve the detail that they all wore American flag pins on the left lapel, over the beating, red-blooded heart. They were the commander, the pilot and the payload commander. They weren't coming to see him. They were coming down the elevator into a green room to check their spacesuits, have a last shit in native gravity, perhaps enjoy a smart cocktail and go straight to the shuttle. They expected that everything was in order.

Doctor Chesky grabbed up his radio. —Rodríguez, hurry up, please, over … Rodríguez, do you copy? The foreman still probably hadn't grabbed a radio. —Turn on the shuttle speaker system so I can talk to him, please. You know what, I'll turn the whole thing on.

The loading foreman left a track of wet footprints down the gay gangway that was like some tunnel of love from an outdoor summer wedding. He arrived at the shuttle door, found it unlocked and went in, just as the whole thing lit up in hundreds of little lights and screens like the video arcade in a pizza parlor.

With one hand and both feet on the nearest ladder, he hung sideways and hunted through the switches and grates and banks until he found an intercom box, conveniently located near the hatch. —You hear me, launch center?

At the moment he opened his mouth, however, the shuttle flooded with the straining strings of the fast second chunk of Strauss' *Blue Danube,* and Rodríguez yelped.

—Turn the fuckin music off! he stabbed at the intercom, —turn the fuckin music off!

—I can't from in here!

—What?

—I can't from in here! Wait for my signal!

—What? The shuttle went dark and silent like a fist closing around the foreman. From the cuff of his pantleg dropped a single muted drip on the sterile shuttle wall beneath him. Damp fleshy wrinkles squinted around his eyes for a moment, then he climbed further down until he could drop toward the payload hatch that yawned open like a bottomless pit, or the anus of a man-eating predator. He landed square without a slip and left two sandy prints on the wall, got down on his butt and dropped himself carefully down into the payload bay, his feet banging against the red container full of pigs.

He cautiously inched down the rope ladder that ran the length of the bay, exposed again now to the loose drizzle and slick metal. Overhead the shuttle lit up again.

—Rodríguez, you hear me? came a voice from three stories beneath him, —Go back up! There's an intercom above you next to the hatch! The foreman shook his head and shoulders out at nothing, then glowered down at the launch center's big window just long enough before he couldn't resist vertigo.

—Okay then, just listen. When you get to the hook, undo it, then hold it loosely with your hand. The chain's gonna pull, and when it gets tight, let it go! Yeah? Rodríguez nodded at the rope ladder. He went down to the bottom where sat the cylinder Zosime had wrangled into its temporary chocks. Standing on one chock, he found the hook and unshackled it, and tossed it with a thumb-up into the air.

From the bottom of the silo Zosime and Clayton watched the ant in the toy shuttle working. Fifteen stories above, the top crane woke up again. Its winch pulled at the chain until it tugged fast at the shuttle, and then the chain swung free. Its hook clattered once against the concrete esophagus of the silo, then gradually made leaner and leaner pendular arcs until it hung like a conquered fish.

—That was intense, Clayton remarked.

Up in the shuttle Rodríguez labored at dragging his beergut up the rope back to the shuttle cabin. He caught his breath at the edge of the second supply box. Then he clambered up along the box of live sedated hogs and swung over toward its brink. —Now how do I get back up in there?

The equatorial heat and the orange fuel tank were mute above his squinting brow. He pulled himself breathlessly up the rope ladder and got an elbow and a wrist up into the hatch. He groped for the handle, not knowing he'd overreached it and had it rolling under his weak brachioradialis. His hand slipped, he lost his equilibrium, and he fell.

He didn't fall fifteen stories to his death, but hit the box of hogs hard with both kneecaps. Below him Zosime and Clayton heard a withering wail. The launch center heard nothing.

—Rodríguez, hurry up, please, came Chesky's voice through the dusty speakers, —We want the crew to have that shuttle to themselves when they arrive.

The foreman blustered curses through clenched teeth and distended lips. He got up and dragged himself back to the raindampened ladder, found two handles in the shuttle's hatch that he hadn't found before, and got himself slowly up through the shuttle. Once more in the gangway, oriented with his stature, he hefted the shuttle's hatch door. It was heavy hanging down against its hinges; he tried to get his weight under it, but the pull went to his knees and he swore again, long and loud, until he had the hatch shut like new, and limped back down the gangway. Passing through the mellow decorated green room he nodded curtly at the astronauts, tracked footprints and drips over their stylish seafoam-green carpet and stalked into the elevator.

He had nowhere to go but the bottom of the silo, back to his listed duties. Zosime checked her clipboard and found that they were only about ten minutes behind. She didn't bother telling the foreman, whose face was red and swollen. Even at the bottom of this damp, fluorescent-lit tomb, excitement was building in the subterranean air.

—What's in that new container? she asked as he found a chair. —It doesn't say on my paper.

—It's a load of frozen food, the foreman sighed.

—Why wasn't that on the description?

—Usually that means it was added at the last minute.

She added it up in spite of herself. He knew. Why hadn't he told her? Was there a rule? Had it remained undecided?

—But there're already supplies in the first container we loaded, Zosime probed, confused.

—It's not 100% Food, it's frozen food. It's meat products, frozen potatoes, that kinda thing. Barbecue shit.

—It's going to Mars? They really will keep the pigs alive all the way to Mars?

—Nope. Not yet, at least. To Star-X's staging grounds in orbit. Then it's goin to Mars ahead of the mission.

He'd avoided her question, just as Chesky had last night. Once again to the staging grounds in orbit that may or may not exist. —When will Mars be ready?

—You like axin questions, don't you? You're like a little kid.

—If Mars isn't ready, it makes no sense to send the pigs now. No one can tell me the answer to this.

—Am I an expert? he thrust his fingertips into his chest and shouted at her. —You figure it out! The fuel's cheaper now, or the labor's cheaper now, or their stocks are high, somethin. Right? Who gives a shit? Now leave me alone, my fuckin knees're killin me.

—You hurt your knees? Concern splashed up against her annoyance. —You need to get medical attention.

—I don't wanna talk about it with you.

—You shouldn't have gone up into the shuttle! Someone else should've corrected the mistake.

—Uh huh. If you thought that, how come you didn't tellem that while I was up gettin my ass rained on?

—I have no idea that I may say that!

—Well, whose fault is that? The most annoying question in the English language rang out against the silo walls. He scowled at her such that she was silent. She wanted to get on the level with him, tell him that she'd almost killed herself as well, that they'd used her and him both! But the English wasn't coming. It didn't make a difference, if they meant to stay on the job. She took her eyes from his and let him be. Above their heads three bulky shadows slowly paraded through the shuttle gangway's lineny yellow tunnel.

Doctor Chesky exhaled a watermelon of damp breath as he watched the shuttle crew settle into the towering shuttle stack. His monitors reported the astronauts' activities multiplied by those of Gopman's digital assistants. Little hourglasses, pie charts and colored bars like piston strokes ran their courses, systems checked each other, electrical circuits ran their tracks, and percentages calculated each other as the silo's brain drew up the shuttle's bill of health.

Once more a few earthlings clever and greedy enough to abandon their fellow earthlings would sail in a gourd of ashes up over the rocketburnt refuse of Olusosun, above all the Earth's landfills, across the infinite lifeless sea beyond, and they'd do it using nothing but math and explosive chemicals. The pilot even took a moment to say good morning through the intercom, his voice warm, fatherly, calm as could be and fatglittered with coffee and pastry.

—That Zosime is amazing, Chesky breathed, —but this is a disaster.

—Dyou fucker last night or what? Gopman demanded suddenly, and Chesky's head shot toward him. —I'm not discussing that with you! We're gonna have to postpone the launch by the time they clean up all this! He spoke into a headset: —Commander Jones, any water damage in the payload bay?

He turned the launch center's speakers on and the astronaut's voice boomed larger than life.

—Negative, chief. Your foreman got filthy footprints on the walls down in here, though.

—Sorry, commander.

Clayton and Zosime were looking at the shuttle again, shuffling their feet, catching glimpses of the payload commander inspecting the boxes. Collected rain streamed down the shuttle's pendulous engine cones and dripped down into the bottom of the silo.

—Zosime, turn your monitor on, please, came Rodríguez' pained voice. She took out her phone. There was another message from her mother. She had to slide it away with the tip of her finger. She turned on the monitor integrated in her work email and found herself face to face with the payload commander.

—Houston, we have a problem, Jones' chiseled face reported to all and sundry with a disappointed smirk, then floated away as the camera turned toward the open door of the hog container. From behind the camera an unsuited bare hand pushed the rustpocked metal door up, and the camera moved in. In their suffocating wire cages the upturned animals looked enormous, much older than yearlings, and seemed to grow upward like slack-jawed onions. When daylight hit the glimmer of their open eyes, their whines and screams reached the bottom of the silo.

Clayton leaned in over Zosime's shoulder, stinking of burnt trash, and noted the wire lacerations pressed into the hogs' hides. —They got charbroil marks onnem already, ah.

The bald payload engineer quietly turned toward the launch center's blasted window, said chief, sir, and pointed to his monitor.

—Then you didn't! Gopman laughed. Chesky held his scowl on him, but he felt no pressure, no squeeze from his chief. —Fine, I'll fucker then, he resolved, —If not bros then hoes. That's basic. That's fuckin not even Python, C-Plus.

—That's enough! Chesky eyed his technicians, who were probably filming this with their phones, —Just a minute, please. Which channel?

The payload engineer told him which channel. —Your behavior has been absolutely unprofessional today. When I say shutcher mouth and focus on yer job, I mean it! You understand me? Or you're gonna be on a plane back to Colma tonight, and you can get a job back in the States, where any job's gonna keep a hiring loan of two months' pay until the day you quit! Got it?

—You can't fire me, faggot,

—Yes I can,

—Only the boss can! We're a team that his people put together, not you!

—And I can rearrange anyone on this team as I find it necessary!

The telephone rang in a flurry of beeps. The chief held his eyes heavily on Gopman as he cradled the receiver under his chin.

—Chesky ... Oh, hi, sir. I was expecting to hear from you soon ...

The technicians were looking at him now, their desks and consoles floating in a misty distance beneath their heads. He found the monitor channel that the engineer had told him. His technicians and his analyst saw horror spread over his face. —Yeah, the welcome music worked. Yeah, I think they got a kick out of it ... well, I'm glad you always ask that ... mhmm ... because we'd better discuss the possibility. We're not behind schedule yet, in case you heard about the last cargo box was stuck in traffic. Yeah. No, but we've got a problem with the payload ... mhmm ... I just saw that the uh, livestock've woken up ... yeah ... is that gonna compromise quality? ... I see.

He glared again at Gopman, then out at the towering orange tank, the white rockets and the scaly tiles of the shuttle. —Yeah. Look, I'm sorry ... I appreciate you sayin that ... so, what should we do, then? ... okay. Well, sorry ... thanks ... sorry. Bye.
—Who was that?
—The boss.
The technicians dropped their gazes, but not Gopman.
—See? You're not gonna say nothing.
—Shut your god damn mouth and close the silo doors, Craig. He turned regretful near-set brown eyes to his two technicians. —We're not launching. Will you get the bridge crane going, please? He spoke into his radio:
—Rodríguez, you're on the forklift. We gotta unload, over.
—I can drive it but I ain't loadin, over.
—Whatta you mean?
—My knees, the foreman hesitated, —I'm hurt. Over.
—What happened?
—I got hurt on the shuttle.
Chesky swore under his breath. —Okay. Just get it to the freight elevator and go home.
The routine was for all staff to huddle in the cafeteria with two bulkheads between them and the rockets that blasted the shuttle out of the silo. Support staff came first, then the launch staff slid in as the shuttle left the ground and forces in North America and Europe took over responsibility for its escape into orbit. There'd be no launch today, but the long launch lunch remained.
Doctor Chesky dismissed his two busy technicians and came down to the tunnel, where he met his loading crew. He was depressed. According to the boss, who seemed to be an expert, it was like this: without enough sedatives on the ISS to cover for this, the pigs would have to endure

fucking space as well as be fed and watered intravenously, and it was too dangerous to keep feeding tubes in them as long as they were fucking awake and could move one centimeter to each side. The order to stall the launch had only been the second time ever that he'd spoken to the boss. The impression was bad all over.

Where this launch was to be, now remained a gaping hole in Chesky's résumé, a blankness of immaturity, virginity, a lost mark of achievement. This was no complex mechanical malfunction, a devil in the material and programming details like when that bottle strut famously failed and killed that early rocket. This was a mundane logistical error, a case of escaped livestock, a human fuckup. And no matter how well he'd done, the fuckup was on his turf. He hoped that the boss and the investors would look close enough to understand.

He had to call headquarters about getting a veterinarian to deal with the pigs, had to find out where they'd be kept, and had to stay late to meet up. Happily headquarters' sleepy night shift informed him that they had just the vet.

He watched his soaked foreman and the new guy help his swift, decisive shift leader transfer the pig box and the frozen food onto the forklift, and she also took the trips driving the cargo through the yawning hall to the freight elevator. The foreman called the private security firm that defended Ibadan's landing site, and soon they would come take the payload away to secure storage.

Gopman came trailing them out of the elevator now, no kendama string around his neck, laptop under his arm. There was no heavy chemical smoke from the launch to follow them down the tunnel; only Clayton wore it in miniature on his sodden garbage-smoked polo and his ballcap as they crossed through the next bulkead into the cafeteria to meet the shuttle crew. Doctor Chesky caught one of the astronauts eyeing his soaked underling, and moved to take control.

—Clayton, you look terrible. Why don't you call it a day? I don't want you to get sick hangin around in wet clothes.

—Alright, Clayton looked up and every which way but at the chief, —is that an issue with the pay?

—No, no, of course not, the chief nodded at his limping foreman, —just get yourself dry and get some rest. Rodríguez …? Yknow what, Clayton, I'll fix your clockout time. Gopman, call the van over, please.

—See you at Bushmeat tonight?

—You know where it is? Yeah, probably.

Clayton gave a nod to everyone and turned back toward the elevators.

The lady had somehow by herself prepared a grand lunch buffet with every kind of meat, sausage, bottomless ground beef, hamburger steaks, hotdogs laid out separately as if they weren't a kind of sausage, the usual lunchmeats bologna, roast beef, turkey, ham, gross microwaved chicken and pork cutlets in broth, rotisserie chicken, tuna and tuna salad, an entire poached salmon with the head and tail intact, the local farmed catfish from Jovana Farms made to look exactly like the tuna only seasoned browner, but no local catfish pepper soup; macaroni and cheese potato salad, local rice and cassava dishes with North American condiments mixed into them, French fries, hard boxed taco shells, microwaved pizza, breadsticks, tatertot hotdish, pasta with tomato sauce, pasta with cream sauce, all of it looking depressed and resigned, like animals born in cages with the aborted instincts of free wandering, their nutritive value shrunken or left at home carelessly, or renounced, all spread out under the bludgeoning fluorescent light. It was a good thing that Clayton the North Dakotan had gone home, for there was no pizza hotdish nor taco pizza.

At the far right side of the great buffet sat an astronomical festoon of condiments, like a baroque garden forced into plastic squeeze bottles, ranch, chipolte mayonnaise (the lady was trained to say and label chipolte because the proper pronunciation, chipotle, contained the pan-American /tl/ phoneme that doesn't exist in English), French, dijon, basil pesto, Italian, blue cheese (bleu, as above), red wine vinaigrette, caesar cheese blend, country barbecue, creamy bacon alfredo, horseradish, fat free balsamic vinaigrette, honey bourbon mustard, four-pepper chili, mayonnaise, zesty grill, guacamole and au jus dip.

Finally she had also put out a salad bar of colored gelatins, baby carrots, baby corns, cottage cheese and machine-shredded vegetables. The six of them would have to eat three meals apiece for three days to eat all of it, yet the lady was to throw all of the leftovers out this afternoon, because if she didn't, the company couldn't write the cost of the food off of their corporate taxes in the United States, even if all this were transpiring in Nigeria. If they didn't write the food off of their taxes, they'd have less money to invest later in finding out how to stage as huge and varied single-day feasts on Mars.

Zosime wanted to sit where she normally did, near the door, but when the blast door sealed the bulkhead according to the timer, she wanted to be further in. More lights were on today and the cafeteria had the ambience of a large parking garage. The astronauts had found a place to sit with a comfortable angle of the neck to look at the nearest screen upon which the Apollo 11 interview between Walter Cronkite, Robert Heinlein and Arthur C. Clarke was about to begin its loop anew. The corporate logos paraded across the screen followed by the bambooish umbrellish word LAGOS!

She returned from the buffet first with a few salads, some pasta and a few soft rolls still shaped like the tight plastic bag that they were shipped in. She sat across from the three astronauts and sipped her bottled water. They were dressed in comfortable clothes, enjoying the conditioned air and ogling the screen shoulder to shoulder over meat feasts. Chesky ate somberly, Gopman figured on his laptop, and the astronauts made friendly and easy despite the abortion of their mission.

—So this is what the launch lunch is like, Gopman put in with great enthusiasm, —totally intense. The astronauts chuckled at him. Zosime was annoyed. If the launch were aborted, why were they sitting locked in here? The timer to shut them in must've begun its countdown much earlier.

At length Chesky commented, his eyes on the television: —See, they're so serious on this show. They don't have a concept of the innovation, the pride. You gotta be cool about it, yknow? They're like … how did old people talk? Like, destiny, superstitious.

Gopman waited for Cronkite to patiently explain something to the audience. —Well, he countered analytically, —there was no social media then, yknow? So they just, like, talked to themselves, for themselves. It wasn't like they were sharing.

When Zosime saw that her chief was done speaking, she inquired without a beat: —Will the pigs be cared for?

—Of course, he nodded wearily at the astronauts, then at her, —we've got a vet on the way.

From the speakers Arthur C. Clarke's voice bounced authoritatively: —Space travel will end war. This sort of thing makes our stupidities here on Earth more and more intolerable ...

—What's your position here? asked pilot Lightyear of Zosime, trying to conceal a rehearsed intimidating tone left over from being a drill sergeant or a corporate motivational speaker.

—I'm a loading specialist, Zosime replied eye to eye with him, —I loaded the pigs and everything into the shuttle. I came from Ecuador, from the sky ladder.

Longnosed commander Morgan bowed his head and shook it twice. —It's terrible news, about that sky ladder. A tragedy. Such a waste.

—Well, that's the kinda security that socialism can afford, concluded Lightyear to his food.

—Have you fellas been with the company long? Chesky inquired to suppress the tension he was smart enough to feel but not smart enough to face productively.

—Only about a month, responded Lightyear, eyeing the screen, —do they have the Disney Channel down here?

No one responded. —I hope, doctor Chesky, growled the pilot, —that there's Disney Channel on the shuttle. Chesky's face puckered, nonplussed. —Was there a,

—Oh, the commander chuckled, —he gets a little testy after a few Salisbury steaks, eh buddy? He patted Lightyear on the back, who sighed, cast his eyes to the center of the Earth and went on scooping food down his order-barking throat.

—So, to answer your question, commander Morgan went on, —We all quit NASA about six months ago, during that government shutdown. Couldn't takem anymore! Lucky for us Star-X is such a great company, we're really happy to be here.

—The government shut down? inquired Zosime.

—Yeah, Gopman piggybacked on her, —I was gonna ask that, too.
—You didn't hear? frowned Lightyear.
—I'm not from the United States.
—Since we're all sittin here, Chesky continued to lean on the conversation's tiller, —I might as well let the cat outta the bag. No use havin anymore secrets to slow us down. Lookit this, it's the company's new plan for the Mars colony.

He handed around his phone, and onscreen was a cartoon of the Mars colony, in which cheerfully wobbled pictures of the five inflatable living capsules on the Pantone 158-C orange ground.

—Now zoom out with your finger, he said. Each person did, passing it around, and they saw a wooden pen erected around the capsules, along the rim of which grew green grass with plump cartoon cows, pigs and chickens happily ruminating, rooting and pecking thereupon. Behind the capsules stood a chaste white aluminum grain elevator and a plump happy barn painted perfect Swedish Falu red. No chestnut tree. At the widest zoom a dash of white and blue color suggested an atmospheric bubble over the colony. The shuttle crew smiled crisp, squinty fatherly smiles and ahhed gently.

—So that's what you're gonna gahead and think about when you're bein really careful loadin the shuttle. This's what we're goin for. We want the Mars colony to remind visitors and the research crews of the central features of life on Earth! And of course once it's perfected, it can be adapted to every space colony.

—Is that real? Zosime asked in disbelief, —they want to keep all those animals to eat? How will they live before they're eaten?

—Look, there's a bubble.

—But the sun still shines through it! The animals, everyone, will burn. The cattle produce methane that they have to remove,

—This is the greatest event in all the history of the human race, up to this time, Robert Heinlein cut her off gravely from the screen, —the human race, this is our change ... our pooberty rites ...

She had to hand it to Heinlein, the entertainer. These men she worked for, oblivious of his existence, followed his creed. The universe is your oyster, obliviously by the grace of your color and sex; here's your space ship and laser gun, go play. —Even if we spoil this planet, the human race will not die, Heinlein assured them.

—What's wrong with experimenting, with innovating? asked commander Morgan, —If we didn't try, we'd never got this far. Yknow? You'd never got this job. He smiled pastorally, his mouth a corncob of perfect teeth.

—What's,

Chesky suddenly arched his head and shoulders over at Gopman's laptop screen, to which Gopman indulgently turned the thing around so all could see.

—This's what I saw last night! he exulted in a raspy hush. Pilot Lightyear grinned and watched the pornographic video intently. —That's how big the guy's dick was,

Launch chief Chesky turned away to his food in shame rather than watch his analyst subject the female employee to porn that didn't expressly respect women.

Gopman threw his hands in the air. —I didn't even get my own whore to fuck. I just stood there and watched that show. I was in, like, I couldn't move! Shock.

Without mentioning it, several present saw an additional blond hair sproing forth from Gopman's regulation college-senior beard.

—Craig, finish your reports after lunch. Join the conversation.

Zosime went on undeterred: —The Mars mission is important. But what's wrong is that these animals don't have a choice to go, like the researchers do. They could find out that the animals get sick from the radiation and can't … she grasped after an answer in English, —can't live at all on Mars.

—A fair point, shared payload commander Jones, and cast an eyeful of humanity at the loading shift leader.

—Who cares? They're animals! countered Gopman.

—You're vegetarian, Lightyear accused the meat-free plate in front of her, —arnchou?

—I knew a guy who was vegetarian, reflected Morgan, —his skin was always gray, he was on his bike everyday … thirty-one years old he had a heart attack and died.

He looked around the table for validation. —Another issue is the longterm health of the researchers. Even with short stints, we're talking nine months to get there, with a light load, and nine months to a year back. He gestured at his roast beef. —We need meat to live. They can eat 100% Food for a while on the space station, and on the way out to Mars, but eventually they'll need real Earth food. I mean, I can't go a meal without meat protein.

—Me neither, Lightyear growled, —and pushing your vegetarian lifestyle on others, on those who're gonna need the protein most to survive this ordeal for the advancement, the survival, of mankind! Is no way to show loyalty to this company.

—I think she understands that, chirred Chesky to his loading shift leader's defense.

—Of course a vegetable diet would be so much simpler, put in Jones, —but there's nothin simple about discovery. And we've barely scratched the surface of growin vegetables in space. Naturally there's a huge business interest. I mean, imagine how big of a cotton plant you could grow in zero gravity, or even Mars' gravity! How big of a cow! I mean, he laughed at his own cleverness, chucked Lightyear on the shoulder, —it's almost a bad idea to grow an atmosphere on Mars, cause you could justisoon pump all the livestock's greenhouse farts out of the bubble, guilt-free!

Zosime's ear was turning. Did someone play this video for these astronauts day after day in their lunchroom as well? Their voices were arching, rising in pitch, becoming more like Cronkite's and Heinlein's by the second, affecting that strange, supposedly-extinct Yankee naïve optimism.

—They should think about this before they send anyone to Mars, Zosime insisted, then backpedaled: —a mistake will cost the company a lot of money. If the animals' waste and ... dead bodies,

—Carcasses,

—Carcasses aren't processed correctly, the entire biosphere could be contaminated. If a pig gets an infection that spreads, you see? There's no way to save the researchers fast enough.

—It's utterly inevitable, Robert Heinlein argued,

—We're going to spread through the entire universe.

—A grand painting, mister Heinlein.

She wanted to scream at them, at the stupid fuzzy video, scream her only true point, that they had no right to imprison animals in their insane dream of Earth-life in space. But she had to talk business, because her point brought too many more points into her mind, and it was unbearable. She couldn't stop or slow down anything, really. Neither could these men see beyond their own plates that they were animals in another space colony, closer to home.

—You can't stop progress, and this is progress, this is where men go, Walter Cronkite insisted, —we know we can't. If we could, we'd probably stop some of the highways built through the middle of our forests and our cities, we'd stop a lot of other things, but it can't be done. And uh, this promises benefits which you can't imagine today.

—Smart women like you should be goin up to Mars, Zosime, chief Chesky offered down his long sausage nose, —yknow, if only you'd been taught to code starting at five! Anyway. In space you'd all be so busy discovering, you wouldn't have to talk about Earth's waste and … sexism and ugliness anymore. He showed her a big smile.

The idiot, she thought silently behind her salad. Every sensible person knows that a man who plays at seduction in every single conversation either has a magnetism suited to it, or is insecure and thinks that he doesn't get enough opportunities to practice. Chesky was certainly the latter.

She no longer wanted to gather information, to probe, to test boundaries. She was silent for the rest of the hour. The men talked about everything, anything, besides what had happened today, what hadn't happened, what it meant. Someone smarter, more of an innovator, more of a disruptor, was handling it all for them far away.

She looked on as the young Americans plotted and fantasized about conquering space, leaving behind all the terrestrial problems they refused to acknowledge, with all the billions of dollars in sponsorship money for their software ideas to protect them. When these overgrown children grow old enough, connected and ambitious enough to influence policy and vie without competition for public office, no one on this Earth will have the right to be surprised when these men legislate disregard for life outside themselves, as generations of aging spoiled boys before them have done.

The film repeated every half hour, seeming always to give a dramatic flourish from the writers' dialogue right in time to bolster the astronauts' or the launch staff's statements, even opinions about bubbly water or the threat of violence from Africans here on the streets.

After the two hours corresponding to the post-launch airing-out and cleanup finally ended, the timer-tamed blast door rumbled open again. Doctor Chesky dismissed everyone and said he'd wait for the veterinarian. He tapped his feet against the glazed concrete floor of their parking garage of a cafeteria. Gopman lingered with him.

—Whatsamatter, chief?

—This waiting for the vet to show up, it's stressin me out. I wanna go to the gym before it gets full of fatties and locals. That intern coulda taken care of the pigs!

—What intern?

—Iyiola, the one that bugs us at Bushmeat all the time.

Gopman's blond head turned toward his chief. —You want me to call him?

—Nnn ... no. Forget it. What's done should stay done. What's this? He looked at his phone. —Oh, she's not even here.

—The vet?

—She's not even in Nigeria. Okay, let's go.

—Should I call him?

—No, no.

Doctor Chesky went back up to the launch center, cleaned up, found the former intern Iyiola Godsend's telephone number and waited to catch the van when it came back from taking the loading crew home.

Zosime cracked the box of pigs open once more, which released a fresh monsoon of screams and stink, and then drove them in the overloaded forklift onto the freight elevator's platform. She left the bare concrete expanses of the silo and its corridors, and with her hand on the box's rusty aluminum skin she rode to the surface and left them in there to scream until the veterinarian should arrive. Her sinuses and the ducts down her nose swelled with hot tears, but they wouldn't come out. It was like being the one person in the empty market square left holding the orphan. Arriving up at the elevator cone, through the pinched elevator doors, she saw the great blue needle of Lagos' sky poking through. The bustle and crush, the smell of rain-dampened garbage and the crowds of scavenging people rose up into her sinuses as the concrete and industrial technology diffused around her.

Olususun was ugly, Lagos was ugly. There were no sublime beaches, no soaring mountains, to make the work enjoyable, as it had been in Quito, no trembling measurements to be found in the wind or the ground. Perceptions and feelings mix together. She hadn't seen the connection the other night, when she compared Lagos with Quito. It was the focus on money rather than nature, not disorientation or nostalgia, that made her suffer. These orphan earthlings stuck in that rusty box were her only connection to nature in this self-consuming nightmare place, and they were slowly prying her attention away from the singularly technical, the invisible, the cheap. She needed the honesty of nature that she'd taken for granted in Corfu, in Quito, even in Utrecht, which was a virgin forest compared to Lagos. She was the true orphan, and the orphanages of university and career had now somehow expelled her.

Doctor Chesky was in the front seat of the van, but they ignored each other, or at least Zosime ignored him and he got the vibe. She didn't intend to take any conversation back up from the two hours of prison they'd put her through in the silo.

Past the scorched garbage truck, through the two violent fences and the new crowd of fifteen or so protesters in Unilag shirts, through the streets stuffed with people, stands, fabric cabanas and small motor vehicles, stopping behind the occasional bus striped with rainy mud, the van bore her down to the middle of Ikeja, and she made her walk to the Protea hotel. Now she finally noticed that there were two bus stops along the southwestern rim of Olususun, and she wondered why she was still dealing with the van, whether the van was perhaps her passport in.

She took a swim in the pool, laid out to dry and relax, but she couldn't relax. Her mind assumed the duty of wondering when the veterinarian would arrive, whether the pigs would be fed, if the drugs'd harmed them. Their owners seemed oblivious that the pigs were suffering needlessly, just as the company would probably never find out how she and Rodríguez had put their lives in danger just to rush all the cargo into place. All thoughts without conclusions.

She checked the time and found it was early in Quito, but right to call her mother. She hoped her mother would take the time to put the video chat on the phone.

—Zosime? her mother's heart-shaped face blinked onto the small screen.

—Hola, Mamá! Their conversation waded in the foamy tides of Greek and Spanish. Her mother still called her dlakam, in Kurdish, through all the languages they'd learned to speak together. Each time she said it, to the spring of her voice returned the young mother, curious and timid, the worst pain of her life certainly behind her. The daughter had never tried hard enough at Farsi; Dutch and English remained behind at work. Behind her mother, yellow sunlight played on happy cornmeal-colored walls and breezy linen drapes. She told her mother the least necessary. Though she had a new mind today, she didn't want to appear to her mother to want to flee her job. She pled that her mother tell about herself.

—I got word from the doctor that the stomach cramps have to do with a pinched nerve.

—Can they cure it?

—If I can remain calm, the muscle can be massaged slowly. Then it may let go of the nerve.

—Why aren't you calm? What's wrong there?

Her mother let out a patient laugh under her breath.

—It never goes away, dlakam.

—Are you eating?

—Olives, locro and chicha.

They both laughed, hid their worry. She hoped her mother meant the non-alcoholic chicha.

—Are you walking?

—Yes, yes, I leave the house! I'm not an old crone. Anyway I'm supposed to stay in the club's pool all day for my nerve. The doctor wants to put me through massages and physical therapy, but it hurts just as much. He stretches me the wrong ways.

—I wish I were in the pool all day. Do you have enough money?

—Oh yes! The doctor accepts Salud. But be happy I didn't have the choice to follow you to Amerikí, because then he would cost too much.

—I know you'd be happier if I were home. I should come back soon.

—Don't say that! You need to work, you need to use your education.

—The job I have is bad, Zosime reflected after a pause, —I shouldn't tell you all about it. But now I did more today, more that I have been, and I can't support what they're doing. They have wasteful ideas about the Mars mission.

—The Mars mission is itself a wasteful idea! her mother laughed. Upon Zosime crept the first cynicism about a job that she'd ever felt. The orphanage of career wasn't just rejecting her; she was rejecting it.

—Then come home, but don't hurry. Midooni ke your ladder of the sky won't be rebuilt for a long time.

—I want to use my education … Zosime asserted, then trailed off, —you should see my workplace. Midooni ke I'm at the bottom of a well that they blast the spacecraft out of. This week I also met my bosses. Both are from California. One is an idiot, and the other lets the idiot keep working there. My foreman hurt his knees today, so I'm trying to convince my boss to find me a better job, in which I could work for the launch of the shuttle itself. In case they need someone who knows the environment.

—That's good thinking! You could create your own position for the needs of the spaceship launch.

Zosime laughed.

—What?

—No, you're right. It's a good idea. The launch was to be today. But it was cancelled.

—Oh! What happened?

—I shouldn't tell you, she repeated. —It had to do with their ideas, you know. What cargo they want the shuttle to bring. It doesn't work.

Now her mother wore concern in the wrinkles slowly settling into her brow, in the strands of gray in the black hair that fell out of her loosely-wrapped scarf. Today she didn't look like a woman that needed to be contained.

—It's fine, it's fine, the daughter insisted, —but now we have to wait and see when we'll try to launch again. I have this long to get myself a better position until the launch, then I'll find some work in Quito and come back. I have my nose full of this place.

—It sounds like you've thought it out. I was expecting you'd be gone a year. Her mother's brows and lips turned up. —I'm happy to wait for you to come back!

—But I didn't finish telling you about the young man who works under me! He's from North Dakota, in Amerikí, and he's like a Greek truck driver. He doesn't know anything, and he used to pump oil. He hates to talk! Her mother didn't respond. —Ypothéto you have to be here to understand. But he's like a clown. He got really soaked working in the rain today. I hope he doesn't get sick.

—Is it raining a lot? Is it warm, like it is down in Guayaquil?

Zosime nodded for the camera. —But these Americans, you wouldn't believe them. They have all this money, all this power, and no brains. They don't realize they're in Africa, so far from their homes. It's the same to them, they do their jobs, they spend money, and that's all.

—How so?

—How to explain it? They only see the surface of what they're doing.

Suddenly she felt angry. —The astronauts didn't like me because I'm vegetarian. She wanted to say more, to talk about the pigs, the frozen meat, to explain why she hated the job, but she couldn't. She was still a professional.

—Don't listen to them, her mother advised her innocently, then remembered something: —but listen, they've arrested two young indios, barely twenty years old, in Ibarra. The police've accused them of being members of Pichincha.

Through Zosime's mind flashed the fall of black night on her monitors, the featherlike path of the invisible ladder's fall, the faces of doctor Wood and her colleagues who never climbed back down from orbit. —What've they confessed?

Her mother shook her head. —There's no news of a confession. But the police insist that they'll charge them with conspiracy if nothing else. People in Quito are talking about convicting them of anything possible.

—I may be the next one they convict, Zosime blurted out, —if work gets any stranger.

—And I'll be next, her mother chuckled, —if the doctor tries to stretch me or make me do anything I don't want to. We're too close to falling into the hands of impatient men, Zosime!

—I wish I could rebel like you do, Mamá.

—But you must know when to rebel, dlakam. You have to be patient with your job.

She wanted to keep her mother talking a little more.

—Have you heard from Behrouz?

—Not much. He wants to leave Iran. She sighed. —I feel for him, I know that this means he doesn't have anything to keep him at home. That's very sad. But where would he go? Where are any of us going? I wish I could keep him and you in a suitcase.

Zosime couldn't hide her feelings, but thanked her mother for the news.

—You look tired, dlakam. Her mother and she searched the shadowy-browed digital blurs of each other.

Time and photographic reproduction were making them look so similar. —I feel so different now. Well Mamá, I'll talk to you soon. I love you!

—I love you, dlakam. Goodnight.

She put the phone down. How much time had she burnt up? Hardly any. Her mother's sudden but not senseless advice about rebelling didn't help; it didn't help to be given a new tool and told not to use it until the time was right, and not to know how to know when the time was right.

She was furious at those three astronauts, at her chief. She was furious at their judgment of her beliefs, and at the same time furious at their deferral from arguing her case for the animals. Was it beneath them to discuss it with a woman? Or were they too stupid, too blind, to see her side? When was the right time to rebel?

Her fury took her nowhere, and soon she wandered back to her mother's story of the arrested youth. The story stunk, through her phone, through thousands of miles of electronic transmission, through translation. Her Spanish was only slightly fresher than her English. After these months suddenly the police stumbled into the iron gate of an Ibarra house and tripped over the two, precisely two, youth who were to have destroyed the sky ladder? And if that didn't stick, they were close enough to Pichincha to be guilty of conspiracy?

No one in Quito approved of the sky ladder. Graffiti against it was removed from walls and sidewalks around La Mariscal while Zosime and her mother shopped for hats and shawls. The bourgeois made pleasant remarks that it was exciting and fascinating but had nothing real to say. From the locals' perspective it could be like nothing other than having a nuclear reactor or a rundown dam right in town. Of course Zosime had remained blind to it;

it takes time to perceive one's place in a new situation, and no one wants to immediately disdain the thing to which one has recently committed one's life. Time brings that disdain soon enough. And besides, travel still excited her then.

She turned on her phone's internet browser and searched for more information on the story. Sure enough, last week some of the protesters against the mine in Peru had been detained without charge as well. As the protest was holding up the resupply of materials to rebuild the sky ladder, there was talk of rebuilding it in California. The boss lived in California. Maybe he wanted it in his stock portfolio as well. The protesters were now accused of conspiracy with Pichincha. The volcano was losing its name to a so-called indigenous terrorist organization that may not even exist.

Why did her chosen profession have to attract destruction, frame-ups, persecution? Questions like holes began to yawn in her memories. If they were working for the Mars mission both here and back in Quito, was similar cargo going up to the space station on the sky ladder's climber? Did doctor Wood know about it? Did ignorance ever confer innocence? Some say that trauma can be passed through the genes to children; Zosime now felt an urge to run. Was it her mother's flight from home, or was it a flight as old as Pichincha, as the birds in the mountains?

Flight to Bushmeat, to the island's Americanized international entertainment zone, was pointless. Drinking alone she wouldn't be hiding or running anywhere. She had to be awake now, figure things out, break out of the ridiculous prison for vegetarians that those American astronauts had built around her. The earth-moving, self-mythologizing force that these men granted to their small opinions! She had to fight back.

4

Veterinarian

Glass-heavy rain drummed against the silo's enormous steel-grated hatch, against the windows of the van. In Zosime's ears echoed raindrops mingled with the muted voices of the protesters who confronted the van outside the public perimeter. The nameless driver rolled his power window down five centimeters and yelled at them the launch was supposed to be yesterday, dipshits. They didn't rock the van, they only shouted and pumped their signs up and down: don't burn up Lagos, spacemen fly back to the global north, Earth's resources for Earth. There was no African Pichincha to make them shy into the shadows, make them fear association, not yet.

She'd checked the freight elevator as soon as she'd come in. It was empty, and the shuttle's ribs hung cracked open and gutted. Her daily work order wasn't in her work email, and Rodríguez and the forklift driver were gone. The foreman was likely rubbing his injured knees in a tight seat against the window of an airplane by now, or maybe even already home with whomever he had there. The shuttle crew had gone without a trace, like a short dream in the middle of the night.

No one in the launch center answered the radio or the phone, and she saw no heads bobbing in its broad yellowed window. Her mind was full of do something, do something, but nothing had revealed itself.

An urgent message from the company, however, was in her work email about monitoring the temperature of the shuttle's huge orange fuel tank. The delayed launch had financial consequences, as the message politely explained, and as such the minimum temperature had to be maintained in order not to overuse the fueling system's refrigeration power. They were apparently supposed to pray that the orange fuel tank's insulated skin stood by its work in Lagos' humidity.

She was anxious to find out what happened to the pigs, but guessed that the veterinarian had likely come and gone. With the flow of temporary workers stopped, Clayton's outline was acquiring a hard black permanence. When he appeared for work, she forced herself to make small talk, as eager to hear something as he normally was eager to say as less as possible.

—Did you see the chief up there in the van? she asked.

—No. But a lady was on board, should be down here somewhere.

—A lady?

—Yah. She said she was a vet.

—She's what?

—A vet, a animal doctor.

—What? Her surprise thumped on the concrete floor.

—The animals are still here?

—Yah. We're launchin again on next Monday. He added when she glared at him, —You shoulda been at Bushmeat last night! I had a nice talk with doctor Chesky.

—About what? She found her professionalism was weak today, crowded by loathing for the job, with useless jealousy, loosened by even the thought of doctor Chesky sharing more information with this insignificant broom-pusher. Always she had to pretend, to conceal.

—Just things, he shucked, —a little bitta everything, he joshed.

—Are you doing anything? She pointed down. —Take a lamp and go down to the bottom of the silo.

—A lamp? You mean a flashlight?

—Take pictures with your phone of how much water is down there. I'll tell doctor Chesky to buy a pump if there's too much. Otherwise, get a mop and pick up as much as you can.

—Where's the foreman?

—Go, we can't have mold in here.

She watched him as he waddled over, got a mop and bucket from the closet far around the silo, and began to climb down the nearest ladder into the silo's dank fundament. Over his head the huge engine nozzles hung a little menacing, as if they'd discharge deadly flame at any time. Just as eerie was the big steel drainage grate at the bottom, like the toothy sucker at the bottom of a pool.

She turned to her cart and picked up the radio.

—Doctor Chesky, pick up please, over.

After a moment the chief's voice came clearly over the radio. —Morning, Zosime, go ahead, over.

—Is Rodríguez coming in today, over? She knew, but wanted to hear it from him.

—Negative.

—I need my daily work orders. And Clayton says the pigs are still here. I need to know what to do with the inventory, over.

The radio was silent while he doubtlessly said um and piped on his teeth. —Why don't you go up and find out? Out at the fence there's gonna be a little uh, a little pen setup, over.

—Affirmative. Clayton's cleaning the silo floor, over.

—Roger that. I, uh … we'll talk later about how we're gonna get you the daily orders, over.

So Clayton had been right, he who now stood with rainsoaked shoulders, gut and ballcap, despite yesterday's soaking, despite the wide availability of umbrellas and forecast information. Perhaps he was scared to go shopping in the gelled traffic that lined Lagos' streets. She went back down the yawning concrete hall, got her umbrella and some gloves from the locker and rode the elevator to the surface.

Routine had made her blind when she'd come in. Behind the elevator cone she'd missed the short rust-red seagoing container, which stood against the western curve of the perimeter fence. It wallowed there in the rain, verily sinking into the plastic trash and mud as the rain soaked in. Drops from the umbrella's points seemed to splash back up on the toes of her shoes, but she approached quickly and deftly avoided puddles. She found a woman's upturned khaki rump hanging out of the container, draped with a heavy green rain slicker and planted in galoshes.

—Hello, she ventured. The woman straightened and turned to her. —Hello, I'm Zosime, I'm the loading specialist. I loaded the pigs.

—Oh! I'm Martha Glass, hi, good to meetcha. The lady gave her hand, then turned and paused as if she felt the need to say something about her work, nodded into the open door of the box.

—It's very sad, Zosime offered, observing the pigs' silence.

—Yes it is, the veterinarian said from beneath her stiff hood's lip, —I'm waitin for your driver to bring some fencing. We gotta gettem outta there before they suffocate.

The woman spoke with a low-pitched monophthongized American voice that Zosime had heard in films, but this time without the bravado and volume.

—Will they heal?

—Heal? Oh sure, but it's gonna cost the company more, now that I'll hafta treat their skin, feedem the right kinda food, all that.

—I'll help you take them out when the fence arrives. She wanted to set them free, to do a magic trick that'd make them vanish and reappear somewhere else, but there was no safe place on Earth for a yearling hog. Still, they would have their native sky, their true blue proof of earthly citizenship, for a week longer.

—That'd be great. Can I call for you?

Zosime gave Martha her radio. —Use this. Will they have shelter at night?

—I don't know what the company's gonna pay for, Martha said plainly, —someone'll hafta loadem into the container when they leave if they want the pigs covered, and if no cabana arrives.

—Give me the radio back, please. Doctor Chesky, I'm sorry to disturb you, please pick up, over.

—What's up, Zosime?

—We need to cover the pigs. Will you tell the driver to buy a …

—A tent. An overhang.

—An overhang for the pigs. Over.

—I'll see what I can do, over and out.

Martha couldn't stop looking out at the strong-hipped women and wiry children picking through the expanse of garbage, rooting almost like pigs, but then neither could Zosime.

—When the fence arrives you'll call me and we'll take the pigs out, and when you treat them I'll take the cages out of the box.

—Sounds good, the American woman smiled, —I'll be here most of the day. Her I'll sounded like all.

—Just call me when the fence arrives.
—Sure thing.

A trip to the surface during work hours was a novelty after a month of routine, and descending back into the silo, even on a rainy day, was stifling. Silently she wondered if this veterinarian would see things her way. As she came into the silo's upturned throat, she found Clayton standing there with his hands empty.

—What did you find? Show me the picture.
—Here, look. I needa pump, there's too much water.
—This isn't a centimeter at most, you can use a mop.
—It's too much! He looked everywhere but at her, puffed himself up and shook his capped head. Zosime frowned at him and strode over to the cart, got on the other radio.

—Chief, can the driver also buy a pump for the bottom of the silo, over?

Clayton loafed back and forth along the steel-lined verge while she waited.

—The bottom of the silo's drained, over. Hold on … negative, Zosime, we don't know where he can get one. The drain'll do its job. Use a mop otherwise.

—Now you heard him, she ordered Clayton. He sulked off to the closet far around the walkway to look for mop supplies.

Her daily orders didn't come, but it was just as well. Within an hour the American veterinarian called for her on the radio. The veterinarian waited six minutes while Clayton let his shift leader finish a mandatory ten-minute break, and then she brought Clayton with his mop, knowing he'd probably want to chat with the woman, up to the surface. The rain fell steadily, but the drops were small as tears.

They set up the fence, but there was no overhang. They watched as Martha Glass slowly pulled the agonized animals from their cages and helped them hobble on doubtlessly asleep limbs out into the drizzly fresh air. She must've given them a mild sedative because they didn't squeal. Or had they cried themselves beyond crying? Across their rumps, distorted at the bottom by their tails, each had a metallic blue number between one and sixteen crudely spray-painted into the wiry blond hair and skin.

Zosime dragged the last cages out onto the paperstrewn dirt and Clayton mopped the muck out. He ignited homey American smalltalk several times but failed to launch. They waited for a passing downpour to fill his bucket with fresh water so he could rinse the box's floor, and then Martha Glass scattered large bags of maíz kernels for the animals to eat. The van driver set up a pitiful wading pool of stiff plastic, the kind for children, which started collecting rainwater as Clayton and Zosime went down again to get buckets of water for drinking. They stood there, then, like a trio of pig farmers in the middle of a landfill, and watched the animals do all they knew how to do.

—We launch in barely a week,

—I know, Martha said, —I'll be here until they go, this time. The boss said it's real important!

Zosime exhaled a withering laugh out her nose. The pigs' lives were important until they were eaten.

—Clayton, I need you to help clean the pen, bring water, and feed them.

—Yah, I figured.

—What do we do with them at night?

Martha took her eyes from a skinny, almost naked black child who'd wandered near the fence and was observing the hogs while wringing a muddy wad of empty plastic bags between her short knuckly fingers. —With no cages in there, at this age they can pile up to sleep in there at night. They're smart enough to keep outta the rain, for the most part. A smile spread neatly across her long bread-square face.

—Let's get out of the rain, Zosime suggested, feeling the rain's damp breath through her clothes. —Clayton and I have been soaked enough this week.

They came down the elevator and Zosime was out of things to do. She checked her radio volume and brought Martha and Clayton into the cavernous cafeteria for a coffee. They sat under Zosime's distant, trash-darkened surface skylight. Sure as hell there was no sign of the feast from yesterday. The lady's aluminum Cambro pots floated empty and sterile on their beds of steam, except for the core of the usual fare. Not even the sauce bottles remained, and surely it'd all been thrown out into the landfill, written off, forgotten.

—How long've those activists been there? Martha inquired with her nose in a plume of steam. —This is the second day I saw them, Zosime reflected.

—Jeez, put in Clayton, seeming annoyed by the subject, —in Nordakota we just have the cops send out a remote control drone and zappem with a taser. No more activists.

—Tell us, Martha, where did the company find you?

—Oh, I was in Florida … I'm from the company! Is that what you meant?

—Yes.

Martha pushed a dull red curl of hair from her brow and puffed her title up in her lungs.

—I'm a life support systems analyst at the launch facility in Florida.

Zosime spoke again before the woman noticed that she recognized the title. —How long?

—Oh, about a month. I was just the medic before that, but they slimmed the program down. I'm here to look at the animals this time, but normally when your astronauts get launched here in Nigeria, I'll be monitoring their vitals from home base! But I'm sure they'll be fine.

Now Zosime had to let a beat pass in spite of herself.

—I see. That sounds like a good job.

—Right place at the right time, Martha clenched her face in a smile and shrugged it down between her shoulders.

The loading specialist found the anger and disappointment from the beginning didn't change now. Someone could've at least told her. But Martha Glass had indeed been in the right place at the right time. She couldn't remain angry at this efficient, humble woman, who held herself like a stoic farmer from back home. Did that stature mark the hidden, worldwide ethnicity of workers of the land?

—Martha, do you know if the boss is angry at the launch delay?

Martha shook her head. —I'm sure it's fine. He didn't mention anything ... You know, he calls before every launch to find out if it's kosher. Your chief probably would've told you if he was really upset.

Zosime was wondering what kosher meant when the radio chirped. —Zosime, pick up, over.

—Go ahead, doctor Chesky, over.

—Are the pigs okay?

Martha nodded yes. —The veterinarian says yes. Clayton and I will help her take care of them until launch, over.

—You heard that we launch next Monday?

—Yes.

—The shelter's okay for them?

Zosime looked at Martha, but got nothing more.

—Yes.

—Alright. When she's done you can gahead and go home. I appreciate you showing up to work the next few days, even if you just go ahead and check on the pigs. We might have new orders anytime now. But the shuttle's already full, so I don't think there'll be any new inventory, over.

—Do you have a new foreman?

—Negative. We'll talk about it soon. I have to ask the boss, over.

—Very well, over and out. She hung the radio back on her belt.

—I can be done with this coffee anytime, offered Martha, —I'm not cold.

—It's fine, we have no hurry today. How can we help you more?

Martha clasped her strong dry hands in front of her on the table. —Well, I'll administer antibiotics and treat their skin. They got pretty banged up in those cages.

—Yes.

—There's no secret to it, it's like putting Neosporin on one of yer own cuts. You can help me with that if you're comfortable around animals.

—Yes, of course.

—Then we'll see how much they ate, put a little more feed out and that'll be that. They need more than corn, but I don't know about … and check how much water they're using. And that'll be that.

—Let's go, Clayton suddenly broke his silence,

—before it starts rainin hard again.

—We'll fill the buckets once more and give the pigs more water.

He stood and pulled his collar up. —I'll see ya out there.

—Wait! The buckets ... from the pipes, not from the rain!

He stood erect, impatient to move. —Oh.

On the surface Zosime looked east for a sign of the protesters, but this deep in Olusosun the unnatural landscape blocked the view. A truck was leaving, having dumped a fresh load of the west's discarded computer parts, and a band of lucky youth was scrambling to liberate the gold, wire and other metals from the electronics before they got competition or got jumped. Some shrieked as they stepped on pointed shards of monitor shells and the toothy points of power plugs. A new smell was coming on the air, past the small pointy noses of Martha and her colleagues, past the fleshy noses of the youth, past the enormous olfactory nozzles of the hogs: the smell of a campfire burning circuit boards and releasing mercurial smoke into the rainy sky.

In the middle of holding a pig still, Zosime received the buzz of a message in her email. She looked at her phone and found that her father had written her. His Greek letters told her that he'd heard from her mother that she may be finished in Nigeria soon, and he begged her to come home to visit before she returned to the Americas. She had to catch a pig around its long neck; she couldn't respond right then, didn't want to decide right then.

When their hands were washed free of ointment and the smell of hogs, Martha and Zosime found themselves in the cafeteria again. The lady floated behind the counter, a blankfaced apparition, and served them lunch. The video of Cronkite, Heinlein and Clarke repeated as always.

Zosime was relieved that Martha didn't take any interest, ready as she was to pull the screens off their mounts.

—Where are you staying, Martha?

—The Ibis hotel.

—Where is that?

—It's right over here in the government ... the place named after the government.

—Yes. I'm nearby. You know, it's Friday night. I invite you out to dinner tonight. We don't want to go where the men go.

Martha's eyes widened. —Is it dangerous?

—Not so dangerous as bad taste.

Now the veterinarian's face dropped a little and acquired that knowing-disapproving frown-grin. Her teeth glimmered faintly behind extended lips. —Is it like a strip club?

—No. They're just not good company. We can eat at my hotel, the Protea.

—That's very sweet of you. Yknow, does the lunch lady over there ever come out with you?

Zosime realized she hadn't thought about the lunch lady outside of work. —No. I've never spoken to her, to be honest! Maybe she has another job.

—Huh. Well, I'll be there, just say when.

The curly-haired veterinarian appeared relieved to pass less time alone, and more time in the presence of westerners. This trip wouldn't be long enough to acclimate herself to Lagos.

For the second week Zosime had to sit down in the locker room and try to make head or tail of Rodríguez' mess, print out the day's timecards and integrate them into the former foreman's logs. Before leaving she sent doctor Chesky an efficient, collegial email about the timecards, the hogs, and their plan with Martha. She was sure to mention Clayton's dourness and lack of cooperation, but didn't suggest a consequence.

♂

The rain had quit, and even small patches of sapphire blue sky, eternally-even equatorial day, lit up the evening. The umbrella-capped crowds packed down every street outside of Ikeja bristled with a cheerful vibe, and blackened iron braziers sweated spiced wavy heat all around.

Zosime read her father's message again. There was more. He said Behrouz was going to cross over from Iran to Greece, and he promised to let her seven years-older brother stay with him.

Her heart, her stomach, her emotions flew in the four directions. She was overjoyed for her family, proud of her generous father, who didn't know Behrouz, but who knew how her mother'd suffered, and who endured the flight in her nature. But she was also terrified for her mother. If Behrouz' journey were to go wrong, and her mother ran after him, or if it went perfectly and she ran after him anyway ... but surely he had a plan. A man with a job and a reasonably good education must be above some suspicion, even a Zoroastrian. If he still were a Zoroastrian; she knew so little about her brother or his father. At last, in Iran the authorities must always be aware of the educated leaving, because they leave for the same reasons over and over.

She answered, told her father she'd think about coming home; she explained that without a plan it was hard to say right now. She didn't say the constant truth, that she was impelled automatically to rush wherever her mother was, though her mother and father now were each a continent removed from her. Would such a reunion heal her mother's nerves? It made sense to collect her mother first, to bring a larger piece of the family back to Greece to meet Behrouz.

She knew her father expected little of her, but he deserved to see his daughter, and Lagos on top of Quito on top of Utrecht made her miss him intensely, made him part of the measure of her life that was passing ever faster by. In a similar way, Lagos had also given her this strange homesickness, this novel habit of comparison to home that pulled her toward home's unchanging simplicity. That plainness no longer chafed her wanderlust's boot, which was now more of a frayed, stretched-out sandal. Her father deserved to see his daughter, with her travel-hardened layers of experience and identity peeled back, so he could see clearly how much she'd grown.

But the new conflict with this job pulled her, too. The momentum of her new resolve to fight back, to stand in her boss's way, had a gravity of its own. She had to wait and see what happened with this upcoming launch, with the pigs, she had to see whether she'd leave this job pursuing her mother or fleeing suspicion.

The loading specialist shift leader met the veterinarian at the restaurant in the Protea's ground floor. It was decorated as any hotel, no stuffed fake plants or fake ethnic masks with long cheeks and noses, no explosive lips and war-squinted eyes, only meaningless abstract color smear art prints and pleasant empty vases. Neither of the women were dressed up; neither had the clothes with which to do so.

—Usually I only have breakfast here, Zosime encouraged Martha as she opened the menu, —all the food is supposed to be good.

—Oh, even just a good hamburger would do me fine. Are they good?

—I don't eat meat.

—Oh … well, you didn't have to help me,

—Don't worry. I like the pigs when they're alive, and I want to help them. I just don't wish it for them to go to space.

Martha leafed through the menu in its plastic booklet.

—Can't say I do either, the way they're goin. But that's what the company wants …

—You knew that they were going all the way to Mars? The pigs?

—Why, yes, of course I did. You didn't?

—Not until a few days ago. I only saw the video to make a farm yesterday.

Martha chuckled, but stopped self-consciously. —I suppose they thought you didn't need to know. It's crazy. But you know how the boss dreams big. I think he likes to show off, even to the lower workers.

All the help was black, red and green, all the clients foreigners. Arabs, Chinese, sundry whites and Mediterraneans. The muzak played *Al Lemoni,* my god, she's like a new lemon! The waiter approached, brought them water and took their orders. Martha caught Zosime listening to two men seated nearby. —What is it?

—Nothing. Those men are speaking Dutch.

—You're Dutch?

—No, I'm Greek. I studied in the Netherlands.

They ate and discussed the excitement around the colonization of Mars that would soon be a reality, while all around them a former colony slowly sunk into poverty and pollution. They wondered at the technological progress being made to try to sustain life on the dead planet, while all around them a fully self-sufficient live planet slowly died of the technological cancer eating its skin and guts. They didn't discuss how on Mars there would be no natives to kill, enslave and conceal, no rivers to pollute, no trees to cut down; ample space to make new landfills, a pollution sink the size of a planet. Olusosun wouldn't even be noticed. There was nothing in the cozy western hotel environment to make them think about it. Martha admonished Zosime that vegetarianism wasn't really natural, that even the paleo diet had some meat protein.

When they finished Zosime took Martha up in an elevator. —Let's go up to the roof, she said, —I used to go a lot when I first came. But it's not fun to go alone.

—Is the view good?

—You can almost see the ocean.

Zosime led them to sit on a dusty aluminum shell near the edge of the roof, like an enormous upside-down wire basket, that housed one of the air conditioning system's pumps. They saw the low unlit sheetmetal of Ajegunle in the south, Makoko in the east, slums that stretched out muddily toward the sea. Above those slums they saw the faintly gleaming glass-faced bank towers above Ajegunle, the minarets of the big mosque concealing Makoko, and in the far western sky a bright planet.

—That's Mars there, isn't it?

—No, Zosime raised her chin at the blazing candlelight, —that's Mercury. But you were close. Mars is there next to it. You can see it better when the moon moves.

—They're so close together!

—That is a special thing this year. They're going to have a conjunction this month. Besides that, you know that Mars is very close. I imagine they'll try to begin the Mars mission soon.

—Is the spaceship ready?
—I thought you would know this.
—I don't know, I don't know!
—I think no one is allowed to know. Amateur astronomers can see the factory they're building, but it's impossible to know if it's finished, how large it is, or what they're building inside it, or when it's ready.
—Wonder why doesn't someone just take a picture and publicize it.
—The trade pacts don't allow it. This would be a violation of many companies' right to competition. Countries … wait. Groups of corporations, I mean, could sue each other's countries, but they're multinational companies. It doesn't make much sense.
—How do you know all this?
—I read. Zosime looked at the veterinarian, then back at the stars. —Martha,
—Yes?
—Would you tell the boss that the pigs can't go to Mars? I mean, if their health is bad enough.
—Oh, I guess, if they were in that bad of shape. But they're fine, Zosime. Once they're in space, there's not much harm can come to them. We don't wanna make waves. You just hafta let go. She squinted at the moon and its companions. —Hard to believe that soon Mars could really be our new home, she breathed, —sure gonna be a long way to go.
Zosime thought of her mother. —Some people go a long way to a new place that they choose, and still can't have a new home there.
Martha's long curl-wreathed face turned from the moon to Zosime, and she expressed a whimsical exhalation. —What would you miss the most about Earth? If you went to Mars? Zosime scoffed, but quietly, and

looked back out at the stars. —What would you miss the most?

—Well, Martha seemed caught offguard by her own question. She squinted up the bread-puffy tips of her high cheeks. —I'd miss seeing dogs chase balls across the lawn, and ... I'm silly ... I'd miss rain. And thunder storms. So, what about you?

—I'd miss Greece. It doesn't matter Mars, or Florida, or Hell. I'll always miss Greece. I'll miss swimming in its beaches.

—Why aren't you there?

The woman had such care in her voice, it softened her young colleague. She told her story again as she had to Chesky, didn't mention her brother, as before. She didn't enjoy repeating herself, but each of the two women silently felt that she needed someone with whom to see herself clearly against the strangeness of Lagos, in whom temporarily to pour a measure of herself. She finally asked: —Where's your family from?

—Well, Martha welled again, this time a little higher,

—we're all just Americans, I guess. I was born in Missouri. Not much of a story to it. So, do you like working on space shuttles?

—I came because they promised me in Quito that if I kept working here, it would secure my job back, when the sky ladder's fixed. Um ... they're not owned by the same people, not the same governments or companies. But you know that the space programs trade employees. I don't like it much here, to tell you the truth.

The words escaped from her, drawn out of her by the look in Martha's eyes. Her character was starting to stand out as Zosime spent more time with her; she carried a sorrow, an agony, in her eyes that was almost unbearable to behold, and it got worse when her upbeat Yankee smile failed to conceal it. —Why not?

—The men I work with are very immature, she said, for some reason unable to put it in more precise words, to expose her superiors' ignorance. —It seems that they don't take the work seriously. They take themselves very seriously instead. The metal creaked beneath her butt.

—That's not surprising, Martha said flatly, hunching her muscular shoulders and big chest forward. —They're not exactly worried about representing the company way out here in the bottom of that dump. Are they rude to you?

—They don't try anything. But they talk in a disgusting way, like I'm not there, like I don't care what they say.

—Yeah, cause probably we're the only two women at this level of the whole company.

—You're at a much higher level than me. They don't listen to me, they treat what I contribute like it's a problem they have to solve. What is that called?

—They, they're dismissive to you?

—Yes, they dismiss.

Martha thought, widened her eyes in the dusk, nodded, as if something had just occurred to her. Zosime reflected:

—I've only met a few American women. But I imagine that most American women are more like you than the ones I met in the Netherlands.

—Oh, I don't know about that, the veterinarian chuckled. —Your English is really good. And you were working in Ecuador? That's Spanish, right? How do you know all these languages?

—It's normal. You know, I was supposed to get the job you have. You really were at the right time. She felt better now.

—Really? They took advantage of you! Then Martha looked away, deeply distressed once more, —Well, no they didn't, they gave you a hand.

—What's wrong?

Slowly Martha spoke, now belabored, each word seemingly heaved over her tongue out of her throat. —I made a deal withem, it was all a neat package forem. They get a life systems analyst, a vet, and ... my baby ... he's goin to Mars too, one of these days.

—To Mars? How? Martha was now barely holding herself together. Above the yellow mist of streetlamp light her blackening form shuddered.

—After he died, yknow, a foundation got him. They found out that he had ... has, a stem cell that fights cancer. They just found out, and it's a big secret. The company wants to send it along to Mars to help the researchers in case they get sick. That's how I talk like I know the boss. I met with him. Over video chat, yknow.

She looked straight into Zosime's eyes now, both of their pupils still starry in the darkness, and their hearts swelled, Zosime's with apprehension, Martha's with grief.

—It'll give meaning to his life, to his death, yknow?

Zosime couldn't speak, but she felt she had to, to take her turn and be done with it, to give the word back to Martha, a word that was too suffocating. —I won't tell anyone. That didn't seem to be enough. —Does his father agree?

Martha shook her head, poking her fingernails under her eyelids. Did she mean no he didn't, or the father wasn't in the picture?

—How old are you?
—Thirty-eight.
—How many children?

—He was my first. The American woman plunged her face into her knees and coughed out long sobs. She bawled between her fingers I'm sorry about this, I'm sorry, and Zosime didn't know that Americans pat each other weightlessly on the shoulder, like fruit flies landing, when saying it's alright. So she sat there, a cold half-meter across the world, and said it's alright. Eventually the woman stood and Zosime walked her back into the hotel, to the elevator.

5

Activists

Saturday morning the rain fell hard, heavier than a nanotube cord from orbit, from a sky strewn with wet tatters of night. Odors of Earth seemed to fall back from it now, as the nanotube cord had fallen back to Earth.

Zosime stood in the doorway of the courtyard watching rain pound on the pool's plastic cover. Clear-edged clouds hung out of the ragged sky's smear, iron-black and arched like the rims of buckets. The Protea wasn't that old; only thin charcoal-pencil lines of rain had scummed over the stucco in the corners of its walls, and the white paint was otherwise still vivid. But no one was going to open the pool for her; the tall concierge gestured to the closed sign and asked if she needed a translator.

There was even less to do on a weekend than on a weekday, though not much less. The drama at work was a dream now, though the lactic acid of resentment for her colleagues, for the astronauts, for the company's plan, made a very real knot in her shoulders. She didn't want to aimlessly ride through the city, aimlessly peruse downtown's stores full of things she had no interest in buying, or aimlessly eat. She felt lonely, because boredom didn't happen to her.

Curious, her eyes found the television in her room, which she'd never used, and she turned it on before laying back on her bed. With the remote she familiarized herself with Nigerian television. All the channels identified themselves as NTA, so the state must control all the television. There were Nigerians playing game shows from America, Nigerians acting in reality shows from America, Nigerians singing pop songs in contests from America, and soap operas.

When she was about to give up, the news came on. Another group of adolescent girls detonated suicide bombs in border towns between the Nigerian north and Cameroon. They killed three or four people at a time beside themselves; this time only one person died when the first girl blew up. Self-defense committees, per custom, fired their weapons into the air to make her comrades panic and blow themselves up, and it worked, so they blew only themselves up. Someone in the world is making a ton of money selling the fixings for vest-adorned explosives to really poor, confused, uneducated people, and that someone is not being held responsible for it. She wondered if there would ever be self-defense committees in Greece to protect the people from German bankers and their pet project the Golden Dawn.

She was about to give up again, but the next report was from there in Lagos. Was that Olusosun's fence on the luxurious flat screen, the unmistakable cyclone fence with the multicolored tassels of garbage bag-plastic tied to the links? The headline printed at the bottom of the screen said DEVELOPMENT GROWING PAINS, no joke. Dressed like in American television news, the reporter reported that activists from the university, who'd attracted citizens from the slums to their cause, were gathered at Olusosun, one of the world's largest landfills, to speak out against the dismissal of an intern from the famous American spacecraft launch site located in the landfill.

The intern, who remains unidentified, reportedly complained to a colleague at Unilag that he'd been dismissed from his position before his contract was finished. He never had a chance to make a salary. The message has run through to the activists at Olusosun, and now the crowds have grown overnight, tensions are high between police and the students. We'll let you see for yourselves what they demand.

The camera moved away from the reporter and the flashy graphics faded away to show heads and arms bouncing under the black rainclouds. Their banners and signs were moving and the camera was moving as well, through the crowd and against the banners, such that their demands folded in and out of vision. A scarecrow vampire with gory fangs and a black widow's peak, marked with Star-X's logotype, bounced on a broomstick. People were shouting demands, opinions and slogans but without a sympathetic microphone it was all indistinct. One could imagine.

One can imagine, the reporter said into his padded microphone as he shouldered back into the frame. Protesters want guarantees of better safety, and controls over development in Lagos. They claim that all the development will displace Nigerians to make way for foreign investors, particularly Americans. City Hall have declined to comment, and insist that the activists call off their unhelpful troublemaking. Activists have responded that City Hall are allowing racist hiring practices to exploit our city's workers in order to appease foreign investors. He sent the broadcast back to the television studio.

Zosime's eyes widened and her hands fell into her lap, let the remote control stick fall away. They were talking about that intern, Godsend. What had he said? How was doctor Chesky, how was the company, going to respond to being in a negative news story? But then she tried to stop worrying when the first scene from *Agamemnon* came to her: we'll know the future when it comes. Greet it too soon, weep too soon.

She put the television off and looked out the window and was lonely again, so far from the handful of people she'd ever got to know. She cracked it open, let the window swing open, smelled the heavy wet gravel of rain, pushed the window to again, turned the handle up, let it fall open from above, reached up and pushed it to, then repeated, like she did when she was a kid and couldn't figure the windows out.

In the distance an airplane's lamps shone under the black rainclouds, and its red beacon and red port winglamp made her think of the sky ladder. For a moment she saw it from above, as it would've been seen by the kids from Pichincha as they destroyed it. If it were kids from Pichincha. Like cutting the mooring rope on an enemy's boat, setting him adrift. That is, if Pichincha really existed; if it weren't a lie concocted to conceal who had blown up the sky ladder's feet.

Paranoia was foreign to her, not something she'd inherited from her flighty mother and logical, moody father. But she knew that this news program was probably lying, if not about the protesters' story then about how city hall was responding. The annoying video from work intruded into her head, when Walter Cronkite asks the writer about the first steps taken by the American astronaut on the moon. The writer says that there's a feeling that this is where we belong. Did these Americans she worked for feel the same way about the developments they were building in Lagos? They had to know that they were throwing someone else out, just as they'd settled their supposedly empty continent by throwing someone else out, just as the Persians, the Greeks and the Turks tried to erase each other's right to live somewhere. Was it necessary to live by deceptions in order to face the strangeness of these endless explorations?

Somehow an hour went by, as they always do, and Zosime picked up her phone and logged into her work email to see if anyone had anything to say about the news. Sure enough there was an email from doctor Chesky, sent forward from the company, in which the boss himself ordered staff not to talk to journalists, and further down the message ordered staff not to talk to any locals at all. Loneliness washed over her indeed. She felt like a prisoner, a refugee cut off from knowing what the locals knew, from what her mother knew, from everyone.

♂

Zosime, Clayton and Martha said nothing to each other in the van Monday morning. She didn't bother to find out what they thought of the television program. Maybe the two Americans were waiting to see what happened next, like Zosime was, or maybe they had drinker's remorse, or maybe Martha was embarrassed of telling Zosime so much Friday night. Or her imagination was going wild and something else occupied them.

They passed through the famous protesters, smaller in real life, whose numbers had thinned and whose vampire was sleeping. Through the public fence, through the silo's perimeter they trundled over scattered trash, to the elevator cone and the pigpen. The sky was almost clear, but altostratus still crouched under it.

—Let's have a look, sighed Martha Glass. She had her raingear on again, ready as ever. The pen was as they'd left it, the pigs milled about, and there was still water in the wading pool.

—Oh ... But then Clayton's oh, deeper than a silo at the Cooperstown Ronald Reagan Minuteman Missile Site, announced the hole cut in the fencing behind the rusty red seagoing box.

—No, Zosime breathed. She approached the hole, found it clipped open with bolt cutters. It hung low enough to get a leg through, high enough to duck under. She looked down, found the trash-scattered floor smoothed down by rain, no footprints. She turned around toward the pigpen.

—We must count the pigs! Someone's broken in!

They herded the pigs into the box as they counted the numbers painted on their rumps. All eight females were accounted for. Males five and eight were missing, so two breeding pairs were shot. Would the two lone females be sent up anyway, as milkmaids, as fresh meat?

—I toldja, Clayton grunted, —just get one a them drones.

—Close the door, Clayton, Zosime ordered him,

—let's go down. I'll talk to doctor Chesky.

Down in the clammy silo the space shuttle hung with its ribs splayed open, like a slaughtered animal, against its huge orange fuel tank. Zosime turned her laptop on in hopes of finding work orders with clues to what was going on, found her radio and called for doctor Chesky.

—Let's talk in the tunnel, Zosime. I'll be down in a minute, over.

—When did you see them last, Martha?

—Yesterday morning!

She left Clayton standing around, uncomplaining, and by the time she walked to the elevator door, the bell dinged and doctor Chesky stepped out, looking exhausted, brown circles under his close-set brown eyes. Things were certainly different; she estimated that the rule about never involving upstairs in the silo appeared to have been erased, now that Rodríguez was gone, now that Chesky probably thought he could get Zosime to himself, even on some misguided professional level.

—Doctor Chesky, there's a problem. With a whisper she touched his sleeve with just enough force as to turn him toward the locker room and the cafeteria, and they walked.

—Besides interns crying unfair labor practices and getting my site packed with activists? He hesitated, waited for her to engage. She didn't. —I'm sorry, that was just thinkin out loud. Doesn't need to be your business. What's up?

—Someone cut through the fence and stole two pigs, both of them male.

—That figures, he breathed after a beat, non-judgmental, unblaming. —Must've been all that negative press. The rest are well?

—Martha didn't say anything, but when we put them in the box they moved better than yesterday. And the cuts look better.

—That's good. He stopped and looked in her eyes,

—Hey, there's nothing you could've done. He sounded like an actor in an American or Nigerian soap opera.

—So what about the foreman position? Without a foreman I can't see the work orders.

—I looked this morning, and there aren't any. I know, it bugs me, too. I signed up to work eighteen hour days, like the boss did when this all started, yknow? His smile wavered. —We should be able to rectify the foreman thing today. Just keep yer eyes on Clayton.

—You read my email?

—Of course, of course. I'll gahead and talk to him. You read mine yesterday?

—Yes.

—Just keep your eyes open. So. Tomorrow the easy week's over, I'm afraid! Without daily work orders I know the cargo is comin back from storage before we know it, and we'll need to get the place ready. I see it's pretty clean in there now, and I appreciate it. You'll have to help the veterinarian,

—Glass,

—Doctor Glass load those pigs up so we can gettem outta here with as little time in that box as possible, with minimal sedation. Yknow?

—Yes, she ejected a polo-uniform yes.

—Thanks, Zosime. His tone had slowly ripened to a personal one. He crowned the transformation by squeezing her left shoulder before he turned his short-cropped head and went back toward the elevator.

She came out into the silo, found Clayton still standing there with his mouth hanging open, looking up at the shuttle. She glared at him, unnoticed, and then the sight of the orange fuel tank made her start. She went to the laptop and ran the refrigeration monitoring system. Even if it were evaporating and about to catch fire, she couldn't do anything but report it. The budget cuts hadn't cut too deep yet, nonetheless. The temperature hovered just two degrees below the minimum, as if the computer system knew and were lazily maintaining minimal effort.

She didn't want to use the system's alarm, and instead wrote an email to Chesky. She imagined that the spoiled child Gopman was probably in charge of the temperature, and she hoped he got the message.

At quitting time the van got halted again. Zosime, Martha and Clayton all spun their heads, trying to figure it out. Some of the people in the crowd must've been protesters, though they had no signs nor banners. The others came from the dump crowd. They'd circled the van so the driver couldn't get through, but not all were clamoring against the side panels and windows. Many were talking to each other. The driver cracked the window and raised a megaphone to the glass. —Get the hell outta the way! Get outta the fuckin way! I'm callin the police!

Voices collided with the glass, some slid through under the weatherstrip. —Let us get these people out! A young woman, young enough to barely be a Unilag student, called into the van through the deafening shriek of the megaphone. —We're here to take people out of the dump!

—Leavem alone! the megaphone squawked.

—Listen! They'll be burnt up when the shuttle launches! We have to tell them to stop coming to Olusosun!

—Tellem later! Get outta the fuckin way! The driver went on swiping his cupped right hand across his chest as if shooing children.

The protesters' message wasn't being heard. Skeletal women were prying themselves from the supple green hands of the youth, and children ran about evading them like chickens underfoot. They wanted to go back into the junk, back to their metallic fires and computer shells full of gold dust, to dragging their long plastic bags full of cans and bottles. The driver hit the gas, the van bucked, and the crowd began to let them through. It was only two, three bodies deep, but he couldn't just plough through. Hands bearing pink halfsheets flew up and jammed the handbills into every weather strip, windscreen wiper blade and body panel seam they could find. Zosime read the sheets as they flapped in the damp breeze. They said close Olusosun, Americans out, don't burn Lagos.

♂

Two downpours passed and shook the metal from Lagos' sky by evening. Doctor Chesky sat under the teardrop green leaves of the Ivory Coast almond, on the faded yellow wooden bench across the dirt patio from the bar. The ground was hard from foot traffic and seemed not to have absorbed rainwater.

The barkeep called hey chief at him, and hoisted his plate of chicken and rice. The chief set his Star down on the chipped yellow tabletop and strode over to get his food and pay. Against the palm of his hand he felt Lagos' humidity as the beer bottle's cold sweat evaporated. On his way back Iyiola Godsend, the famous young former intern from Unilag, caught him once again.

—Doctor!

The chief sat down and leaned in over his food, not sure what to say. —You've got some guts being here, Iyiola.

—Why? I know my city well. The young man was emphatic, fearless. —Is there a reason we shouldn't be seen together?

—You know it's not good for either of us, the doctor obliviously tried to colonize the young man with his province's fear of impropriety. Godsend sat down and folded his arms. —I don't like being in the spotlight either, doctor. I said what I said in confidence to a colleague at work. I didn't tell him to tell the press.

—So the activists're just using you, huh?

—Their demands are reasonable, he insisted, —but yes, I'm caught up in it.

—Why should I believe you? You see what your little rumor did to my fuckin launch inventory? They stole my pigs?

—How do you know it was the protesters?

—It doesn't matter, they put me on the map!

—The map? Your spacecraft launches were already on,

—Don't try to play with me, huh?

—It was you who were making fun of me! Iyiola countered, raising his voice just enough, —When you offered me that job on Friday, shoveling pigshit!

Chesky, momentarily terrified, was too slow for his humor. Generously Iyiola calmed his voice. —I saw on your company's website that a loading foreman is needed! Why don't we work together and put the story behind us?

—You what? Oh! So it's that easy? And what, you're not too highly-trained for the job now, huh?

—The ride from the university to here is very long, Iyiola grinned, —I had time to reflect. I was guilty of pride before.

—That's uh, that's an automatic thing on the website, Iyiola, because we've gone through so many people lately. I don't really need one. I've already got a replacement. Look, I shouldn't even be talkin to you!

Godsend kept his gregarious smile and his educated gaze leveled on him. —Can your replacement make peace with the protesters at the landfill? Intently he watched Chesky's facial and infrahyoid muscles for a response.

—What you need is a connection with the city. Let me help you!

—That's impossible, Iyiola. I think your tenacity's great. The chief downed the other half of his Star and set it aside. —And if things'd gone differently, I'da taken you instead of all these drama queens I have workin for me. But now it's impossible! I can't even be caught talkin to you, and you oughta know better than to talk to me!

—You don't understand, doctor. This is my home, Iyiola gestured around him with open arms, —I can talk to whom I want to talk to.

—But you know it'll get complicated. Chesky's frown deepened and he dropped his brow so low that the whites below his pupils were showing. —The activists'll disappear when we don't launch again for a few days. There's no way they can know our plans, I don't even know our plans at this point! They can't … but what if someone sees you talkin to me and thinks you're on my side, instead of the activists' side? One of the locals? Yknow … who're pissed that we're takin over their dump?

—Their dump. Iyiola Godsend laughed and shook his head. —Their dump! This is not a war, doctor! You talk about sides as if we're at war, but you don't know what a war looks like. Listen to me. He shook his head at the yellow tabletop a moment. —They may not disappear. They may intend to cause delays for your launch. They may only have to block entrance into the landfill when you expect your spacemen, or supplies for them. The space station can hardly wait for you. I could talk to them. I'm honest, doctor!

—I guess you are, Chesky muttered to his beer bottle.

The kid rose and smiled politely with his full lips closed, though his eyes were diffident.

—You'll see. I can see you like to please as many people as possible. I hope this keeps working for you. And I hope it works for me. See you around?

—Yeah, seeya around.

Doctor Chesky watched him leave and heaved a sigh. He raised a finger at the barkeep, who was still visible, as it was early, and signaled for another Star. The beer arrived, and he sipped it and looked up at the almond's little twinkling leaves and their glowing, blood-red, almost animal young stems. He got halfway through the beer before Gopman showed up, kendama ball bouncing, wavy blond hair greased up to the stiffness of ripe wheat.

—What's up, chief.

—I'm eating. The chief avoided Gopman's arrogant grin.

—Just you here tonight?

Chesky almost said something about the visit from Iyiola, out of familiarity, but stopped when he heeded his own advice. —Until you showed up. You get your computer fixed? No more videos?

—Dude, Gopman sucked his teeth, —I'm never givin my computer AIDS again. That fuckin lop from North Dakota's not here?

—No.

—God, like everything he wears has like, fuzz on it, like sasquatch padding, like, for the cold, I guess. Hey. He sat down across from Chesky, —Hey!

—What?

The analyst leaned in close. —Do you have, whatsernames, Sucky Sucky, her number?

—Who?

—You know!

—Who, Zosime?

—Yeah!

The chief put down his fork. —You can't talk about your colleagues like that. You know this! And even if I have Zosime's number,

—You know you have it,

—Stop! Even so, I wouldn't give it to you!

—Jesus, chief, put yerself in my shoes, Gopman pleaded, but with condescension, like in a badly-written film, —you know how hard it is to meet anyone here. Hey! Did you know it's illegal to be lesbians in Nigeria?

—Please go get yourself something and let me eat.

—I just wanna get myself something laid, chief! Fuck me ... exactly, fuck me, that's all I want. You know! Just lemme try an caller.

Chesky glared at him, hurt in his eyes, a strange internal vulnerability that he nevertheless could expose, like a frog regurgitating its stomach. —You think it's that easy, Craig? You don't know.

—I do know I can't just get skizzy whores from Craigslist here. I'm buyin these houses, though, so that's gotta count for,

—You think that's what it takes? Then you don't know. You haven't been rejected, patronized, by women, even when you're on their side!

—There's no sides. You just gotta have balls, chief,

—You just gotta have anxiety issues, like me! Gopman didn't soften, back off, as people usually did when the topic of anxiety was raised. He persisted: —You think you can just give Zosime a booty call, just like that? I'm sure she's aware of the sexual harassment and misogyny in tech! You haven't,

—You're fuckin ay I can just give her a booty call,

—haven't been to sexual assault prevention workshops! Have you? Have you? Where you get made to feel like a predator just cause you wanna relationship! When you know you might never have a relationship cause women can't trust you!

—That's a little intense.

—Yeah? Too bad it's reality. Women look at you and they see a potential attacker, it's called,

—It's call cohonays, chief!

—That's not funny!

—I'm gonna go take a shot.

—Go. Chesky's right hand automatically sailed up to his brow and rubbed it. He took a few bites of food, someone batted at a colored hanging lamp and little yellow stars spun across his tabletop, before Gopman returned. —But Craig, get this through your skull. It's not funny. The whole workplace is tilted toward women!

—I'm the software engineer, Gopman thumped his thumb into his chest, —I'm the important one here, women irregardless!

—Listen, dammit. If she cries harassment, it's all our ass. And I will not be the one who has another tech sexual harassment scandal in the news! So you can't! Okay?

—I'll take the risk. Serious shit! I didn't get here by being a pussy. Gopman took his whole right sleeve from wrist to shoulder to wipe his mouth.

—How much've you had to drink already?

—So what? Gopman abruptly turned sour. —You fuckin drink. You're in charge of all of us.

—You know what, Craig? I'm sick and tired of yer fuckin attitude!

A warm, moist ribbon of air drew across their jawbones from up in the night sky. —I don't need assholes like you around me when I'm eating, and I don't in my launch center neither!

—What? You gonna cry?

—I'm gonna call the boss and get you fired!

Gopman seemed to swell up a little, leaned across the yellow tabletop a little too close, and dropped his voice.

—You're gonna fire me? I'll take my beautiful launch analysis program with me when I go,

—Shut,

—Yeah, that's right! I'll take it with me! I don't give a shit about yer launch! I'll sell it, I'll get the Python genius award and make my own startup back home, have a billion capitalization, and you'll be back changin fuckin tires at Tesla and suckin Vietnamese dicks in Hayward! Huh? You need my fuckin program! You think you're pretty tough for a little bitch who jacks off all the time.

Chesky shouted back in his face: —And you need your Python thing on this launch before it'll mean shit to anyone! Think about this, genius. I'm callin the boss in the morning and by Friday I'll have the smartest people on the planet lined up to replace you. Or that kid from down the street! You can still get fired for being a shitty team player and a little spoiled,

He swiped at the kendama as Gopman sent it sailing up to do a trick. —Put that fuckin thing away!

—Peace, gentlemen, you're scaring my drinkers!

A chorus of dry laughter responded to the barkeep. The two Americans' eyes swivelled out into their beery peripheral vision, which glinted and blurred like a glass jar, and found themselves in possession of the other clients' attention, including the inhabitants of the windows and smoking balconies of the houses overhead.

—Sorry. Chesky turned back to Gopman. —Listen to me. Put that fuckin toy away!

—Fuck you! I'm the best!

Chesky reached over his food and seized Gopman by the wrist, and the wooden kendama ball went plunk against the tabletop. —You don't talk that way to your chief. Ever. As soon as this launch is over, you can do what you want. But until then you listen to me,

He tugged even harder as Gopman tried to free himself. —Or I'll throw you in the bottom of that fuckin silo and run your genius program myself while you fry, and what's left of you'll just melt down the fuckin storm drain! You hear me?

Gopman was shocked for a moment, then started laughing.

—Don't laugh. Don't laugh! You're a psychopath!

—Which one of us is talkin like a psycho, faggot? Burn me alive,

Chesky hauled his weight up behind his shoulder and shoved Gopman off the bench, then took up his fork to eat. Gopman would never understand. He obviously didn't know that the boss had fought against macho jocks, too, that the chief was more like the boss, because the boss called out sexist language.

—Seeya tomorrow, uh chief? The analyst brought himself up from the dirt, untangled his knees from the angular space between bench and tabletop, holding his phone intently and searching with his eyes while his thumb swiped. —You're so gay, he reported as he read, moved, chose, —they asked you for a sperm sample so you farted in a cup.

Gopman turned to go, but his way was blocked by a large cart driven by the pattering shaven-headed barbecue man in his stained undershirt. Gopman almost ran into the cart by the time he got his eyes off his gay jokes.

—Fresh pork suya! Name your cut, name your cut! The barbecue man repeated the pitch in Yoruba. —Fresh pork suya and yams, three hundred naira!

A hungry grumble rumbled forth from the bar's clients. Chesky squinted: on the cart sat the entire carcass of a barbecued pig, a yearling of one hundred pounds. He'd already sold off most of its back and ribs, and the spine, flapping with redstained tissues and greasy shining cartilage, hung like a bridge span between the big burnt-out head and the glistening hind end.

—Aburo, he called to the barkeep, —may I offer you a sample?

—Leave me alone, Barbecue Bros, this is my kitchen.

—Hey! Chesky stood and called out at the man,

—where'd you get that pig?

Barbecue Bros turned a defiant glare and a toothy grin to the foreigner. —Why? Did you lose one?

The locals laughed. Someone asked where did the Unilag guy go. Chesky rose and trod forth to confront Barbecue Bros, but the carving knife rose just as fast.

—You're not gonna rip me off, white man. This is my pig! Mind your business!

Gopman took off at a trot, and the barbecue man deliberately, patiently turned his cart around and left as the barkeep waved him off. The other local men now stood; to the launch chief it seemed they were ready to back up their fellow local, their fellow African, whatever. Chesky stood there just long enough to elicit laughter from the small group gathered at the place, including the demure Chinese and the once-scary locals, and then he saw the crush of people, vehicles, umbrellas and mud on the street absorb the man and his roasted pig.

—Has he come here before? Chesky demanded of the barkeep, to which everyone gave another hearty laugh. — Never!

—I'll get it back! The red-faced chief hesitated, looked at his plate of food, which made everyone laugh again.

—Calm down, the barkeep ordered him, —you don't even know about him, then you can't find anyone in this town. You don't know how to get around, and you'll never be following a guy who knows the district. Listen! Don't get yourself in trouble.

Chesky paid him no mind, tried to follow the greasy smell. He pushed through the waltzing rings of people, over fallen bicycles and children, through faces spinning in and out of shadow under the streetlamps. He directed himself here and there after a glimpse of what he thought was Barbecue Bros' head.

The trail, the smell of barbecued pork, but not sweet barbecue like in north America, rather the local bitter kick of cayenne, ginger and peanut, not that he could discern them, ended at the Agege station's terminated tracks. The crowd stopped at the tracks' end bumpers, their voices gave way to the bell, and the train trundled off, the barbecue man nowhere in sight.

The chief returned to Bushmeat. His plate of food remained unmolested, the fork at seven thirty-eight. As he sat down, casual laughter closed around him, died down slowly, and he started drawing on a suit of shotglasses and liquor to protect himself. He would drink his way home.

♂

Zosime woke from a dream about a white, dead sky glowing like a computer screen over a dead rocky landscape dusted with red powder. Words from Stanislaw Lem's *Fiasko* were in her head. Rather than see an exciting visualized dream of images from the book, she trod over the boring red dream landscape on sticky, heavy legs while a voice in her sleeping head narrated paragraphs from the book, or dreambabble that was supposed to be paragraphs from it. Her father had recommended the book to her.

She was a little dizzy, but rose as if mechanically to the buzz of her phone. Was it her mother? She picked it up. No calls, no email. At the last moment she found the instant message function in her email account. Her colleague Gopman was instant-messaging her, the lowest form of communication, one that destroys the intentions and importance behind the message. It said come hang with me. Then, as if he hadn't finished his thought before he sent that message, a new one arrived, continuing the thought: I just bought a condo in Morocco, I want to show you the pitchers. What is a pitcher? She looked it up on the internet. Why did he want to …? He must mean pictures.

She made the grandiose mistake of replying, saying that she was asleep and was not going out. Quickly, too quickly, he replied, ha ha I got some property in escrow right here down in Ajegunle, to. They finally cleaning up the degenerates and trash. Building soon. Come hang with me. Midnite snack.

She logged out of her work email and tossed the phone back on the nightstand. She couldn't sleep. As long as she was out of her work email, she grabbed the phone back and logged into her personal mail. There was a single line of Greek from her father: Behrouz in jail. It was as if she'd imagined it to life.

She stared up at the ceiling, wanting to know more, knowing that she would've heard from her mother, from her father, if there was anymore to know. Fate wasn't inviting her back to Greece now, but pulling. But that pull wasn't fate, after all. It was the pull of what her mother might do when she found out.

♂

At the end things went automatically for doctor Chesky. The autonomous nervous system labored against alcohol, basal ganglia drove his legs through foreign territory to the threshold of familiarity, up barely-learned steps into a vaguely-familiar elevator, until his hand reached into the uterus of his pocket, grabbed the door key at the roots of the placenta, and he bore himself into the cradle of his bed.

He dreamt of outer space, not a suffocating tunnel of darkness narrow and blurry as human vision, like in real life, but a wide starry field like in the movies and the wide-angle telescope photos. He drifted drunkenly, a terrified alcohol-isolated particle rather than a singular glimpse of everything, as on better substances. The sight of each star violently ricocheted against his corneas and eardrums with the sound of marbles falling on steel.

Space's trillion stars turned out not to be balls of flaming gas whatsoever, but a single nebular mycelium stretching its spores all through the Blue Mountains of Oregon and from there out across the universe.

From within the vast star-birthing nebula crowned a tower of sandy cooled hydrogen and tumescent dust like that found in the Carina and Eagle nebulas, a pillar of creation that had a big puffy star-filled head, a galactic mushroom.

—Brandon, it spoke to him with hardly time to perceive whence the voice came.

—Who's there? Chesky's mind stammered.

—Who's anywhere? It's me, dummy, the mushroom, everything. Its voice was calm but firm, North American accent, perhaps a reflection of his own identity, perhaps a voice from television. It was a friendly enhancement affected on Chesky's behalf through the mushroom's eternal wisdom.

—Oh.

The mushroom let a few more stars spin out of the folds of its turban and dispensed with the pleasantries.

—What're you looking for out here, Brandon?

—What am I … I don't know! … Mars?

—What do you hope to find in the stars, Brandon?

—I said Mars … well, the whole point is for people to live on other planets. So we can go out into the universe.

—That's no different from what you're doing, Brandon.

—You asked me twice! And no one calls me Brandon. They call me Buddy. Only my mom calls me Brandon.

—I don't know your mom, Brandon.

—Okay.

A hangover was coming on, dryness, seasickness. The mushroom must've been testing him somehow. In another reality an electronic signal delivered a message to his phone that said she's gonna morocco my sockos off.

—Try again.

—Well, the point, I guess, is to find other life in the universe! To prove that we're not alone!

It was the most dramatic reason he could think of. The mycelium responded coolly, —You won't find life out here, Brandon. This is not where living things live. You would know that if you paid attention.

—We can change Mars. We can terraform it,

—You're bullshitting, Brandon. I mean life lives on planets, like Earth, not out here. And what good would it do to make Mars like Earth? More to manage, that's all. No nearer contact with other life. Just an extension of your own.

—The world's got too small!

—You won't find life because you're looking for it in the wrong place, Brandon.

To illustrate its point, the mushroom called up a little cloud-bordered dream bubble containing a vision of himself. He was working his twentieth hour in a hundred-hour week for Star-X, enduring verbal abuse and weird coldness from the boss when he fucked up a small calculation, day after day, year after year, for hundreds of years. The mushroom courteously skipped the moment of death, and instead doctor Chesky now saw his work desk, tenanted by Gopman or someone who was supposed to be him, enduring the same endless workdays while the doctor lay buried under his former workplace, eternally staring up and watching his replacements scratch their balls.

—Wait. That was the wrong place?

—As we speak, your astronauts aren't the only living things searching through space. Right there on your homeworld there are billions of extraterrestrial living things. They're moving through everything all the time.

His mind squinted into a mental wind, a harsh, icy plastic sheet of unknown. —There are?

—Beings of every kind of living energy, both what you call material, and otherwise. You're just too stupid to look.

Chesky protested: —How could I possibly be stupid? I've got a doctorate! STEM rules, it's undeniable!

The nebula darkened for a split second and then turned inside out into the drooling glazed head of a barbecued pig, triangular mandible, huge indecent snout bristling with brush hairs, breath of regurgitated Jack Daniel's and chicken fat-soaked charcoal. The only thing left of outer space was the infinite black of its moist dead eye tunnels.

—It's not enough, the pig croaked, —extraterrestrial life is beyond where you've looked, but it's also inside.

Have you ever asked yourself, Brandon, how much of your body is you, how much is bacteria from Earth, and how much is the children of the stars?

—That ... I'm drunk ... that doesn't make any sense.

—If you understood that human consciousness is unique to humans, you'd know that vegetable life, electron life, is all around you. Tell the boss, Brandon.

—Tell the boss this? Are you crazy?

—Save him money. Tell the boss, Brandon ...

Doctor Chesky fell out of sleep, his mind already on the boss and the job, before sunrise. Last night's steadfastness, the pride, and the carefree liquor were gone. Failure was collapsing in on him. Someone was frying pork down on the street, but the launch chief thought that the rain-dampened stink coming in his ear was the rotten breath of the cosmic hoghead. Was the Barbecue Bros, alleged pork thief, following him, still trying to humiliate him, clueless white kid in an organism he couldn't comprehend?

Eyes pressed shut and head turned away from the window, he endured two waves of nausea, heard the word failure, failure, failure, pounding behind his kneecaps in his diaphragm, distracted himself, calmed down, tried to jack off, felt sick again, got out of bed, into the shower, and vomited an oily red muck, like the Niger delta, through his mouth, nostrils and tear ducts.

# 6

Loading foreman

Zosime climbed out of the van, as the driver still swore about the protesters, and went immediately to the pigpen. Beneath the sun reeling up its even tropical thread, the landfill smelled like battery acid and fish tailings under morning dew. She threw her weight against the door and it slowly opened, grinding against its track and probably harming the retrofitted pressure seals, and the pigs rushed out into the daylight.

The box's interior stank of urine, and surely the carbon dioxide alarm would be flashing if it were turned on. She took the heavy grain sack from the hook on the ceiling, unwrapped its scent-concealing plastic caul, and poured the rest of it out onto the spongy ground. As she observed the pigs ate, but patiently, each leaving to each a portion, grunting with satisfaction. Their hides were scored but no longer swollen; they looked healthy except for their spray-painted brands. She didn't know when Martha usually came, but knew she was early, likely second only to the chief. They'd got their wading pool-trough filled with shit and mud, so she tipped it over. The hole in the cyclone fence hung beyond the pigs, staunched on this side with a roll of the fencing and on the other side with a tumble of razor wire. A breeze came from the east, saddled with a strong sewage smell.

She rode the elevator to the bottom of the silo, looked up at the distant gray bulk of the shuttle, and turned on her devices. There was a dimness in the silo today, a pronounced lack of natural glare, despite the blinding fluorescent lamps installed in the wide circular walls. She looked up and saw the silo doors darkened. Had mud flooded over them?

She called on the radio up to the launch center to see if anyone was in yet. By the time her laptop came to life and was ready to work, there came no reply, and no work orders were in her email. The external tank's temperature remained just degrees below dangerous, and the silo's floor was as dry as could be expected.

She couldn't think straight now, not about the banal details of the job, and not with as little sleep as she'd got last night. Was Behrouz safe, and where was he in jail? Was her mother well? Would she be sending these traumatized animals to space, locked up like her brother? Was there any alternative? She knew, despite doctor Chesky's candidness nights ago, that she had no real connection to his mind, no openness grounded in real respect. She knew that she was only an employee. Her chances were thinner and more invisible than the sky ladder had been, and could collapse just as easily. Her hands shook with the urge to act, unable to do anything for the pigs, for her family, for anything but her job duties.

At length the radio chirped and the chief's voice came over. —Zosime, good morning.

—Good morning, doctor Chesky.

—Put the code in your mailbox into the elevator and come up, if you could, please.

The invitation took her by surprise. The last time he'd given her an elevator code it was to risk her life climbing on the wet crane. —I'll be there in a moment.

Doctor Chesky thought ahead of the handshake, the touch of Zosime's hand, the proximity and intimacy of their conversation. It shook him out of his winsome reverie from looking again at the boss's email to him. He'd written a simple response to the activists, a quote from Arthur C. Clarke, who of course was in the television broadcast that he and the boss loved so much. The quote was really deep for him: any sufficiently advanced technology is indistinguishable from magic. It was the perfect response to the superstitious Africans. It would help build a bridge between the innovation blooming at Olusosun and their primitive standard of living, which they apparently were afraid to lose in the transition. The boss's response, a curt do not fucking publish, hurt him, hurt his sense of self-confidence and made him wonder if the quote was bad, or if the boss didn't trust him after the failed launch. Only Zosime could save him from the anguish.

Preparing for the handshake, he hurried into the bathroom in the foyer between the launch center and the elevator. The guilt from his hangover reminded him of qualities of character that he felt now he'd neglected, like thoughtfulness. He wanted to be considerate, but efficiently so. Things that would fall under the rubric of common decency if they ever came out except under a hangover. He squeezed some liquid soap into his left hand before he peed, and handled all the tucks and moves of peeing with his right hand, so he could wash his hands faster once finished.

The elevator doors slid open and Zosime stepped into the launch center. The dusty fast-food grease atmosphere rippled against her bare arms. There was a long, finished console desk below the yellowed windows, strewn with computer monitors, electrical switchboards and papers. There were four smaller but equally cluttered desks, office-supply dull beige, cut from big sheets of plywood with formica facias, one for each of the launch center's crew, overgrown with two flat computer monitors apiece. In the back a large print on panel of the Star-X mission control center in America. Only doctor Chesky was there, upstage left, waiting for her in his starched white coat, tan slacks and iridescent striped running shoes.

—Welcome!

She'd never been up here before; she'd learned that she was to be a loading specialist in the lobby of the Sheraton hotel on the southern rim road of Ikeja. Now she saw what the tops of heads up here saw when she looked up at them from below. He stepped toward the window and gestured for her to sit at the big console. They each folded a knee over the other and sat with the shadowed shuttle and its rockets between them.

—The silo doors are covered by something. Did you see if they flooded?

—Impossible, the chief sighed, —the hatch isn't flush with the ground, by a foot or more. But I know. Someone broke through the fence again last night. They didn't touch the pig box, but they spread something all over the door … it smells like, like animal feces. Didn't you notice when you came down?

—Yes, I guess I did for a moment. I didn't think anything of it, because it's a landfill.

—Well, I'm guessing they poured feces all over the door so we'd have to clean it off. Is the door leaking?

—I didn't notice.

—Well, go ahead and look again when you have the chance. And then you'll have to get up there and somehow clean it off.

—I can wait for the rain.

—Don't, Chesky insisted, his eyes darting back down upon her from the shuttle's nose. —That won't necessarily save us any work. Just, yknow, think of it as cleaning a big toilet.

—You're right, she started. —The pigs ... their water was full of mud this morning.

—They put the feces in their pool, too, then. He sighed again, looked at his bitten-up knuckles. —Other than that, the silo's lookin real nice, and according to the systems, he tapped on the plastic frame of a busy monitor,

—the shuttle stack's in great health. Ready to go anytime. How're you?

—I'm fine. I'm used to the weather. Somehow the weather, of all things, was a strong enough cork to contain all the changes her life had just undergone.

—Yeah, it's wet, he said to his crossed knee. —Happy with the work?

—Happy to have the work, she said, and sounded to herself like an imitation of an American, like the astronauts. —Are we going to talk about work?

—Yeah, he smiled through his hangover, —as you probably figured out, Rodríguez went home. His injuries required ... yknow ... care in a place where he was comfortable. So he hadda go ahead and go back to Arizona. So that leaves us in need of leadership, but not really in need of more hands on deck. I know you understand that, even if our former intern didn't. You've shown that you're more than capable of doing everything down there.

Zosime held her poise, eager. —Yes.

—So what I did is, I went ahead and sorta created a new job for you, that fits. Yknow?

—Yes!

—So you'll be inventory analyst, it's the same work as before, no special jobs,

—And I don't climb up on the crane,

—No, no! Of course not! I really appreciate what you did, but that … that wasn't normal, uh, regular. So it's the usual duties, only you'll have access to the daily work orders, so you don't wait to receive them. And of course, since you can see it all, you can keep up with all of it.

Zosime nodded, feeling cooperative, engaged, despite the distrust he'd dropped at the end. But then the bait and switch began to sink in, and she didn't know the phrase bait and switch with which to describe it to herself.

—Have you read my mails about Clayton?

—Yes I have. And that's why you're inventory analyst, and he'll be foreman.

—What?

—Cause he's just … he's not really hands-on, yknow? It's better if he just be a quarterback, for information, yknow. Just handlin the lines of communication between up here and the silo, and you can still go ahead and shine as the star of the show.

And still clean rainwater from the bottom of the silo, and sewage from its roof. Zosime bristled; her ribs and the skin of her back, her hips and knees, drove her backwards away from him, toward an unknown future at home, but she kept them seated.

—Let's see, what else … uh, and in terms of salary, with a smaller staff I can make it worth both yer wiles. Of course you're housed at the Protea, so that affects cost of employment. He sighed, wove his fingers and reverse-cracked them. —Unbelievable about Godsend, huh? That intern?

—It was him, in the news?

—Course it was. He seemed to swallow her playing dumb, as Gopman had in the bar. —I was about to givim another chance! Now everyone wants a piece of us, wants us to share the company's wealth with the whole city just because we're successful ... just unbelievable. It's like dealin with the mafia. I just gotta find out more. Like the boss said, you just don't wanna talk to anyone around here.

—You could respond in public, so the people would understand the company's side. Otherwise they have a reason to believe that you fired Iyiola because of his race.

—Yeah, who would listen? He sneered with one end of his mouth, his throat bubbling with what he and the former intern said last night. —There's no time to talk about race now! We're in charge of sending humankind to space! What difference would it make tryin to talk about race when all these people care about is gettin to eat some pigs they stole?

—You should let those pigs go, she let him change the subject, ever angrier, looking for where to make him see her side, —out here you can't do anything more to keep them from being stolen.

—We've got surveillance now,

She took her chance. —You see it. Something else could happen tonight. They'll cost the company too much money while they suffer. And they could die on the way to Mars after all.

—I can see you've got attached to them. He leveled his eyes on her, leaned forward as if to protect what he said, clasped his hands in his lap. —I'm upset that they got stolen, too. But this is why they had so many,

—I'm not attached. This idea is going to fail.

—Well, we're just launching the thing, so relax! I told you the night we first talked, we're not,

—We're only launching them, but they're still living things. They'll have to be put to sleep on the way to Mars, and no one will look after them if they get a skin infection. I said before that they don't have a choice to go to Mars, like the researchers do, and their health is not to be ass,

—And I,

—Why should they,

—And I heard you. He waved out the window at the scaly old shuttle stack. —Has it occurred to you that those pigs're the only reason we're here, that you or I are employed here, in Nigeria, instead a somewhere decent like California or Florida? The company can't send up livestock on the little new unmanned rockets! That's why they bought this expensive, dangerous shuttle, and that's why we're here. To move big, complicated stuff up, to support the Mars mission, that the cheap and easy rockets can't do. I accept that you don't like it. But we've gotta follow the plan. Of course it's uncertain. We're innovators here.

—If we're innovators, we should ask what the boss would do. If he saw what happened to the pigs when the launch was delayed. This is no different from having faulty components on a rocket!

—I think the boss … he actually tipped his chin back, looked up, and thought. She could see that he didn't know what the boss would do. He was working for innovators, but was none himself. This young man was erasing the whole operation with his ignorance.

—I think … the boss … it's all about teamwork. If the boss knew it was the plan to send the pigs, even if, please let me finish! Even if they get sick! If that's the team's plan, we gotta stick to it. It's a matter of morale. And science. And I object, Zosime, I object to you trying to impose this, like, vegetarian social justice belief system on this whole mission.

—This has nothing to do with my diet!

—No one in the world has any plan for some vegetarian future in space, and your fussing about the pigs makes this job that much more stressful!

—It's stressful that they put the Mars mission's plan in danger if they contract an infection before the crew eats them! You could be telling the boss these ideas, and you get the credit for finding problems. Instead you talk like the shuttle crew talked.

—How'd they sound? Now he was circling her as much as she was circling him. —Loyal to the mission?

—Will you criticize me for loyalty, when they left NASA to make more money?

She had to fight with him, to make her peace. As long as they were bearing their feelings at work, she hoped he'd fight, not evade her like a coward, nor jealously strip her of the safety of her model minority, not reprimand her like a temp worker. He responded by doing that nodding, chin-circling thing that Americans do when they're really putting a strong point together.

—Well, the shuttle crew is loyal to, yknow, efficiency! And that's our team's job here!

—Will we still have this job, we'll have this team, when people find out? If a pig gets an infection and it spreads to the others … when they land on Mars, and the infection, like a pig flu, becomes trapped in the capsules? Will we have this team when people discuss in the news how the researchers are making bacon to fight a flu, and building American red barns on Mars?

—Instead of what? Teepees? There's no point of discussing that, it's above our heads. How they plan the thing, how it looks, we have no control over that! And who's gonna come out here, all the way to Nigeria, to stop us?

—The boss will run out of money if no one supports him. These pigs put the company in danger!

—You've made your point. He leaned back now, put on his sternest face, something neither of them were old enough to have, something the boss was too far away to confer upon him.

—Zosime, you think way, way too much. Keep thinking about it, you're just gonna drive yerself nuts. No one here can do anything about it. And there's something you need to understand about working in America.

He was about to do it. —And working in an American workplace, like here. We don't talk about issues at work. We don't do anything about it outside of work. Yknow? That's how we end up on the news and a little piece of our private business now belongs to every Tom, Dick and Harry in,

—This is Nigeria,

—This is an American operation. See that number of dollars on your paycheck? I know it's gotta stretch pretty far here, and in Ecuador, too. You wanna see how far that number goes in naira? American influence and money are what keep us here, not anyone's opinion over the pigs, or whether someone stealsem and putsem on the internet and TV for people to discuss. He dropped his voice, conscious of his tone. —I'm asking you, cause I like you, and I think you're valuable here, please do it like we do it. And after this launch, who knows what's gonna happen anyway. Okay?

He slid a clipboard with a one-page contract clipped to it, like the one she'd signed weeks ago, only with a different job title. His hangnailed fingers came as close as they'd ever come again to hers when she took the clipboard up. She signed it and looked at him. He seemed to be looking for the words.

—After all, I'm glad we're still working together, Zosime. He sounded regretful. —I thought ... I thought we could connect on ... on a deeper level, and share our love for the job. But it's okay. We just can't communicate.

—We communicate well, that's why you're giving me this new job ...

—I mean communicate about us! Then a flash of terror went over his face, and in an instant his eyes seemed to run over every last object in the room. Her Italian colleague at the sky ladder hadn't exaggerated. This young American was blaming her for arguing with him like an adult, blaming her for his fear of the consequences of talking, for the softness of his feelings. —I mean I hoped for a better understanding. But it's fine ... I don't know what I wanna say ... you think I don't really consider the things you say.

—How do you know what I think?

He avoided her glare, turned the mole on his cheek to her. —You said that ... you said,

—What did I say? How can you tell to me about my opinion of you?

—You said when we were talking that you didn't want to be around any of us colleagues, around men.

Her face widened. —At the bar? I answered your question about men! You're telling me your imagination, not what I said!

He sighed, lost the focus in his eyes. —It's ... we're just two different people. Look, thanks for comin up. I'll send an email, and that'll have all your new permissions in it.

She stood, nodded at him, which to him made her eyes look even more elongated, exotic, fiery, and went to leave the launch center. —Oh, and send Clayton up when he comes, okay?

The chief watched her go. He'd wanted to say something to her, before Gopman did, to be in control of the situation. He wanted so badly to secretly practice connecting with her, with no risk or pressure. But it was hopeless. Why was he striving?

Now he needed to deal with Gopman, before he arrived, before the conference with his new obedient foreman. He checked the time in Los Angeles. It was ten fifteen in the evening. He thought of a pleasant thing to say about the order not to publish his response, opened a video conference call on his computer and called the boss.

Before the elevator doors opened all the way Zosime was back at the bottom of the silo, looking for something to do, waiting to see Clayton, wanting to strike her annoyance onto his narrow Scandinavian nose. In Quito the job bore with it a prestige, a respect for the operation, a collegial climate. Here those didn't exist. It was like working in any gyro stand. Why hadn't she said that to Chesky, to make him see? Obviously Americans were oblivious to dignity, that could be seen almost anywhere. She'd abased herself to his level, had begged for crumbs. She had to get out of here.

She was angry now, fed up with these Americans obligating her to bear their emotions for them as she worked. As long as she'd thought Martha's unforeseen gush of grief was a fluke, it felt acceptable, something to help her with. But now she asked herself whether she'd always have her colleagues' feelings to trip over from clock-in to clock-out. Whether this neediness would be carried over to Mars, out into the universe, while the even-tempered of the Earth looked on from below.

It may indeed be like this always. But always didn't matter, because always was now getting much shorter. The chief had simultaneously given her what she'd worked for, a position made just for her, while busting down her rank. It was funny. She felt released of obligation, of responsibility.

She wouldn't fight back against these overgrown boys' contempt and abuse of her, whom they didn't understand. She'd fight back for the pigs who didn't have a choice, for the youth being rounded up for Pichincha members, for the people of Lagos who didn't have a choice, for her splintered family.

This path she'd been on had to have a destination! What point was there to studying and working, if not to gain a choice? She wanted to choose her family, to choose to renounce her inherited refugee status, to free herself from the compromise of success in a place that dispensed success but didn't want her. In order to become herself, she had to stop buying survival by acting out the model minority.

While she was at it she may as well free the pigs and disappear without a trace. She knew nothing about sabotage, but didn't need to. If she set it up right, these men would ruin the launch by themselves. They weren't the men to catapult the human species into space.

And who was ever supposed to be the right kind of person, who explores space while children and old women pry gold dust from discarded telephones in Olusosun, while illiterate warlords' child armies blast themselves and Earth's only history into oblivion? Was this rocket experiment really our puberty rites? Were we really supposed to evolve into the right kind of space explorer, as Robert Heinlein implied?

It'd be a break in tradition if we did. For who explored the Earth and gave birth to the mentality of those who created space travel? The Americans, the British, the Spanish, the Ottomans, the Arabs, all of them had their the blind and gold-sick, plunderers, conquerors, rapists. She didn't know how she'd stop them, but to stop this launch would be better than nothing.

She checked the oil on the huge doors in the bulkhead, which had only been closed for an aborted launch, so the grease wasn't blasted off their tracks. Clayton strode through the bulkhead then, hair still curled up in wet points, face as doughy and whiskery as ever. Zosime began scribbling on the corner of the nearest paper, and tore it off. —Clayton, take this code to the elevator and go see doctor Chesky.

Clayton froze with his eyes deadened in defense but his face open in terror. —Why?

—Come take this paper and go!

Woodenly he wobbled over, took his ticket and went the way he came. Come to think of it, not everything was bad. She'd doubtlessly still dominate the North Dakotan through the proper steps of his job description. She may need to move him in order to help the pigs.

While Clayton was upstairs she rushed down the yawning hallway into the locker room where Rodríguez had his improvised office nook. Clayton may eventually use it, but she needed to clean the important information out before Chesky inevitably directed him to touch it.

The most time it took was going through the existing stacks of daily work orders, inventory sheets and timecards to make sure there was nothing mixed in with them. His laptop was secured with a password. It was remarkable how he seemed to truly know nothing about the pigs; the only evidence she found was an inventory slip that said exactly what he'd told her: eight live pairs of hogs. She threw away paper takeout cups, plastic bags of convenience-store food, old advertisements and fragments of newspapers. No new information.

She restarted her own laptop back in the silo. She found an email with a secure link to install the work order and inventory programs, and set them installing and rolling out her new permissions. What could she help Clayton to screw up, to delay the launch, to keep the pigs on Earth? There was nothing happening yet. She found herself leaned in intently, straightened, and stepped away from the cart as Clayton entered, grinning faintly to himself.

—Mornin!

—You were right, Clayton. They just move people's jobs and salaries around however it suits them.

Clayton grinned wide, his one crooked bicuspid seeming to slide with his upper lip. —We got our promotions, ah? His promotion was deeper than Devil's Lake, particularly the penultimate syllable. —Got a nice chunka change comin, ah?

—Yes. And without much of a raise.

—I got a raise. You didn't?

She wondered if he'd assumed that or if he'd seen it.

—Not compared to what he makes!

—Howda you know?

Zosime glared at him for the stupidity of the question, and he was growing accustomed to her glares, and he was getting sensitive to them. —What?

—I was wrong to assume, I think, that the promotions came in order of who had worked longer, and harder.

—Don't get pissed at me, Zoseemy. They made their decision for the good of the Mars mission. Why're you pissed off when you could be back at the sky ladder at any time, and I wanna stay here?

—The sky ladder may never be rebuilt. Not in our life. They are different from this company, because they are serious about their mistakes. And I know why he made you foreman, and so do you, so you must not be defensive.

—Yeah, why's that?

That he dared to ask her, the idiot, drove her close to losing control. —Because men trust each other not to talk! Not to complain. It's so you don't have to trust each other for anything else. You won't take any more responsibility if you can be afraid of breaking the rules instead. Now I have to go and clean the mud off of the silo's door.

The radio hissed. Martha Glass was on the surface and requested a response. Zosime told her they were coming, and they poked their subterranean noses once more out under the layers and grottos of the cloudy sky. She wondered if Clayton was thinking about what she'd said, or about something else.

—Mornin! He called to Martha when they came into the pigpen. Martha was professional and pleasant with them, but looked terrible, aggrieved, as if she hadn't been eating or sleeping.

—The pigs look real good today, she reported, —no worse for wear. I appreciate you doin the lifting this morning, Zosime.

—Of course.

—Not a lotta trash out here forem to eat, Clayton remarked, —so that's good.

Zosime turned to him. —By the time you came here, Clayton, you never could see the fire burnt on the ground around the silo, when the last shuttle launched. That's why it's so clear.

Clayton turned his hips and trunk around toward the elevator cone. —It didn't burn up the elevator?

—No.

—I got some real food for the poor darlings, Martha continued, —there's enough for them to eat well for two days. Then we hafta cleanem out a little, before we givem the sedative. She trailed off, exchanged a miserable look with Zosime, and shook her head. Clayton raised a hand.

—Ah, I'll need to see a receipt for that feed, there, Martha. To see about if the silo's gonna pay ya for it. Martha looked again at Zosime, then back to him. —I didn't use this site's account, Clayton. Don't trouble yerself. I used the boss's numbers.

—Oh. Uh, okay.

—He's the foreman now, Zosime said with a glass voice.

—I see.

—Anything else we uh, we can do for ya?

—No, Clayton, it's handled. Thanks.

—Okay, he suddenly grinned wide and pointed his thumbs back at the elevator cone, —I gotta go an make a phone call. His phone was rounder than Goose Lake.

Zosime helped Martha clean the area up and set the feed back up where it'd be safe, then inspected the container itself. It'd probably need mopping again tomorrow for the faint acrid stench of piss gathering on the floor. The walls and ceiling, nevertheless, were space-worthy, the pressure seals looked good and the electrical system hadn't suffered any in the rainfall and humidity.

The two-twenty plug hadn't been tampered with during the break-in, and remained clean, so it was a good thing for the door and the plug that the box had been left unlocked that night. As Zosime saw it, her bosses weren't gaining or maintaining anything, but rather were getting luckier and luckier not to lose.

She heard Clayton's rotund vowels bubbling up from within the shade of the elevator cone:

—Hello … ? Hayyy! Oh, you were awake right? … well, arncha glad to hear from me? It's African phone service, can ya hear me okay?

—Martha, she turned her attention back to the veterinarian, —may I ask you a favor?

—Sure, honey.

—When you're done with the pigs, may I borrow your boots? She pointed at Martha's galoshes. —I need to go clean up some mud that flooded the silo's doors.

—Oh, I didn't see that, Martha observed, or didn't observe. —Sure, go ahead. I'm through.

Clayton had gone down into the silo. Zosime gratefully put on the veterinarian's galoshes at the elevator door, took the pushbroom she'd brought with her and excused herself to go remove the shit from the silo's hatch doors.

In the dense canopy of computer windows, doctor Chesky's email service warbled a noise at him, indicating that he had a chat request. It was a video chat. He started, found the right window and turned the video chat on. Was the boss calling him back already?

Onscreen Gopman's face was frozen, lips spread in a pickle-shaped rictus filled with chiclet teeth, and halting jets of spittly breath spouted from between them.

—Where've you been? The chief wasn't actually upset; he'd needed the time to call the boss, and he'd got it.

—My dick is the size of a cucumber, the pixelly analyst reported just as the bald payload engineer strode into the launch center. The chief exhaled, exasperated, and nodded at Baldy.

—That's great for you, Craig. I'm glad you finally measure up.

—No. Really. Gopman stiffly leaned in, his waist and thighs totally immobile, his chin hung up in the air, eyes wide and staring straight down his attractive nose. His blond hair sported an unhip, basic part with windblown wheatrows flowing erect along it. —I'm on antibiotics. I can't feel anything beneath my bellybutton. I can't ... I needa not move.

—Is ... Chesky didn't want to know, —is it serious? What happened?

—Last night. That bitch Zozowie turned me down. I don't give a fuck, I was already on my way to a whore.

—Craig, Craig, enough with that. This conversation about your personal life has nothing to do with Star-X business,

—Star-X? Gopman squealed, his eyes widened, his hand temporarily covered the screen of what must've been his phone, and tapped at something.

—You wanna talk about Star-X? Lookit this. Lookit this fuckin link.

A link appeared in the chat bar of the video screen.

—We needa talk about Rape-X, chief.

The chief opened the link as over his shoulder Baldy peered. Onscreen was a photo of a piece of plastic, solid enough to stand up on its rim, condom-shaped, in cross section. Inside the condom were columns of barbs, like fishhooks.

—I been at the fuckin hospital all night. Serious shit. I don't even know if these African doctors speak English, all I hadda do was pull my pants down,

—Did it smell like come, or like your regular dick?

Gopman's peeled eyes crinkled into a scowl, his rictus of chiclets unmoved. —I know he said vagina, lots of times! Vagina and then always some African word, like dendada, dendada boo ...

Chesky shrugged again, slapped his palms into his lap. Gopman hissed forth: —I'd already paid her. She did it ...

after I paid her. She didn't take it out. Or she put it in! The words shrieked from the rim of his lungs like air from a leaky bicycle tube. —She did it on purpose, chief!

Chesky shook his head, mouthing who. Gopman's neck vibrated: —The whore! He took a deep breath. —All that fuckin Greek slut hadda do was come kick it with me, just hang with me. Can't even fuckin walk without tearin something.

—Jesus. Staying home, then?

—Do we fuckin have … do we get sick time?

—Iyeee … I gotta look into that, Craig. Just take care a yerself. Is there gonna be any legal action?

—No? No! It was a whore! Baldy quietly padded away to his desk. —Yknow, last night was my fuckin twenty-seventh birthday, Gopman whimpered, —fuckin almost thirty … look, I'll be back Monday for sure. Don't touch my controls till I get back! I'll be the one doin the disrupting.

—I won't disrupt, then.

Zosime washed off the veterinarian's galoshes and they exchanged shoes again. She asked Martha Glass if she were alright, and Martha insisted that she was alright, thanks.

When the silo's tiny staff was all gathered in the cafeteria once more, doctor Chesky and Baldy arrived. The chief was all smiles and had his bitten fingers woven together in an upopening cornucopia of plenty.

—Hi everyone! Good to see you again, doctor Glass.

—Hi, chief.

—So, is the coffee here good enough?

—Sure is.

—Great. So. I think what the boss'd do, if he were here, is go ahead and make sure we spend more time together. We're all so busy. Doctor Glass, have they been takin care of you, showin you around? He asked as if showing her around were another unlisted duty, a courtesy elevated by authority.

—Well, yes, Zosime took me to dinner the other night.

—Okay! He gurgled a forced, no-confidence okay. He wanted to get his message over with; the Rape-X device had made an impression on him and transformed into the irrational fear of what Zosime might say if she took his plans wrong. —The good news is, the boss says that not only are we launching in a few days, but the Mars mission is on schedule to leave the ISS and blast off toward Mars in about two weeks! It's finally happening!

Everyone gasped, wowed, sucked their teeth. Perhaps Rodríguez truly hadn't known when Zosime had asked him. Walter Cronkite was enumerating the timetable of the Apollo crew's plan to open the hatch and step out onto the moon.

—That means we wanna go ahead and look to the next launch, now. I know we've had challenges with the locals, what with the activitsts and the pigs got stolen, but that's small stuff compared to the part that we hafta take in bringing humankind out into the universe! So the next launch we've already got some companies interested. I know, he grinned, —that the shuttle crew were joking about growin huge cows and tobacco plants in the Mars farm module, but it's the truth. We've got Monsanto on board, we've got Philip Morris, Simplot … and by on board I mean they wanna use our shuttle. As well as, yknow, the other delivery systems. So that means more investment, and it means more money for all of us!

The chief returned his attention to Martha.

—So, doctor Glass, that'll keep your trip really short. You'll be on your way home in no time. So we'd like to go down to Victoria Island, there's tons of places to eat to remind us of home. He met eyes with Zosime, as if anyone saw him do it, or cared that her home was different. —There's Korean, there's yknow, steaks, Indian, there's even a Johnny Rocket's. Seeing's how the week's gettin away from us, I'd love if we could all go ahead and go out to celebrate before we launch. Whattaya say?

—That'd be fine, Martha smiled.

—I was just gonna say the same thing, said Clayton jovially, —thank gad we're gonna get some steaks! It's time ta celebrate!

—Should we say tomorrow night? We'll check in toward the evening for a time?

Everyone, including Zosime, agreed.

—Great. So, doctor Glass, who you see is who you get. The chief gestured with open arms and palms to his loading crew, —this is our core team. Anything you need, just go ahead and lettem know, and Clayton'll put me to work. Zosime, you should have daily work orders now. He gave a narrow smile, turned and went back up to the launch center.

Baldy returned from his journey to the coffee counter, sat and smiled politely. —Will you be joining us, sir? Martha asked Baldy. He shook his head, never taking his cold, polite gray eyes and blanched closed lips from her.

—I'm very busy nights. He sipped his coffee and regarded the lurid shadows between the cafeteria's pylons with calculated satisfaction.

Walter Cronkite asked Arthur C. Clarke if he thought that we civilians would get out to the moon. Clarke replied in all seriousness that the procedures would have to be drastically simplified, but Cronkite assured him that there'd be all those moon hostesses to help.

Zosime got her phone out and searched in her work email. Now she had work orders for tomorrow. The first supply cylinder was coming back from storage. Presumably the pigs and the cold cylinder would come early Monday morning, right before launch. There was another unlisted duty, too. She was to deliver a plate of crudités, cheese, crackers and milk, just as it said in the order, from the lady to the astronauts' green room.

It would be another early-quitting day, and her mind wandered. She got the feeling that she should go over to her personal mail. There was a new message, this one from some doctor at Hospital Metropolitano. Her Spanish wasn't as good as it could be, but the context made it clear that her mother'd been admitted that night, and the time of day wouldn't allow her to learn more just now.

Zosime became frantic, moved by frustration with the rigidness of time, and it came out in frustration with her work's computer and how limited her access was. She wanted to know everything, to throw a wrench in something. If only her mother knew how serious her daughter had become about her advice to know when to rebel. Then, all of a sudden, it came together: all the company wanted was for her not to talk to the locals. The intern, Godsend, had been working on the computers. Therefore A plus B, she could ask him how to see more of her bosses' plans. This was one right time to rebel.

She had the van driver drop her off right outside of Olusosun where Abayomi Abelaja Drive, which crossed the landfill, hit its dead end at the bus stop. She waited five minutes for a bus or a taxi, in which she looked on her phone and found that the E1, which conveniently passed right along the opposite end of Olusosun, wouldn't get her anywhere near the university. She didn't know the buses that might connect from the Ikorodu Express Road even if she did take the bus rapid transit, so the short afternoon gave her no choice but to take a taxi.

She walked, feeling stupid and lost like a tourist, southeast along the express road, and soon she was in a taxi forcing its way down to the Mainland. The hour of travel in impossible traffic gave her time to doubt. She tried to distract herself with the radio, but none of the stories were familiar. Finally she met the coastline lapping at the broad lawns of the university. The Mainland was like its northern neighbor Ikeja, older, colonial. The buildings were planned and made of precious material, surrounded by greenery, not slapped together to store a mushrooming population, not cracked and corroded by relentless rain, as up in Agege.

She walked onto the campus where students were calm but moved fast. Below the unmistakable red-grid façade of the Senate House idled a few students with old unheeded Occupy Unilag signs. She felt bad for a moment, asking them only for directions to the library, and not for information about their cause, so eager were they. She felt her own eagerness from the interview with Chesky still spiraling down the drain to disappointment. The palm trees waved in a green breeze in which rain was reforming.

The library looked from the outside like a concrete prison, and the inside wasn't much different, like anywhere else in Lagos, crammed with people, like the busiest beach of a Greek summer, but everywhere, every day. The woman at the desk told her that there was no Iyiola Godsend. Before it sank, Zosime's heart tensed up, holding itself by all limbs above the void. She asked if he'd quit, testified that he'd said last week that he worked at the library. The woman said maybe he was at the Education Library, down the road at the eastern edge of the campus. Of course.

She found the place and called for Iyiola. The day was getting late and she didn't know his shift. She waited a few minutes while the young lady searched, and then he appeared, smiling wide and wearing a knowing look in his eyes. What did he know? Was that just Nigerian humor? He motioned for her to follow him. As they approached the stacks, he shoved a book into her hand. *For Women and the Nation* by Ransome-Kuti. He was slender and not tall, like her.

—I'm very happy that you're here, mister Godsend.

—Please, Iyiola. They strolled through the stacks at his insistence. He was probably gauging her intentions.

—I've come to ask you for help.

—And you work at the launch silo? Doctor Chesky decided he didn't need my help!

—This is why I've come to you. I ... she had zero plan for couching this thing so it appeared that she had some benign technical problem, that she wasn't planning capital fraud, that she wasn't asking him to be an accomplice. —I wanted to tell you that they think you may be involved with the theft of their pigs. The pigs that are going to Mars.

—That's absurd!

—Quiet! Listen. I know it wasn't you. But you shouldn't have anything to do with the launch silo until he forgets about it.

—I just saw him last night.

—You did?

—That stupid white man is,

—Please, listen.

—I have a right to be upset!

—Yes you do. This is why I came to you.

—Let's sit down.

They found a study booth away from the other students, sheltered only slightly from the blinding fluorescent lights. He gestured for her to open the book, threaded his fingers before himself and knit his brow.

—The truth is that the police already came to question me. Barely two hours ago. Of course I don't know the first thing about their pigs. He hesitated. —I want to be honest with you, but I don't want you to suspect me. He left one message with me, and he asked if I wanted to watch his pigs. I thought it was a joke. I told a friend of mine, and over the weekend we have this big story in the news. He paused again. —Now that I think of it, it could've been someone beside my friend that talked. It could easily have been the barbecue bros at Aburo's.

Zosime's tension eased, knowing now that none of his openness came from her luck.

—They've also insulted me. They've changed my job as they needed to, just like they did to you!

The left corner of his mouth rose, and his eyes narrowed to patient attention. She went on.

—And besides that, I fear that the pigs will suffer terribly during the launch, but I can't find out the answer, because I don't have the correct permission for our computer system. I need your help. You have expertise with a computer, don't you?

She must've sounded stupid to him.

—I don't want to engage in anything illegal, the young man intoned without a pause, a pause that would've told her that he didn't already know what she was thinking.

—I don't want to be arrested, either. But I have to help. They want to send pigs to space, but there is no life support for them on the way to Mars!

—It sounds like you have found out the answer. How can I stop a cockamamie thing like that? He dismissed the idea wearily, as he probably did with every new idea the westerners brought down into his hometown. She sighed, aware now that she was vulnerable. —Please don't tell anyone I've told you this. I can pay you, if that will make you trust me more.

Iyiola Godsend leaned back, looked to the side at the rest of the basement, was aware of the volume of his voice. —I must tell you something. It's not just about them insulting us. I knew doctor Chesky would dismiss me because I was the last person left from the first launch staff.

Zosime's fear evaporated off of a hot surface of surprise. He saw it and smiled. —Did you ever ask yourself why this is their first launch? The first staff quit after last month's launch, and they didn't finish the inventory. They refused to launch something. The chief was an American woman, and the rest were Germans from the ESA. They built the launch center from the ground. There were twelve people in the launch center when I began. After doctor Chesky took over, there were four. Is it still so?

Zosime's eyes were firing in front of him, like rocket engines. —Gopman boasted to me that he was the reason the company was making space travel cheaper …

—You see. I wouldn't be surprised if the company were hiring as few people as possible, who won't ask questions, who can be remote-controlled.

—You're right! And doctor Chesky is angry with me for asking questions because of this!

—And now you want to spy behind their backs?

—Yes.

Iyiola Godsend pinched the bridge of his nose between his fingers, but kept smiling. —What exactly do you need from me?

—I need passwords, user names, so I can see what my chief sees.

—You can learn how to hack into someone's password on the internet,

—I have no time to learn! I need passwords, and you may need to know ... to know ... what is it called? The computer program with the name of a snake!

—A program? It could be anything!

—I don't know! It's very popular and famous!

—A program or a programming language? He waited.

—Do you mean Python?

—Yes!

He hesitated, looked again, frowned under the surgery-bright lights. —I know it.

—I have a lot of money, and in dollars. Zosime began pleading, and her ambition grew, improvised itself. —I'll exchange my whole salary for naira and give it to you. You can go anywhere and do anything, do work where you'll be respected. We'll both leave and they'll never know what we did.

—I can see you mean it. Iyiola waved his index finger. —But I'm not just gonna leave Lagos. I'm gonna leave it better than I found it!

—Good! Do that, then. You're brave. Please, use it to help someone, then.

—I'm not so brave. I know I can get into your chief's computer without leaving footprints. I don't want to know what you'll do with the passwords, but maybe I can help you help me.

Zosime raised an eyebrow, leaned in so he could drop his voice. —I tried to tell doctor Chesky. I could've made an attempt to mediate, if it meant getting the job, getting his money. The students want the people to stop making their living in Olusosun. They bring illness and pollution into the city. You know what chemicals and materials they burn in there, roasting computers and garbage.

He leaned back. —Of course Chesky thinks it's all about his launch, that they only want him out of the landfill. Yes, his launch is the worst part, and I don't want to support his displacing my people. But it was bad before he came, and he's only making it worse.

Zosime's heart soared. She couldn't believe her luck in finding someone who believed in something. Did he think the same of her? —So you can help me help you?

—And I have to help my mother, he added obligatorily after a pause, lest his mother find out he didn't say it.

—I'm caring for my mother, too! She's in the hospital now, because my brother has gone to prison in Greece! I have to do something, I have to help those pigs, and then I'll run home.

—To act for those who can't act, Iyiola mused. —I was born in Ajegunle. They just kicked my mother and my sisters out, with no notice, no legal process, and now they're building luxury homes there for the foreigners. An NGO from a high school student in California was supposed to give her money to find a new home. The student's NGO got her accepted into a prestigious university, and the money hasn't come, not that this is surprising.

Zosime nodded, remembered Gopman's message from last night. She didn't have the heart to tell Iyiola about it; he may advance from hacking to murder. —If it helps you and the people in the landfill, so much the better!

—Now my colleagues here at the university want to start an information service that tracks foreign investment and aid, to make sure every penny goes to the Nigerians who need it the most. Perhaps I'll use some of your money to help them, and maybe the venture will take off. So fewer people will go through what my mother, my sisters, went through. It won't be much against your boss's billionaire investors, but it's some help.

—Yes, Zosime said from a subterranean, world-birthing place, —You see why I want to do this. I want my family to be proud of me.

The young Nigerian nodded, his left cheek in a sustained crease. They knew each other now, and were, in a way, stuck together in this deal. But how free did he feel to help her? She wished she knew.

He showed her. Without a handshake, without a let's do it, Iyiola took a small notebook from his pocket, a pencil, and started writing a list. What computer programs to run, settings in her own computer she'd need to adjust, programs she'd need to install. In a library hush he briefly explained each step to her, its place in the process.

—How many are there since I left? Doctor Chesky and who?

—Chesky, B., and Gopman … Gopman, C. And now Hieb, Clayton.

She spelled it for him.

—Who's he?

—The loading foreman. He just got promoted today. I don't know if he has a work address.

—Fine. Is Gopman the one with the Python program?

—Yes.

He nodded. —Launch systems analysis. He's shown me his program. He may have built it in Python, I have no idea. But its user side is very easy to use … What do the Americans say? Bingo. What time do they begin in the morning?

—I don't know. Don't you?

—I was never there at the beginning, nor did they let me stay until the end. What's a safe timeframe?

—I was in the launch center talking to doctor Chesky before eight this morning.

—What's a long day like?

They hadn't had one in a week, almost. —He probably leaves last. But I've seen him at Bushmeat in the evening! Close to six once, I think.

He smiled at her again, kept writing. —Bushmeat. Did he make that up by himself?

—That's not the place's real name?

—No, it's called Aburo. Uncle's.

—They have slow minds, it doesn't matter what way you see it.

—Eight to five. Short hours for a technology job. Maybe the position I lost isn't as important as I thought.

—I used to be an analyst. In my old job. Now I pull things with chains. The rules are so that only they in the launch center deserve respect ... no one is stopping them. You lose your home so they can build; in Ecuador every young person is suspected of having destroyed the sky ladder.

—You see! If this launch silo won't try to make peace with the people of Lagos, someone will do something stupid, and it will end up the same here.

Zosime bit her lip. She couldn't out and tell him what she wanted to do. She couldn't expressly involve him. She didn't even know for sure what she would do. She felt he could see through her hesitation. But Iyiola was figuring. He waved his right hand, weighed his pencil a little as his eyes counted something up in his forehead.

—The proper time to break in'll be a close call. But I'll send you more instructions when I succeed in getting into your chief's user side. If I don't send more, it means I couldn't get in and out safely, and you're on your own, and no one owes nothing.

He tore the page off its wire spiral, pushed it toward her with two long fingers, started another. —These are the steps you take to log out of his user side securely. Do not change any program. Know what I mean? Only look. Don't ever save. His programs probably save and back up all the times you save. There will be a date and time. None of that. Understand?

—Yes, yes, I understand so much.

—And don't ever let these notepapers be seen at work. Any fool will know what they mean. I suggest you memorize them.

—I can rewrite them in Greek,

—No. We must be able to each know everything. We can't afford to lose any technical information in translation, or you could do something that sends up a red flag. We'll get confused and they'll catch us.

He shoved the other paper to her. She folded them both in half, then let them hang between her fingers.

—Thank you, Iyiola. I want so much to tell you more, but I can't.

—There's no need. We're both the same now, as they say, shuffering and shmiling.

He looked pleased, excited. They didn't need to say what was possible now. They both would enjoy the view when she finished her work. The whole world likely would see it for a moment.

—Tomorrow night my colleagues and I will go to Victoria Island to eat American food.

—The Mega Plaza?

—I don't know, maybe. We can meet then to discuss what you've found, if you can obtain access by then.

—Not there.

—No. We'll meet here, if you want. I can go on my way. But one colleague may ask to take a taxi with me, and I don't want to make her suspicious, or involve her in this.

—Fine. We'll be fast about it. You can step out to take a phone call from mother and we can meet. Just tell me where to be. But I don't want to be seen by doctor Chesky.

—I'll email you!

—I don't have a smart phone, so if you're late telling me where you are, you have to wait. He sighed, kept his eyes on hers, —I wish they employed more women in this industry, Zosime. You're a very smart, inspiring woman, and beautiful as well! I could write a poem about you!

She smiled shyly, but then a brilliant bolt flashed in her mind. She looked down at the light blue paper in her hands, the information she could never confess to knowing, and then cast glowing new eyes upon the handsome young Nigerian. —A poem …

Her phone chirped cheerily and she jerked it off of the tabletop. It was her mother calling

—I'm sorry, Iyiola, I have to go!

—Write your email here for me, so I can get a hold of you! She wrote her work email quickly down while saying hello mother, scratched it out, wrote down her personal address, waved at him, said thank you and I'm sorry I have to go, and rushed out of the library. He closed Ransome-Kuti back up and strode innocently back to the desk.

—Are you alright, Mamá? She asked in the stairwell.

—I'm a little better. But I can't calm down, can't stop a spasm in my back! Her mother's voice was wreathed by the murmur of a nurse.

—What did you try to do?

—Nothing! I started to feel pain on my walk home from the market, and I ended up here! They had to drag me in a taxi.

Zosime came out of the library, was striding north up out of the university as fast as she could without running. —Have they run tests?

—Only a few. I don't know anything.

Zosime was wiping tears away from the corners of her eyes before anyone else would see, losing her grip on her mask of strength. —How much will it cost?

—I don't know, dlakam! Salud will pay for most of it!

Zosime's strides rose up on a wave of panic. She knew that their medical insurance was cheap. But in Europe they wouldn't have to pay anything no matter what happened to her mother.

—I'm still coming home soon, Mamá. We can move home to Kérkyra! I know Baba will help us begin.

Now her mother said what she hadn't said before, what Zosime knew she'd say. —Don't panic and rush away! You have no work planned in Greece! You've never worked there.

—I don't care, she waved at a taxi after a previous one missed her. —I don't care, I'll work anywhere. She didn't say that she had decided when to rebel, that she was about to resign from her job and run.

Her mother's voice fell out of the Spanish hayloft, through the Greek olive branches and onto the dusty Farsi path. —I'm not letting a woman of your education work in a gyros place for a hick who donates his tips to the Golden Dawn! Now let me tell you what I called to tell you, so I can get back to calming my nerves. You can call me on the telephone here.

Zosime withdrew the scrap of paper from Godsend that she'd stuffed hastily into her hip pocket. She wrote down the number, and then her mother went on: —Listen. Your brother is in jail.

—I know. Baba sent me a message. How did it happen?

—He jumped the gun and went on a train trip through Turkey, before his visa was arranged. He got on a boat in Mersin, Turkey, and was arrested on Kúpros with a bunch of refugees!

—Arrested? For what?

Her mother's voice was eroding under tears. —He's been in a jail for illegal immigrants in Korinthos for four days! They only contacted your father today!

He must've gone as soon as he heard from Zosime's father in Corfu. Questions sprayed out from her mind as if from a firehose. Why did he rush? Why didn't he wait until he had a visa?

—I want to get out of this hospital so I can leave now.

—You can't just run from the hospital. I will leave here and,

—And you can't just run from this job!

Zosime sighed. She couldn't prove it to her mother, not until she showed up in Quito. —We'll go together, Mamá, you can't travel in so much pain! Baba can help him now. You said you'd be happy to wait for me!

—It's different now. Your brother,

—I'll call you again tomorrow morning in your time.

She hung up and told the taxi driver to take her back to the Protea. The taxi driver drove incredibly dangerously, yet expertly, with heel-toe movements that felt like the gas pedal was doing the steering, weaving through a solid writhing pulsating sticky mass of city for a short eternity, and she came home with plenty afternoon left.

7

Inventory analyst

Tomorrow night, with its vague leaves, disappeared in a windy torrent and came out of the tempest stripped down to tonight. The weird greenish tropical glare was back in the silo's air, and the shuttle stack looked like an unexplainable stone carving hidden in some Guatemalan jungle. Zosime spent the day puttering, preparing, polishing the silo, preparing it for what visitors and celebrations may come. The grunt work didn't bother her, and she wore the greasy work polo that she hadn't washed in days; she might as well've worn a kerchief over her hair, a chaste hijab, a French maid's lace ruffle. Salary and social respect notwithstanding, there was never shame in cleaning. She monitored how her new foreman Clayton wobbled around the silo, when he left his user side open on the laptop, where he laid things. She clocked out for her mandatory, unnecessary breaks when he told her to, as he faked Rodríguez until he made it. She stared up the concrete tunnel to the surface in the cafeteria and formulated how she'd use him first, as much as she could, for as much as the system would let her.

She finally thought to investigate the work orders she'd received that morning. Surely enough Clayton's email address was included on the mail string. She carefully exited her work email, entered her personal account, and sent Clayton's address to Iyiola. Then the first cargo cylinder came back from storage and she set it up to be loaded by the computer-guided crane, into the scaly old shuttle's chest cavity, without incident.

When he was away on his break, she took Iyiola's note out of her pocket and installed the programs and adjusted the settings he'd told her to. In the fifteenth sweaty minute of doing so, she cursed herself for not taking the programming class that some of her girlfriends took in Utrecht. But her panic was unfounded. He came back from his break and looked right at her and the computer, with no idea of what she was doing. She wondered if they even had internet in Dickinson, North Dakota. She tore the part of the notepaper off with the instructions she'd carried out, and destroyed it.

She barely felt a temptation to go see the pigs. There was nothing more to see. Once again logged into her work email, she found that she'd need to show the courtesy, after all, of escorting Martha Glass to dinner. She'd have to sneak her meeting with Iyiola into the trip back down to the southern end of the city, between ferrying Martha and arriving in time for dinner. She didn't try to call her mother yet, or find out about Behrouz, just hoped that the hospital tied her down for a few more days. She was now in her most alert posture, listening, her muscles light as hairs. The flush of purpose, of resistance, glowed in her heart like a newly-opened rose.

The weather cleared up midafternoon and soon the smog reascended its throne. With a flight-risk mother, a father to meet again, a brother in prison, a massive fraud to commit, a billion-dollar business to ruin and a spacecraft full of humans and animals to avoid killing, this was no time to skip a swim. Against the burning chlorine and dead insects in the Protea's pool she let herself imagine.

With her eyes closed underwater she communed with Corfu's diaphanous waters, with its cave-studded beaches walled in by wavy layers of white rock, with the cravings and tiny worries of the childhood whose departing she'd barely stopped to notice. She did pool strokes and ocean strokes, though the chlorine and lack of tide stole the ocean strokes' strength. Her body tightened, flexed, inhaled and exhaled, her mind cleared up and focused.

Martha Glass would come ringing soon. She took the single suitcase that she'd brought with out of retirement in the closet. She recopied Iyiola's remaining instructions onto hotel stationary, but tore off the Protea's logotype, folded it neatly and put it in the suitcase's innermost zipped compartment.

The veterinarian arrived and rang. Zosime descended to the lobby and they shared for a quarter of an hour the endless waiting for a ride that was life in Lagos. Martha still looked pale and exhausted, but she put on a positive attitude that Zosime knew was fake. Outside of the workplace it was hard for her to think about anything in Martha's presence besides the woman's dead child.

They rode together through the endless city northeastward, not southward toward Victoria Island. This taxi driver, a little gray-haired old man, was a little more cautious, more irregular, not interested in talking like some other chauffeurs. Except in the relatively fast stretches on the expressway, his tempo was halting, surging, loping. Long, arching pauses in forward-backward rocking movement let his passengers take long swigs of the scenery, the faded advertisements, the people, the ginger and cayenne smoking in the braziers of evening.

Rain came down twice, poured for a minute, halted to a drizzle, gushed, sent crowds of people flexing inward away from the rain and the taxi, back out into their paths, as if the taxi, the rain and the people all throbbed to the same mysterious airborne palpitation. Over the two passengers' right shoulders glowed the moon, Mercury, and Mars. They escaped out over the water on the E1 and, with unbelievable luck, reached the thirty-one kilometers to Victoria Island in a little over an hour.

The island smelled different than other parts of Lagos. The warm, spicy barbecue, road dirt and people smells were gone. Martha Glass' nose unconsciously registered that it smelled like America again: new rubber, the chemical additives in fast food, molten beet sugar, that certain frying grease, scrubbed concrete. Despite repeated emails they didn't know where to meet doctor Chesky, so the taxi driver tooled around the island and showed the two women the sights.

Martha remarked that she could see living down in this part of town. Luxury hotels poked up into the air above so many palm trees. She oohed at the ostentatious dome of the Galleria that faced west at the lagoon and the treeless sunken slums beyond it, and ahhed at the silly brick and gilded glass of Bella's Place, a flattened and capped version of Pynchon's golden fang, not that she'd read it.

At last they heard that doctor Chesky had made an executive decision and they were meeting in some steakhouse around the Mega Plaza. An observer could clearly see Zosime's chin twitch westward when she read it; Iyiola Godsend's guess about the plaza had been spot on. As the taxi headed back west she quietly sent him an email of her location, and insisted he take a taxi. The mall's façade was a grid of squares as if it were a pile of blocks, also bright yellow. They strolled through the mall at a saunter as if Martha were actually shopping, which annoyed Zosime, and finally they found the launch chief in a coffee shop.

—Hi, hi! You're early! He shook their hands and they sat.

A young redskinned woman with her reddish hair in short natural curls strode over and took orders. Martha got a coffee and the chief got another espresso.

—So, Chesky suddenly introduced, —we've just got a nice promise of cooperation from the army here. I know that I said I'd do something after our pigs were stolen. We're gonna get some help. As we all arrive, I want you to tell me if you want a security detail. So, who's in? Doctor Glass?

The veterinarian shrugged, lipped a pinched smile.

—Sure, why not? Like she'd been offered an expensive spa treatment that she'd secretly been yearning for.

—Okay!

—Zosime?

—No, thanks, I really don't think that it's necessary.

—Don't be shy, the chief pushed, —there's no money being spent! Not yet. They can start tonight.

Zosime panicked a moment, then scrambled for the words. —I have an appointment tonight before dinner, and I don't want to be followed.

Doctor Chesky turned blue, looked shocked and confused, but then hung his smile back on below his long tube of a nose. —Okay, sure, fine. So one, then. We'll see what the others say.

He rubbed his dry palms together, swiff scritch swiff. —When do we wanna give up waitin and eat? About an hour and a half?

Everyone said sure. Zosime, who hadn't sat down, excused herself. —I should go now, then.

Chesky reached out toward her, his voice low.

—Another date? Will you be coming to dinner?

—Yes, Zosime stammered a little. She looked at the nearest mall map and saw an ad for a massage. —I thought I would get a massage.

—Oh! Great idea. I should get one, too.

—See you then, Zosime said, and left. Martha and Chesky chatted pleasantly about American concerns while Chesky fitfully tried to learn who was coming. He exchanged a short string of text messages with Gopman:

—U coming?

—Can't move.

—Hope everyone comes. Zosime says she has a massage?

—She probly geting a fuckin abortion.

Chesky sighed and looked back up at the veterinarian, logged out of his work email for the evening.

The inventory analyst was making exaggerated turns around corners, taking the maximum possible turns around walls, avoiding parking and open areas, pursued by nothing but the fear that Chesky was jealous, that he was having her followed against her wishes. What did she know about getting in trouble? She'd snuck out from under her mother's nose a few late nights to meet boys when she was a girl at lyceum. She was bad at feigning innocence.

On top of the aimless maneuvers, she was checking her email for a sign from Iyiola at the risk of tripping. As she passed into the open, into Akin Adesola, one of the island's major north-south bridge roads, a message arrived in her phone telling her that he was down the block and around the corner in Karimu Kotun Street.

They found each other near the doorway and silently she followed him, five meters behind over pale sunny puddles and chipped paving stones, into a place called Munchies. They found a spot on one of the overstuffed couches and sat close, whispering once more under bright lights, though Zosime would've preferred to shelter their secrets in darkness.

—You came!

—Of course.

She rasped: —I wish you didn't have to know this. But doctor Chesky is carried away with the protesters. He says he has security from your army now, and they offered to be my bodyguard outside of work. I'm afraid that they're following me. We can't let anyone see us together.

She didn't want to tell him the whole story, and it occurred to her that Chesky had Iyiola's home address at work. How much could they bear to know together?

—How do you say Mars in your language? I'm sorry, what is your language?

—Shango. Shawn, go. I speak Igbo. But I'm Yoruba. Well, my father is Yoruba and my mother's Igbo. Everything is possible.

—I think I see. My mother is Persian and my father is Greek.

—You see! Did you meet doctor Chesky just now?

—Yes. He's waiting for me to come back to the Mega Plaza so we can have this company dinner.

—Good. He wasn't on his phone?

—No … she hadn't noticed. Had he been talking with his bitten hangnailed hands? —I don't think so.

—Because I was able to get into his account about an hour ago.

—Did it take you long to get here?

—It wasn't that bad.

—Here, she pulled her billfold out of her slim-cut jacket's underarm pocket and handed him a stack of naira.

—For the taxi, and your mother. Much more is coming until I leave for Ecuador.

He accepted the money, never taking his eyes from her. —Thanks. It's about more than money.

—I know.

—Listen. I heard from some people about the sewage they poured on the silo.

—I cleaned it up.

—I was afraid of that. I'm sorry that happened, I wouldn't have,

—Don't be ridiculous. You couldn't know. Could you stop them?

—No. I'm not involved. Not that much.

She raised her head from the couch and looked around. —We don't have time. What did you find?

Without a word he pressed a new folded set of notes, same blue, green-ruled paper as before, into her palm. —I hate to tell you Gopman's password.

—Why? She unfolded the paper and looked. Pussylips10. Chesky's password was there, and Clayton's, too. He pointed below the password to a short paragraph framed by a black box in ballpoint ink.

—This is how to get into the mailboxes. Be sure never to click that you want to stay logged in. He logged in and out while I was watching him,

—That's a rule at the job.

—Good. Stay in the account for as short of time as possible. I don't have to say it, but don't read any new emails.

She scanned the paper once, twice. —I understand. Are these programs?

—No, they're like folders within folders, only the whole system is like a folder.

Now he cocked one eye at her. —What do you really want to do? Only to read?

—Yes ... she hesitated ... I don't know. I only want information. If I know what their plan is, I can try to use the information against them. But I wonder if I'll have to change my daily work orders ... she tried to grasp her ideas, —how do I use Clayton's work order account behind his back?

She'd forgotten already that she'd lied, told him that this was about information, when he'd already given her the control that she really wanted. But he just nodded. —I thought you might want to try that. How many people see it?

—Only he does. But he receives messages straight from, you know, the center, where all the information comes from.

He gently took the paper from her, unfolded and turned it over, and traced his fingertip with its bright pink nailbed around the notes on the backside. —This is how you delete the logs in the email database. Don't do it unless you absolutely have to, if you make a mistake. I will try to do it for you, but you should know how. You'll need time, and I don't know how you can do it without the foreman noticing.

—I don't think that he knows anything about computers.

—I hope you're right. If you need to use Clayton's account behind his back, that's much safer than using Chesky's. But you can't just put the message in the trash. You have to remove the whole record of the conversation.

She let that sink in, and nodded. —Remember to commit that to memory, or else make it so only you can understand.

In his eyes she thought she saw once again that he was going to extravagantly compliment her —Alright. I wish I could stay, Iyiola, I really must go. I just don't want you to be caught with me.

—I know.

She smiled by way of apology, of acknowledging how unprepared they were, how easily they could be swallowed by the river they were swimming. —I trust you.

—I trust you, too. You're right, we should go our separate ways. They're waiting for you.

—When will we meet again? I need to try these things.

—Yes, and when you know what you need to find out, I may need to help you take the right steps so you aren't discovered.

—On the weekend? Saturday?

—Very well. Where?

—Where do you live?

—In Awoseyi street in Lagos. It's a new building!

—Where is that?

—The express road and the hospital are right nearby. The rapid bus stop is called Onipanu. Write it down.

She wrote it down, then took and pressed his hands in hers. —I'll send you an email on Saturday. Then we have to stay apart, and I'll go back to Ecuador, or to Greece, I don't know. When I'm gone you can tell the protesters anything you want. Goodbye for now.

—Until Saturday, then!

They rose and left before the cashier, finally noticing them, could come out and take orders. Zosime turned right, back toward the Mega Plaza, and Iyiola, thinking ahead, turned left. She felt brave, supported, a real human in the current of history, not just a model minority fulfilling an archetype in Star-X's hierarchy.

She hurried back on foot to the Mega Plaza as evening fell like a final curtain of black rain upon the damp city. Once more she spent a quarter of an hour weaving from place to place, pausing to look like she had nowhere to go, meeting eyes with darkskinned merchants and spying headlines about extremist violence and real estate.

Less than an hour had elapsed since she left. She ventured into the steakhouse and found doctor Chesky, Baldy's silent long-eared co-technician, Martha Glass, Clayton and some young frazzled blond, stuffed cozily into a broad-shouldered booth upholstered in brown leatherette. It was either sit next to the blond or doctor Chesky, so she stuffed herself in at the right side of the devil she knew. Up close he still looked sorry to exist in her presence. Immediately a glass of ice water appeared in front of her.

—How was the massage? doctor Chesky asked without missing a beat.

—Oh, it was very good, replied Zosime, realizing that she didn't smell like oil and probably didn't look any more relaxed. —Clayton, what's in your mouth? she demanded.

Clayton already had his right cheek stuffed with some bright green vegetative shit, enough of it such as he couldn't close his big grinning mouth. —Iss khat! Iss allsome! He thumbed at the jetlagged youth and labored to speak out the other end of his mouth, —Zoseemy, iss is Brittney. Chew, tongue, chlick. —Ash shoonish I got the good newf yefterday about my promotion, I putter on a plane! She'f juft come in thish afternoon!

The blond sucked on the black plastic straw in her water glass with a thin purse-lipped mouth, like a miserable all-white blond Barack Obama, not yet making eye contact with anyone.

—The water's so clean in Nigeria, she commented.

Clayton still had his filthy ballcap on over his scraggly dark hair, the cap that had a foreign word on it, Tapout, that Zosime couldn't place. It must've been popular, because the same word was embroidered on Brittney's sweatshirt. Both Clayton and his girlfriend had that slightly translucent, white skin that must be a North Dakota thing, like the cheekflesh of a crappie. Brittney looked deeply, long-term exhausted, worse even than Martha, her haggardness in sharp contrast to her age. She took her eyes off of the young woman before anyone should notice.

It was an American-style steakhouse, distinguished essentially by the offering of reheated frozen steaks; the stakes were low; in another weird coincidence, the menus were delivered by a remote-control drone complete with a big camera eye on the front end, its broad back modified to be a plastic tray that sat between its four enclosed propellers. That's how, by the time Zosime looked back from greeting her colleagues, she didn't see who delivered the water. Clayton almost lost his reserve, he was so pleased by the drone.

—See! I toldja they were useful! He turned his eyes to Brittney and repeated see, as if he were butt-hurt over a prior disagreement and now had the last word.

—Where're you comin from, Brittney? Chesky's wounded little boy was tucked away from Zosime and he was all cool charm once more.

—I was in Williston. Zosime found her voice harsh, dry; frozen, she supposed. Doctor Chesky was all charm.

—Well, welcome to Nigeria! It's not so different from home. I mean, yknow, from the coasts. Did you ever go to San Francisco?

—No, her no went deep as an ice-fishing auger, like Clayton's, only hers was reproachful. A human waiter appeared, a stout man with the green skin of the east, and served two glasses of beer.

—Thanks so much, Chesky smiled, —So what're your plans while you're here? Beside watching the launch!

—Oh, I don't … I don't have any yet. Her eyes were trying involuntarily to meet with his and Clayton's, but she was holding back.

Then the drone reappears, just for show, and delicately lands on the table in front of them all, and on its tray a tall glass boot of beer.

—Ah ha! Here we are! Chesky claimed the boot and toasted Martha and Clayton. —Oop, we gotta get you one, too, Zosime. Brittney, can't I get you a drink? Don't be shy, the boss is payin!

—No, again that reproachful no, regardless of race, creed, origin or sexual orientation. —I'm a former addict. I haven't used since I was nineteen.

Her used was also deep and liquid, yuwuzzed, unsettling to the uninitiated.

—Oh, Chesky's mandible scooped, —well, that's great, too.

—So it's pretty awkward that Clayton discovered this new drug about an hour ago.

—I'm not gonna quit. Clayton's tone was final, or nondescript, which in their North Dakotan dialect could either be simply declarative or awesomely aggressive. Only the two of them knew which. His khat grin, at once crunched down in some primeval defense, now rose again.

Chesky smiled at Brittney. —Enjoy yourself, in any case.

Zosime heaved a sigh. Clearly tonight would be another marathon of holding people's emotions for them. She put up her index finger and ordered a Star from the waiter, and they ordered their food.

Shortly huge steaks arrived on droneback, dressed with little spherical potatoes or a baked potato or mashed potatoes, a dash of oil and rosemary, precisely one enormous piece of broccoli, and a bottle of A-1 steak sauce for each, with which to overwhelm all other flavors. Zosime received a dish of mushroom ravioli with cream sauce, probably the hidden gem of the menu, in a medium of finely-chopped sautéed vegetables in a demi-glace. The earthy, oily mushroom scent traveled with nutmeg and coriander. Clayton reluctantly stood and went to the bathroom to get rid of his faceful of khat, or perhaps preserve it in a sandwich bag.

Zosime felt small gratitude for eating with colleagues in a cleaner, quieter place for once. She almost felt bad for what she was about to do to doctor Chesky's mission, though she didn't yet know what she was about to do. She listened to what all the Americans talked about when they were together, and learned. They mostly talked about money, the prices of things, plans for their money, scary stories about former and expected problems with money. Sometimes they spoke with the same excitement, samely devoid of content, about the Mars mission, just like people did in Quito when the sky ladder was still standing.

Brittney complained of wanting something good to drink, so Clayton, who'd finished eating first, stood and excused himself to go find something. He didn't go out, but rather to the bar, and had a Long Island iced tea by himself.

Martha, who'd got up to let him out of the wide booth, said she'd better be going.

—No, doctor Chesky protested, —stay! Why don't we go to the bar, get some fresh air, and hang a little longer? It's early!

They said okay and followed after Clayton to the bar. They distributed themselves comfortably on stools at small tables, Martha and Zosime, the two North Dakotans with the chief and the long-eared technician.

—Have a drink with me, Zosime told the veterinarian. She activated her inner good host, her party instinct. It may hold off the emotional storm these Americans seemed always to be under. The veterinarian got a glass of red wine and Zosime found herself once again nodding ever slowly at a gleaming shotglass of Pernod.

—Is that yer digestive?

—Yes.

Clayton presented to Brittney a spritzing glass of bar orange juice and dry bar grenadine, like a tequila sunrise. Brittney said she was tired and wanted to get some sleep.

Doctor Chesky ignored their weird invisible bickering and reflected a second. Watching Zosime be herself, the movements of her face and body that he found so hard and foreign, there and then he gave up his illusions of her, and gave up trying to get closer to her. He was just going to accept their relationship for what it was, for the good of the mission, so she'd stop criticizing it all the time. That would do it. Because she'd been criticizing him really, and not the mission. After twelve tries in five years, he reflected that trying to get relationships from work hadn't really worked out.

He excused himself from the technician and leaned over to Zosime's table, the boot of beer starting to course through him. —Zosime, thanks so much for being on base for doctor Glass.

—Of course, chief.

—Listen, he did that drunk listen thing, as if his life depended on her hearing something and he'd got the unnerving signal that she wouldn't listen. Then, secure that he had her attention, he took another swig. —This launch operation is my life, Zosime.

—It's not your life, doctor, it's only a job.

He took that hard, still not knowing her plain manner of speaking. He whispered: —Yeah well. Listen. You were right about the pigs.

A shock went through her that she couldn't hide. Her brow rose slowly for him, she was so calm and collected! —Then you will let them stay on Earth?

—Mmm ... well, hear me out. I just wantcha to know, in the future, when this is all over, I'll remember that you were right. Yknow?

—Thank you, chief.

When what was all over? When low-gravity giant tobacco and space pigs became normal, a cultural necessity in the Americans' short memory, when he no longer had his hands in the matter? Or perhaps he meant that he accepted the potential failure of the pig experiment.

She turned back to the veterinarian and took her hit of Pernod. Chesky's emotions couldn't touch her. He smiled once more at Martha and went back to his boot and Long-ears, who was absorbed in the televised sports.

—How's the wine, Martha? Zosime asked.

—Oh, it's good. I never had Italian wine before, it's pretty good.

—Is that so?

—Yeah, Martha pinched forth a smile, —I like the stuff from Napa more, though.

—Napa, where is that?

—Oh, it's in California. It's very famous!

—Of course.

Martha finished her glass. Her wide, dark eyes shone under the large-screen televisions, reflecting the motions of athletes waist-deep in her gathering tears. —Zosime, want to go to the restroom? The women's international SOS code: a request to go to the restroom. Zosime nodded and stood, zipped up her jacket. They headed back toward the kitchen, pursued by the technician's cry that sounded as some sports thing happened.

In the restroom two older white women with dyed-blond hair and enormous obsidian insect sunglasses were bent over the sink doing those gestures that make it impossible to know whether they were crushing and snorting makeup or applying fresh antipsychotic pills. They didn't take heed of Zosime and Martha. Martha led her young confidant by the sleeve cuff into a toilet stall.

—I need your help, Zosime, she whispered, —I need you to get me information about your launch inventory. Can you do that?

Zosime's automatic response to the cry for help wore off and she found herself in a toilet stall speaking her fourth language. —What do you mean with that?

—If … I just … if there's a medical supply container suddenly added to the cargo, will you tell me? My boy … you know?

—I don't know, Martha, I can't help you. I don't have a list of anything that's added to the shuttle. It's been full since you came.

—I know you don't! He's … the cell samples aren't documented anywhere. They promised me it'd be anonymous. But if you find out, I need to know. I'm scared they'll sit on the cells, that they won't sendem to Mars! I just wanna know.

—You should ask doctor Chesky, Martha, I don't know.

—Doctor Chesky! Some desperate idea in her brain cavity pushed her eyeballs out of their sockets. —I could tell him, Zosime! That the pigs can't go. I could do that for you! I could tell him they're too sick! To make room for my boy! Zosime, you understand what it's like to have something in this launch that means so much to you!

—You can do what you want, Martha! I don't know if your … if parts of you son are here or not. You must ask him if you want to know.

—Please, Zosime. Will you tell me that you'll at least try? I can't have this all go to waste …

Just as Martha's guilt came unleashed behind her first glass of wine, so Zosime's patience unwound. —Martha, did they not pay you for your baby?

Martha's bread-square face shrunk inward in horror and she looked out at nothing. —You're right …

Zosime's heart fell into her stomach. The veterinarian was taking her reaction too far, just as Chesky had moments ago. —Of course they paid me. I needa suck it up.

Martha Glass turned her head away, then the top of her body. She was going to flee, as she had on the roof of the Protea. This party would be over soon. One of the women at the sink squealed, and the tiles echoed as she probably landed flat on her skinny ass, perhaps her black alligator skin boots even flew off as in a cartoon, exposing her somehow indecent wrinkly-tipped stockings. The two women from the launch center didn't turn to look as they exited.

They came out back into the bar and doctor Chesky was drinking something colored with bar orange juice, his glass boot and technician gone without a trace.

—Everything come out alright, ladies? he chuckled at them. Martha, blinking back tears, said she really must be going. The chief turned to Clayton and Brittney. —You two have plans?

—Oh, we're goin out fer sure!

—Zosime?

—I have no plans.

Doctor Chesky took a look at Martha and reckoned.

—Okay. How bout I see Martha home, then, and you guys get on with your night.

He shook everyone's hand, said thanks and this was fun, and with his hand on Martha's shoulder went out to find a taxi. Zosime watched them and felt awful for a moment. Maybe the veterinarian would make her request now and have it done. Clayton then appeared at her left with a big grin on his whiskery face and presenting a red foil bag of Arbor Mist daiquiri mix, which he foisted upon Brittney. —So, let's go back up nort, yah?

Zosime followed them into a taxi as not to be alone. The driver tried to take them to his brother's night club, even almost coming to park in front of it, and showered the place's business card upon them with a toss behind his shoulder, didn't stop talking about it the whole time and what a great guy his brother's wife was, who either danced at the place or served drinks or managed it or all three. They convinced him to move on before he parked to keep heading nort, as Clayton said while he and Zosime exchanged an unfinished disagreement over whether they were bound for Ikeja or Agege.

Zosime sweated in the heated back seat between Brittney and the fogged-up window. The foil daiquiri mix pouch jiggled in the girl's lap.

—I wanna go to sleep, Brittney moaned.

—Soon you will, Zosime said quietly to her.

—Do you like this job? the girl abruptly asked.

—I like it alright. It's not very interesting. I only load boxes into the spacecraft. She exhaled and rubbed her brow. —And I miss my family.

—You don't even know.

—I do know.

—Well, I know a lot, too. Brittney's rebuke, and her too as deep as permafrost, told Zosime that she didn't have a right to talk to the young woman about having problems, —My brother's disabled and stuck in the youth corrections in Bismarck, and my mom died. I was born addicted to meth. That's why I was using, not cause I liked it! If you miss your family you should try therapy, I don't know why everyone's so scared of it.

—People don't like therapy in America?

The girl looked at her, confused. Clayton's disquieted straight-ahead glare wavered once toward Zosime. This girl was adamant that her personal problems were so much worse than hers, that she didn't have a right to criticize, to discuss anything the girl knew about in a way unfamiliar to her.

—So where to, boss? Ikeja or Agege?

—Ageegee! Clayton hooted, —I can't wait to get some bushmeat!

The car skidded to a halt. The driver's right hand grabbed the headrest of the passenger seat and his head swung around. He was young, and in the absence of his affected sales pitch he had an alert, critical face. Maybe he was a student. —Get out of my cab.

They got out, Brittney looking terrified and Clayton absorbed in his aloof silence. The taxi turned around and went back the way it came. They were on some anonymous curb glistening in the rainy moonlight, in front of some low anonymous building that probably had a dentist's office in it, desolate at night, melted by constant humidity. The street was brightly lit from lamps hanging over the expressway on the other side of the fence, but empty as a country road. A cloud could burst any second and drench them.

About ten such seconds passed in which they all looked at each other, but then wouldntcha know it, up pulls a blocky black truck with the windows down. The three stranded travelers squinted and found a Nigerian's dome-lit brow over benighted eyes. —You're Star-X? Doctor Chesky?

Zosime thought yes, idiots! No one said it, so she did.

—Come aboard, came the impatient bureaucrat voice.

Once they were on the expressway the soldier shifted his right eye toward Zosime, who'd got in the passenger seat beside him. —Where you going?

Zosime guessed he must've known her address, but she didn't want to be watched going home anyway, if she could help it. She turned her head toward Brittney, felt sorry for the girl again, and replied: —We're going to Agege. To near the stadium.

—Little watering hole, the colored soldier's colorless voice demanded, —little dancing spot?

—Just a kitchen open late, she explained softly.

She hated Chesky. This felt like a kidnapping, a coercion. Her mother's words came to her from the dewy grass and bare winter trees of some park in Utrecht: never let yourself get into a situation where only a man can guarantee your safety. She led him from the E1 over the slums and the edge of Olusosun into the Isheri road, substantially north of Agege, that turned back southwest into the city and dumped them into the narrow, still-busy Ogba road. The spiky air of peanut, spices and alkaline mud returned through the truck's air circulation. She got Clayton and Brittney out and the soldier wanted to leave to find a parking spot. That would give her a few minutes of privacy.

Clayton strode into Bushmeat like he knew everyone, shouted hey at the barkeep, and ordered Stars for himself and Zoseemy as he said it. It wasn't crowded, so they sat at the bar.

—Hon, let's getcha straw for that daiquiri! Boss! Howbout a straw?

The barkeep turned efficiently and brought back a black straw. Brittney threw the pouch of daiquiri mix on the bar in disgust, and he obligingly poked the straw through the pouch's top after Clayton's instructions. He was indeed a skilled barkeep. —Good to see you tonight, madame, he crooned to Zosime.

—There! Now it's like ah … ah … he laughed,
—whattaya call those drinks?

Neither of the women responded. He stuttered on it, undeterred. —Ca … caprice sun! Ha ha ha! Cool, huh honey?

Brittney dropped her face and sipped the thing deeply, then brought her face back up under the strings of chili lights and asked the barkeep for a glass of water, catching the long strands of blond hair that fell over her brow. They sipped their drinks, only Clayton drinking with enthusiasm.

After a few minutes Clayton ordered a cocktail and it was clear that his previous drinks were starting to add up.

—I don't wanna stay, Brittney protested, —this is so inappropriate.

—Alright, alright, lemme just relax a little longer. Boss! Two more.

Now he had his cocktail in front of him plus a double of vodka. —You don't wanna take in the scenery?

—What scenery? Brittney gestured around the soggy-floored bar, —take in all the men who're thinkin about raping me?

—Shh! Jeez, he fastened his lips on his straw again and sucked down some cocktail. —Okay, lemme take a piss. Boss, still no bathroom?

—No. Try around the corner.

Clayton lumbered off. Brittney shoved away her pouch of daiquiri mix and turned a shocked face to Zosime. —There's no bathroom here?

Zosime sipped her beer. —No. I've got used to it.

—When's he comin back?

—I don't know. Relax, everything's fine. You're not used to how many people are in Lagos. I'll take you home soon.

—I do not wanna be here.

—I'm sorry.

Clayton came back and sat down again at his drinks. —Just wait'll I show you the silo tomorrow, hon! It'll blow yer mind.

Zosime wanted to question whether she'd be allowed in, but let it go. —Yknow, this is a new career, guys. I wanna go up the ladder and get a chance to work in space, seriously!

Brittney spun on him, suddenly furious again as she'd been in the taxi. —Really? Really.

—What?

—I just get off the plane, and you're talkin about leaving?

—I'm just makin conversation! You're all so stressed if we don't talk, talk, talk,

—Just finish your drinks, then, and don't talk.

Clayton obliged his pale young girlfriend and threw back one of his shots.

—I'm gonna go get some air. And he stood and left again. Faintly he was heard repeating the word khat, khat, to people on the street as if they couldn't speak English.

Half a second later Brittney, as if waiting, spun now upon Zosime, her dead-serious eyes full of destiny. She did a no-look and reached for Clayton's other drink, pulled it down through her lips before Zosime could respond, never taking her gaze from her boyfriend's colleague.

—Zosime, she said the name correctly, —I need to talk to you.

—What is it, Brittney? She couldn't sound patient, but the girl didn't care.

—You're the only one here who's smart. I can see that.

—I don't,

—And you're incredibly beautiful. Where're you from?

—Greece, she reluctantly answered.

—Let's go, let's just go while Clayton's drunk. I'll wait till he's good and,

—Go where? Should I ride with you until your hotel?

—I don't have a room, I was gonna stay with Clayton! But things're speeding up now.

—Things? Zosime thought she'd reached a new level of travesty. But this girl was terrified.

—I have a plan, Zosime. She steadied herself, probably sick from the vodka after her period of sobriety.

—Since I left home I've realized that I hafta make a clean break. She grasped Zosime's forearm, rubbed the leatherlike material of her jacket nervously with her thumb, —I'll just end up using again if I have anything to do with home, and that includes staying with Clayton. I'm gonna run to Paris and become an actress. If you'll let me stay with you tonight, that's all I'm asking! I have money,

—Brittney, I don't think Clayton will have problems,

—Please. She took Zosime's bottle with her free hand and drank down the rest. —I can make it worth your wile. I won't get in the way. Just tonight. Why don't you kiss me, and I mean really kiss me …

Just then Clayton came back, smiling again, and sat.

—Shh …

—I thought I had another drink yet, he said, mostly for himself. —Zoseemy, djou take my drink?

—No. Perhaps you dropped it.

—Dropped it,

—Time for bed, the barkeep nodded to him, —she's tired. The pouch of daiquiri mix lay dejected, impaled on its straw, in the bar's rubber-lined gutter.

—No, no, Brittney belligerently blithered, —you stay out as long as you need! I got my ride home, she caressed Zosime's arm again. Clayton adjusted his hat, his eyes wide, and looked at them both, one at a time.

—Is that … is that cool with,

—And maybe I'll stay with her instead!

Listening to their rotund, deep-voweled accents was hard on Zosime's stomach.

—Babe, you just got here! And don't be draggin her into,

—You can drink as much as you want, her voice had acquired a weird pretense of agreement, —it's fine. Party on and celebrate. And then you can blast off to space and strand me here in the fucking Congo! With the cannibals!

Clayton stood, enraged, and raised a finger. —Why do you assume that ... He doubled over and his knees shook.

—What? You can't even,

—Plehhh ... eeeeehhh! Eeellgghgghhlluhhhh! The final remnants of North Dakota emptied out of his guts onto the ground, a putrified puree of Culver's frozen custard, butter burgers and cheese curds, McRib sandwich, Pizza Ranch Texan, Hardee's bacon cheese thickburger and the like, all festered in his lower large intestine and bloomed by a fresh sauce of spicy black stomach acid. No one could tell in the red and yellow chili light that the force of reverse peristalsis had also made him piss his pants. —Huurrrrellgghgghhlluch!

—You're so weak. Brittney stood by and let him have it. —You're disappointing everyone. You can't even commit after all this time, and our friends're using and ending up in jail cause you can't set an example. I can't believe I wasted the best years of my life on you!

Now the broad umbrellas, spread out for the occasion, couldn't keep the streams of rain off the bar's clientele.

—Let's go, Zosime stood, —all of us.

She found that once again they had the attention of the rest of the bar, as for the rest of the bar was becoming custom, and many phones hung at eye level, likely filming the thing. Barbecue Bros, not working tonight, leaned over his enormous cocktail and snuck the barkeep a grin.

Behind them in the taxi Zosime saw different headlamps through the rain. Some were low like those of sedans, some were broad-set like on a bus, some were high and functional like a soldier's truck. As it'd turned out in Quito, so here the persecution was beginning. She steeled herself against what destruction and frame-ups may follow.

At length she arrived at the Protea, hoped she wasn't being watched entering the building, and didn't feel safe until she made her way alone in the elevator to her floor, alone down her hall, alone into her room and found that no one was hiding behind the shades, in the shower or under the bed.

She shucked off her jacket and shoes and fell upon her palmfrond-patterned bedspread. It was only going to be Thursday. What if Clayton hadn't vomited, and those two had turned aggressive, if she'd had that Paris-dreaming child in her room right now? It would be like a television show. How did Americans do this night after night and not suffer nervous breakdowns? She was exhausted, yet wanted to run away this moment, back to South America, back to Greece, away from these insane people, this insane job and the insane things its economy was doing to this city.

Her phone had gone neglected the whole night. She had a voice message from her mother; it was only midday in Ecuador. Before she called back, however, she played the message.

Her mother was out of the hospital. Nothing more. She had to slow her thoughts down. Could her mother just pick up and move? She'd never had the time to look beyond her own preparations to know whether her mother had a Greek visa that would allow her to move freely. Was she in Ecuador as a refugee? Slow or fast, it was too late, she was too sapped of energy by her colleagues, for these thoughts. She stared at her phone. Either call or don't.

Her mother didn't pick up the phone. She got into her personal email and sent a message to her father. She'd never really answered his pleas to come home! She explained that she now wanted to come home but had to find out where her mother was, and could he please tell her immediately if she showed up in Europe. A messy response, but surely he was used to that.

She was happy again when she remembered to empty her pockets. She found Iyiola's instructions in her suitcase where she'd hidden them, and added the new ones to them, even if she would take it all out again tomorrow morning. She now had the instructions, all the user names and passwords. Tomorrow something could happen.

8

Innovators

Poetry was not her thing. Certainly not in lean, unlovely English, and likely not at this early hour. She was glad that the disastrous after-party had ended early, for it'd allowed her to rise early without a struggle. But creativity of this kind was a bear. All she had so far was a packet of tea drunk down and a couplet about breaking into email accounts:

> It's not enough to burn the words,
> But messengers' steps from the path, too.

Terrible. Functional poetry, one could call it. But then, the oldest folk songs began in the rhythms of physical labor. The really hard lines were the multiple steps to entering her chief's side of the computer system. How to safely conceal the meaning of a user name and a password? Poetry was really about telling the truth, and not concealing. Should she be more bold, then, like Dante? Finally she had to just make a code for the important words:

> After the bread and wine are ripe,
> Bread and wine what makes the party,
> The farmer forgets the hours of work,
> Or else he wouldn't work hard again.

That was alright. Bread and wine for user name and password. She realized soon that the point here was the process, having to write these silly couplets. That would make her remember what to do, and not the couplets themselves. Though she'd finished the bit about the password, she stared at it for five minutes, unable to think or move. Maybe Iyiola really wrote poetry, and perhaps he was writing it about her. Writing poetry must be some skill, because this was impossible. Finally the four lines of her own hand released her back into waking. Why wasn't her mother returning her call?

She wasted ten more minutes trying to imagine whence doctor Chesky's password was derived, and trying to tell a story about its possible place and time for her to remember, before she got confused and quit. She just spelled Clayton's out, turning tioga98 into a fantasy:

> Tiny islands,
> Over ground again,
> Nine months at sea,
> Eight days of rest

That was much more fun than serious poetry.

Now she'd be late if she didn't get to work, and today was not the day to get fired. It was probably too late to call for the van. She closed her blinds and turned away from the high smog-gritty overcast against which scudded fluffy, mostly rainless clouds. She took a final look at what instructions she'd decided to remember, and then copied the ones she couldn't, and went down to try to write in the taxi.

Folders within folders. That's where she'd find her work orders, inventory lists and any existent explanations. She wrote out euphemisms she intended to use for the former two, and then tried to write. It was no use. She'd have to quickly copy whatever she found and then turn that into poetry, at work.

She found herself first in the silo, as ever. Eagerly she descended the elevator without a look toward the pigpen, turned her laptop on and opened every account she could. She got into her new work order database, then into Clayton's, then, not knowing if her interface would accept it, she typed in doctor Chesky's information and remembered not to store it, without even looking at the poem.

To her wonder, it was all there. Gopman's lauded interface wasn't unique to their computers upstairs; just as in Quito, anyone with the permission, onsite or across the world, could get in. A little too eagerly, she went into the chief's email, which was nested in the interface, as hers also was, now that she had permission to get in for the work orders.

There was an error message. The huge orange fuel tank was too close for comfort to evaporation temperature. There was her answer: it seemed that neither Gopman nor anyone paid the temperature much attention. She accidentally opened the message, so she deleted the message and burned the messenger's footprints from the path by clicking delete forever in the program's trash bin.

There was also a message from commander Morgan, the astronaut. Subject: Disney Channel. Just wanted to follow up on the Disney Channel on the shuttle. Lightyear wants to send a video to his family from orbit, and if the TV is on he wants it to be the Disney Channel, because in his house the girls aren't allowed to watch anything else and his oldest will call him a hypocrite if she sees him doing it. Zosime followed the words, but couldn't make any sense of the message. Maybe it was something only

Americans understood. She deleted the message, and permanently.

Suddenly a wave of anguished terror came over her, as if she were already caught, and she logged out, typing herself back into her side of the interface. Were there cameras down here now, since the protesters had brought the operation to grief, and could they clearly see what was on a computer screen? She tried to act natural.

She listened hard for the sound of the elevator and kept darting her right eye up at the launch center's singed window to see if each lamp's second set of tubes came on, signaling that the launch heads had arrived.

On her own side of the interface she took the time to acquaint herself with the work order service, since she'd only seen her new information in her email yesterday. She read through her work orders and found the descriptions she'd asked of Rodríguez. On Monday she was to load the two containers to go with the one she'd put in yesterday. One was labeled pigs, eight pairs, life support container. The order apparently hadn't been changed despite the disappearance of the two males. The other said food and medical, refrigerated. Their stupid frozen food was coming back. No mention of Martha's baby, or at least not that she could read, and no mention of the shuttle crew's deli tray.

It was worth a try to delete the order for the pigs. By the time the company figured out where the message was lost, the launch would be delayed again or scrapped. The lamps came on in the launch center. She glanced once more at Clayton's poem on the blue notepaper squeezed in her sleeve cuff, and went onto his side of the interface.

She saw a similar assortment of windows in the interface, and the work orders were in the same place. The only difference was that, where she had boxes to check labeled with finished and hold, he had finished and hold, plus assign to. No delete buttons were anywhere in sight. She hit the assign to button and found only her own name in the menu that dropped down.

She was almost certain that she saw what Iyiola meant by folders within folders; she didn't need a poem about the setup of the interface. But she should make a poem for Chesky's unfamiliar English password. It looked like her only hope to jam the order for the pigs lay with the chief's account, if at all. Except for perhaps this early tomorrow, she was likely out of safe chances to look. She needed a second plan.

Clayton finally waddled into the silo, bleary-eyed and pale as always. Zosime found herself without her work polo and with her jacket still on, and decided to find out what anyone'd do about it now that she was inventory analyst. If the temp loaders were gone for good, as they seemed to be, she wasn't setting a bad example for anyone.

—Hey, Zoseemy. Whatta night, ah? He didn't seem to notice.

—Was it long for you, boss? I went to bed. She stayed logged into his side of the interface, defiantly, and leaned against the cart to cover his view of the screen with her upturned forearm.

—Yah, it was kinda long. Weird that the army guy showed up in the nicka time, ah?

—Yes. I hope he stops.

—Bettern gettin soaked. His soaked was deeper than Lake Audobon. Then something occurred to him. —So! First day as foreman. You know what yer sposed to do?

—Yes.

That was enough for him, who didn't know. —So, just get it done and help Martha if she asks. Let's not be needin the boss upstairs to come down for nothin.

There was noise coming out of Clayton's phone, an angry voice. —What is that sound?

—Oh. Just checkin in on Rush, ya know.

—You should go and make sense of what Rodríguez left behind.

Clayton listed to one side, his dark-bearded chin up and arms at his sides like a penguin's wings. —You think I need to?

—I think I don't know. That sounded more like American. —And that is why you should find out. He had everything of him in the locker room.

He turned and went as far as the huge door's bulkhead before she called. —Clayton?

—What?

—Didn't you bring Brittney to see your job?

—No.

There was nothing else to do about the memory of last night but grin for herself and suppress a laugh. In the echoey silence of the silo one of her mother's proverbs rang in her ear: there is much hope in hopelessness, for at the end of the dark night comes the day. She dragged a stool over, logged out of everything, put the laptop to sleep, and tried some more poetry.

Half an hour later she remained undisturbed by the launch center nor her new foreman, when the radio crackled and Martha Glass summoned her to the surface. She grabbed some blue gloves, her rake and bucket, and went back up once more to be a pig farmer.

The sky wasn't ready to rain, but the clouds looked threadbare and pulpy as if they'd been used to rub smog off of cement. She found Martha, looking as exhausted as last night, tending to the pigs.

—Good morning, Martha. Are you alright?

Martha turned, once more the archetype of a farmer, overalls, high galoshes and raincoat, and nodded at her.

—Just fine, Zosime. Can you take that knife right there and open this new bag of feed? Since we're three days out, let's just strew it out and lettem pick at it, cause after Saturday night we can't lettem eat anymore. Thanks.

Zosime opened the bag. It was stupid to pour the pellets of expensive, formulated dogfood onto the muddy ground, but there was nowhere else, so she emptied it. The mud would consume the bottom two centimeters of feed and give the hogs something to root after. They seemed calm today, in their routine, oblivious of what'd been done to them and how it'd soon be repeated.

—Not in a pile, honey. Go … that's fine.

—Zosime or Martha, come in, over, the radio hissed suddenly. Zosime answered.

—I'm listening, chief, over.

—Can I have doctor Glass when she has a free moment, please, over?

—I'm on my way.

—She's on her way, over.

Martha patted hog number five on the numbered rump. —Ever cleaned a pig's ear?

—No.

—Wanna try? Here, the veterinarian presented the inventory analyst with a cotton stick like an oversized cosmetic swab. —He's almost done. Left ear. Just dig what you can out. Don't push, just like you don't with yer own ear. When yer done, put the swab in the shopping baggy I got goin in the container.

Zosime obliged her, took the swab and went to work. As Martha walked back to the elevator cone, the shiny black American utility vehicle parked outside the perimeter caught her eye.

Would the ear muck float out in space? No, by rights it'd be held in hairs and against the flesh by surface tension.

The hog resisted, worked its neck free from Zosime, and wandered into the rusty red container that would bear it to outer space, drawing the accompaniment of its buddy number fourteen. They were gregarious, caring animals. Number five casually pissed on the floor, then let Zosime work after she shooed fourteen away. She dug a pretty good wad of hairy brown dreck out of its left ear. It grunted at her and shifted its weight on its hind legs, but didn't try to run again. Its triangular mandible curiously produced a pearl of drool, as if taking outside temperature. She shooed the hog out of the box and then tried to find the plastic bag Martha was talking about.

Before she heard the metal door grinding against its track, daylight expired and she was in the dark. She rammed her shoulder against the door to open it but it wouldn't budge.

—Hey! Open this! Martha! She slapped the door with the palm of her hand. —Martha!

What trick was this? Was Martha exacting some kind of revenge on her for not cooperating with her desperate panic last night, for not vowing to find the remains of her dead baby in her inventory? Or perhaps they'd seen what she was doing on the computer downstairs. All her effort could be precipitating back down on her now.

Her own panic went in waves over her, accompanied by troughs of waiting, like an animal saves energy between assaults at the bars of a cage. Five, eight minutes' worth of these waves rolled over her, hot and stinking of ammonia hog piss, until finally the door slid open a crack.

—Zoseemy?

—Clayton! Open this!

The door slid open and she found Clayton staring stupidly back at her. In his right cheek cowered a small bundle of khat.

—How'd you get in there?

—You locked the door!

—They ast me to! His arms flapped. —I didn't know you were in there!

She strode quickly past him, and didn't wait for him at the elevator, in which she shuddered and spluttered. The courage with which she'd spoken to Iyiola two afternoons ago was trapped under a rock now. Why hadn't she seen this coming? Anyone who wants to work for the Americans should have to take a class on surveillance, spying and jealousy to know what really underlies their passive-aggressiveness. Her Persian mother would be disappointed.

She arrived at the launch center's door and passed through the foyer. Rather than barging into the launch center, it somehow seemed less transgressive to knock. She waited, and a perplexed doctor Chesky opened the door.

—Zosime?

—May I come in?

He hesitated again, confused. —Sure. Siddown. What's up?

—Where is doctor Glass?

—She's not up there? I finished talkin to her.

She couldn't say why Martha may have locked her in the box. She couldn't safely untangle herself from Martha's pleas from last night. —She told Clayton to close the pigs' box, and he locked me in it! I cannot feel safe here if we do not communicate. Also, I said last night that I didn't want any security to follow me, and I demand that you respect it, or else it's harassment!

—Okay, he said quietly, —you got it.

The hairs behind the chief's ears bristled, and the nerves on the back of his head lifted, giving the sensation that his skull was opening up so his brain could flee. She said harassment! But he had to be tough now, to stay his course. — I'll talk to Clayton. Sounds like what he did was uncalled-for.

She didn't understand that last word, but she trusted its meaning. —The work orders are complete until Monday, and the silo is clean. I want to finish downstairs and go home.

—Okay, sure. Clayton can pick up anything left over.

—There is nothing left over.

He nodded again. —Sorry about this, Zosime. It was never my intention to have you feel unsafe. The opposite, yknow?

—Thanks. She took a deep breath. He could be lying. She wondered suddenly if he knew that she'd been in his interface account. He would tell her if he knew, wouldn't he?

—Is everything normal up here?

—Yeah, yeah, he looked around the launch center,

—Gopman's sick, but it's fine. Monday's comin on fast!

—On Monday I have to load the pigs, and the cold supply container. It's a good idea to bring it in tomorrow. Can you do this? There are cooling tubes in the silo to maintain it cold.

—Yeah. Good idea, I'll call the storage right now, and then check in with the astronauts …

—Where are they?

—Oh, they're in Germany. I guess they've been stayin with some friends, yknow, colleagues, at the ESA training center.

—I'm going now.

In the end she didn't know what he knew, and there was no way to find out. Maybe Chesky and Davis were working together to push her out, and maybe the chief, like Rodríguez and Clayton, knew as little as he seemed to.

She almost went up to the surface to confront Martha, but she'd only be repeating herself. Instead she descended, took her laptop off its cart and carried it with her to the cafeteria. Might as well eat on Star-X's tab.

Fear didn't overwhelm her. Against the beaches of her chest the tides of her new anger, born in her after a month on this job, born of confusion, of new clarity of vision upon the manifold nightmares that sustained the job, crashed as powerfully as the tides of fear. She wanted to finish something today, to know what was possible from doctor Chesky's interface. It was reckless to look. What would her Persian mother do now? She'd run. Then what was the equal but opposite action to running away from danger? She might as well run into it, and find out how bad it can get. One look likely wouldn't ever be noticed or sought out. She took a pen in case more poetry was in order.

In the bunkerlike cafeteria there wasn't even pasta left. Besides meat products and breads there was only lettuce, tomatoes, pickles and sliced onions. She took a bottle of water, sat under her high trash-darkened window, which still didn't have a buried black face stuck against it, and recited her poem in a whisper. The lines she'd written before Martha called her were no good. She crumpled them in her fist and stuck them in her jacket pocket. She took a deep breath and logged into doctor Chesky's side. In an instant a line about his password occurred to her:

A tree-lined road many years ago.

It had internal rhyme. But now she couldn't stop to write it down. It was an image from her own home, anyway. She didn't dare move her finger on the trackpad or hit any keys. Instead she gripped her bottle of water with both hands and looked. In the work order window was the usual information, and above it the buttons for finished, hold and assign to. No delete. It was impossible to remove the order to load the pigs. She could've asked Iyiola to find out this much!

What else could she do with this power? She looked at all the words stacked down the left side of the screen, each one a menu item that could be opened. Were these the folders within folders? She didn't dare open them. She couldn't think of what to look for.

—Zoseemy!

Clayton's voice, more forceful than she'd heard before, rang out through the pylons and shadows of the cafeteria. Her head snapped around. —What is it, Clayton?

—There's an alarm! Cmon!

She logged out of everything, closed her laptop and trotted down the long hall into the silo.

—Now what?

She looked at the cart, and then up at the shuttle stack. A red light, visible as well to the launch center, blinked on the cart and from two flat lamps installed into the silo's walls, one a story above her head and one five stories up.

—Fix it!

—Let me open the laptop!

It was the refrigeration system alarm. The laptop wasn't waking up fast enough. She ran over to the other side of the shuttle stack, pushed buckets and rakes and ladders to the side, and found the governor panel. It took a key.

—Clayton! Bring me your key, now!

He hesitated, like he didn't want her to know that he had a key. —Bring it! Run or this rocket will explode! She gestured with a flying hand, realizing that a shrill siren silenced her voice. He waddled quickly around the round rim of the silo bottom.

—Give me your key! Give me it! Stick it in here, then!

The fat foreman awkwardly fit the key into the slot and turned it. The governor panel lit up and Zosime jammed her finger on the refrigeration control until the mutant freezer compressor behind the concrete and steel wall bellowed its way up a gear. A vibration ran through Zosime's knees and ankles. Their eyes darted between the launch center's window and the red lights, which soon were extinguished along with the alarm.

—Whatta ya been doin down here?

—Clayton.

—What?

—Shut up. She pointed. —This is the cooling governor. She pointed high up, stretching her arm and her shoulder even. —That orange tank is full of liquid hydrogen and oxygen and it needs to stay cold. That is part of your job! Understand?

—Well how do I know it's workin? he shouted back. He was being honest; he knew nothing about spacecraft, nothing about nothing.

—You should have a message before it gets too warm.

—A message. He stepped back, his eyes lingering on her, and then turned away. She followed.

—Why don't you look? Now that you know this, I'm going home. She walked ahead of him, got her back to him, and sighed away the memory of deleting the message from Chesky's side.

Before she could go through the bulkhead, the radio chirped.

—Clayton, Zosime, everything okay down there, over?

—Yes, doctor Chesky. You can reset the alarm, over.

—It was the cooling system?

—Affirmative, over.

—That's funny ... I don't have any warnings today.

—The company should not worry about the price of cooling, over. She tossed the radio down and walked, within herself running as fast as she could, to the elevator. She didn't look for Martha, only looked straight ahead at the van driver, who would take her to the front gate.

As Clayton watched her go, the radio chirped again.
—Clayton, please respond, over.

—Go ahead, over.

—Clayton, yknow you can fix that from yer laptop, right?

—Oh, can I now?

—Yeah. Go into your menu, at the left, you'll find it. Just gotta put in yer password again before the controls'll show up. You need me to come down and show you?

—No, no! I'll figure it out.

—Yeah, try it out and see how you like it. Save you a trip around the silo in a pinch, over.

No one followed Zosime out of the landfill except the eyes of a few locals. Those eyes were a deep, clear brown, yet they held the blue of the sky, the true blue root that held them fast to the ground of this planet's landfill. Zosime tried to clear away the terror of confinement, the tangle of her colleagues. Only once outside the burning trash and terror of Olusosun, riding down to the express road in a taxi, did it occur to her that the silo's cooling governor was her only hope.

On the way home a brief, heavy rain fell over the city, warmer today than since she'd been in Lagos, and she took a swim as soon as it moved on. She couldn't transmute her place to Corfu's beaches this time, for there were other guests in the pool for a change. East Asians, probably Japanese by their stature and demeanor, swam laps and splashed each other gently but eagerly. An American and an Englishman chatted loudly about wine and various European cities' subways from their deck chairs, both of them bald, the American tanned like leather.

When she arrived in her room once more she checked it, still feeling violated. She had to get out of here soon, if not even her hotel room felt safe. There was no way to know if anyone had come in besides the maid.

She found in her phone that her mother had called. It was barely morning in Quito. She called back and her mother answered.

—Mamá, what're you doing up this early? Why're you're out of the hospital already?

—I'll answer you if you let me speak, dlakam! I'm not in Quito.

—You're not in … where are you? She couldn't help shouting. —Why are you speaking English?

Her mother's voice hushed and changed languages.

—I'm in the airport of New York, in Amerikí. You can't speak Farsi or Greek in an American airport if you ever want to leave. I'm on my way home, dlakam!

—I told you to wait for me!

—Your baba made contact with Behrouz. Her voice was raised against Zosime's, but it was resolute, not angry.

—He's got sick and hurt in prison. Your father and I have to go to him now. We have to make noise and cause problems so they'll let him out.

She waited for Zosime to reply, but her daughter didn't. She went on: —I need your address. The European Space Administration sent a letter to me in Quito last night.

—Do you have it? Just open it!

Her mother's voice and the background noise went away, and the receiver went quiet as if the call had been disconnected. —Mother?

—It's here. They offer you a job at a telescope in Chile. You can start,

—Throw it away. I'm not taking it.

—What do you mean?

—I'm coming Monday to meet you. Tell me where to be.

—Don't be a fool, dlakam. You can quit your job in Nigeria, this job will be much better. I will send this letter to you and you can reach out to them.

—I'm coming home. I'm finished helping insane people go to space! They're throwing people out of their homes, blasting pigs into space, and watching everything I do. I want to make things work with Baba and you!

—Slow down ... I have to get off the phone, dlakam. My wheelchair is arriving now.

—Mother, what wheelchair? Are you in pain?

—I'll be fine! I'll take a pill when I get on the plane and then I'll go to London.

—Mother, you must stay in London until I get there, until I can take care of you. What if you wreck your nerves and can't walk? You can't have it your way with the doctors! You know better than to rebel right now!

—And you know better, too, Zosime?

Zosime looked out over Lagos, at the streams of traffic, at the slums lining the waterfronts. A high steel building's skeleton was rising between her and the big mosque. —I know how I'll rebel now, mother, so you need not feel obligated to do it.

—It's too late to lecture me, Zosime. I'm already gone. I want to see my family again. I know it's too late to help anything by running away.

Her mother's words were so strange, it was as if her voice had changed. She didn't just sound like a younger person, as sometimes escaped from her mouth. Her voice made the wheel of Zosime's life clear. Before she felt that she'd inherited her mother's need to escape. But now she heard her own knowledge in her mother, not her mother's knowledge in herself. She couldn't say, before her mother said goodbye, that she wanted to see her family again just as badly.

—My chair is here, goodbye.

—You'll call me when you reach London?

—Bale, bale, dlakam.

She dropped her phone on the bed, fell backward onto the smooth soft palmfronds, covered her face with her hands and lay there for a long time.

She cried, snorted, gurgled, gasped through her slim fingertips, felt her face heating and cooling against them, as the hard white Nigerian monsoon day wheeled from bright to night. She slept sometimes, mostly when it was dark. Her oath to her mother about swearing off this work had been the first time she'd really decided, just as the news that her wandering mother's flight from the hospital was the first time she really faced the woman's frailty. She endured the separation of hope from her body, felt herself in freefall, a skinless skeleton falling with inflamed tendons through frozen wind.

When her morning alarm sounded, an echo from another planet, she grabbed her phone, saw that her mother had called, she was in London and had to wait. She sent a message to doctor Chesky. What was wrong with her? She had food poisoning. That was never questioned, not even on a Friday. She would deceive him from the comfort of bed today.

She realized that somehow she'd got under the covers. She cried more, and then the ancient meditation of tears revealed its truth: in a moment she realized that she didn't know anymore why she was crying. It could be fear, or grief. No. It was nothing, just tears and sobbing, like sleeping, like breathing. Whether her mother paralyzed herself or not, Zosime realized that there was no final trial coming ahead. She was free. She lay in a daze, shook more sobs out, laughed, somehow somnambulated down to the restaurant and back, and Friday was gone already.

Saturday she woke up renewed. Where had been confusion, the shock of change, loathing for the silo and its staff, and endless fear, now there was just her body and the empty sine wave of daylight that surrounded her mind, plunged down and drew up against her belly and breasts. She called Iyiola and they made plans to meet in the Mainland.

Danger was not done with her. As she came down the elevator she saw a black American luxury truck parked across the street from the Protea's lobby. Why risk finding out if it was the private soldier, persecution, frame-ups, destruction? Her sublime oneness irrigated with tears folded its fronds back up, and she had to be muscular and fast once more. She noticed that a group of women in hijabs were hanging around the restaurant and the lobby, either arriving or departing. She rushed back up to her room, improvised a hijab from her only blouse, and left without her trusty jacket.

She joined up two paces behind three of the women as they went out to the sidewalk. Furtively she watched the black truck. Its running lights were extinguished, its windows were up and it was impossible to tell if someone were in it. Two taxis shouldered up to the curb and she ducked into one while the Muslim ladies climbed into the other.

She stopped at a bank, hoping to throw eavesdroppers further off. The bank gave her the choice of accessing her domiciliary account in America using the Maestro chip in her card. This was probably another reason why Star-X chose Lagos for their silo. She took as much naira in cash as the banker would let her take, and leaving the bank she wished she had her jacket with its hidden pockets. She stuck the envelope full of bills in her waistband and hoped Iyiola could help her empty it soon.

She traveled down with the rapid bus until the Onipanu stop, and walked past the sprawling, weathered orthopedic hospital and its enormous parking structure appendage. She didn't know how far she'd be walking, but she felt safe now. Following her phone she found the bar, an expensive one, where she was sure they served Pernod and not just Star and Ogidiga. Iyiola was there, hiding in a dark booth, overdressed and smiling as usual, just as she'd found him in the van at work not two weeks ago.

His smile clenched into an O as he pointed above her head. She looked up, blushed and pulled the improvised hijab off from her chin. She sat, close to him as always, so they wouldn't need to raise their voices. She liked being near him anyway.

—If they are following me, they could be watching.

—I know, he nodded to her, —a white man came asking about me at work on Thursday. My manager is a wise woman, and she said I was sick. I'm going to have to quit this job.

—Don't. It will look strange. You can't be afraid of them.

—That's easy advice to give. So, how'd everything go?

—I saw everything, she whispered with him, —there's not much I can do from the computer. You know, everything I learned, I could've asked you to look for.

—I knew it! I was wondering why you didn't ask!

—I wouldn't dare. I needed to see for myself.

An older, fat woman in a fancy turquoise pantsuit came over and they placed orders. Iyiola got an iced tea and Zosime ordered a Pernod.

—There was no time, last time we met, to tell me what you meant to do with your powers.

By the time he caught her eye she knew that he could see it, that she had a plan.

—I don't want you to know. No one will know that you showed me how to do it.

—Because they won't catch you in their computer system, not in the act. And they won't catch you soon. But if you do something serious to their launch, and they find out you were meddling with the computers, they'll find you in Ecuador,

—Yes, I know! I didn't change the computers at all. I couldn't. She smiled her guilt away. —I deleted some messages to the chief. They weren't important. But I wanted to read them. All told, I won't be able to do this work ever again. I don't care anymore, not about the sky ladder or any of this. I'll rebuild bridges in Greece, or sewers, or plant trees ... I'll do something that matters.

—Are you sure you saw what I meant by folders within folders?

—Yes, but there was nothing for me to do with them. I tried to write poetry about it, but there was nothing I could do. I mean, it would be too clear.

He laughed. —Poetry?

—That's how I was remembering what to do. Without them finding out.

—I see, I see, he laughed again. —So we won't be needing to trade poems, then.

The drinks arrived. Iyiola now saw a real piece of Zosime, a part of her secret life, as she slightly reclined, put her shoulders back, crossed her ankles under the table, and eyeballed the Pernod like she was waiting to pounce on it. He sipped his iced tea, moving the sprig of mint away from his teeth with his lips.

—You meditate on your drinks?

She watched the light bending in the glass's meniscus, regarded the image of it for a while before she snatched it up and drank it. —That's part of the enjoyment.

—You can drink so much!

—It's only a small drink. You'll have the next one with me.

—I don't drink very much. I can't afford to, working for the university!

—My father's also a ... what do you say ... a professor.

She ordered the drinks as the woman came past.

—And your mother? She called when we met, in the library. You said she's in hospital.

—She's sick. Her nerves are hurt, and it makes her sick in many ways. Now she's in London. I think she's waiting for another plane. She's trying to go to Greece before me.

—And your brother, who's in prison?

—I don't know. But this is why my mother isn't waiting for me to return to Ecuador. She says he's sick from being in prison.

—I'm sure he'll be proud of you for coming home instead of taking the money from this job.

—I don't know that, either. But I'm afraid that my mother ... if she has any problems to get him out of prison, she could have a nervous breakdown, and I don't know what it'll do to her health.

She found her eyes wide, blinked them, found his hand and squeezed it. —I feel bad from telling you this. I'm so tired of hearing my colleagues' problems,

—No, no! This is what I'm here for! You have to talk to let go of your problems.

—Is that how you live, here in Nigeria?

—I mean you. You have to talk. I can tell.

—I almost never talk.

—That's why.

The twin glasses of Pernod arrived, without Zosime's preferred short stems and little feet, but in flat-bottomed shotglasses.

—What does it taste like?

—Licorice. Smell it.

He ran it under his nose, raised his glass and met eyes with her. —Kara o le.

—Kara o le!

They drank.

—Do you like it?

He smiled and nodded as he set the glass down. —Do you like Star, too? He shook his head this time. She turned over toward him, got the envelope full of cash from her waistband, and unfolded it in her hands.

—Order one more. I want to pay you for helping me, now.

He sighed. —I knew you said you wanted to, but I couldn't imagine it was true.

—Don't feel bad. I know you'll use it to help. You need help, too, for yourself.

He waved at the waitress and she went to pour two more drinks. Zosime put the envelope down between their laps and spread its opening with her thumb. His eyes widened at the sight of the cash, which to her looked almost the same as euro. He took the envelope, folded it in half again, and slid it in his back pocket.

—Thank you.

—Don't be shy! You deserve it. This is how we should be spending our money. The Americans took your neighborhood away, now you take their money.

—It's not fair, exactly, and I don't think of this as a trade with them.

—No. But you have some of what they took from you.

The drinks arrived. They toasted again, kara o le.

—I didn't go to work yesterday, Zosime confessed,

—I'm too scared of being watched, of being questioned. The army scares me.

—Now you see how hard it is to take your own advice. Must you go back?

—Monday only. It's the best chance I have to either help the pigs come away from the launch, or do something else. They still have no idea what I can do. They think I only care about the pigs because I don't eat meat.

—You don't?

—No. Listen. They don't understand how they make those animals suffer because they want to pretend to be on Earth when they're on Mars.

—You care about those pigs a lot, in order to put your work and your neck on the line for them.

—I've learned that living things, all the living things in the world, are worth more than this stupid job.

He shook his head at the seat cushion, as he did when considering things. —Your colleagues could never understand that from their place of dedication to the mission. And it's also that you're special.

She shied away a moment, then looked at him again.

—I am?

—I mean it. Very few people understand the concept of subjectively caring about something, without anything material to gain or lose in return.

—You're right, Iyiola. So I'll keep the pigs on the ground and then I'll leave. I'll go home!

Iyiola let that be the path away from worry. —What's the first thing you're going to do?

—I'm going to put my mother in bed, hire a therapist for her nerves, and then I'll go swimming.

—I'd like to see you swim.

She smiled at him a long time, though her chin dropped instinctively. —I like you a lot, Iyiola. You are the best thing about Nigeria. She saw a couple of women come down a staircase she hadn't noticed before, and wet daylight flooded in with them. She signaled to the lady. —We want to pay! Finish your tea. Maybe we're done hiding.

She led him upstairs and they found a roof patio. A warm, dry wind had curled up off the ocean through the sodden rotting city and it blew against their necks and cheeks. Zosime grasped the handrail and hung her face over into the gust. —Do you feel it?

He did like she did, and for him, too, it was sweet to let the wind carry away care for a fleeting moment.

—Let's go somewhere before we never see each other again. We can't be outside.

Iyiola watched her think as she spoke. He couldn't conceal that look on his face like I can't believe how lucky this situation is going. —We can go to my house. It's only five minutes away.

The strange and vivid Greek woman went into the restroom while Iyiola waited at the door, spying for military vehicles or concealed military vehicles as she'd instructed him to. When she came out she had the hijab improvised out of her blouse back up on her head. They walked quickly, trying to look normal, to his narrow street and rose up to his second-story apartment.

The place had a kitchenette and bathroom adjoining a single room occupied by a bed and a tiny desk, a stack of library books running like dominoes under the picture window, and a computer with speakers plugged into it on the desk. A student's room. Out the wide window the university's Senate House was visible, and to its left spread the slums of Iwaya and Makoko floating between the creeks on their garbage foundations.

Iyiola crossed the room and drew the curtains. She caught him on the way back and they introduced themselves anew with a single kiss. He served her water and they undressed each other. She unbuttoned his immaculate shirt and pants, he slid up and down her few athletic layers, and they took to hiding behind their closed eyes in the infinite darkness between their bodies. His hands washed over her limbs, breasts and belly like warm tidal flows. She made new places in him, tied her ankles into new joints around his calves, twisted his knees and groin into multiplications of her own, thrust back at him and pulled, each time waiting for him to thrust again, their chests and chins met before their hips did, multiplied out new bodies that surprised them both.

When he kissed her he felt the acidic heat on her lips and the tip of her tongue. He flexed his groin and abdominals tighter and harder when he felt her fingers around his buttocks, concerted his limbs to encircle her gently after each time she let loose a tiny laugh. His mind was silent and empty, and each suggestion she made sent light coursing through the dark down his meridians.

Together they pulled more and more life up from the abysses within them and poured it out into the one between them. Together they met the door into the other world and jumped through it, together.

When they were exhausted Zosime found herself hallucinating. She hadn't died, that was real. But she kept hearing her phone vibrating in her pocket, now that she really didn't want to rise and answer it.

—I think that is my phone, she whispered in the familiar whisper, not needed now, that would be the voice of their every conversation the longer they should stay together.

—I don't hear anything, Iyiola's lips responded from under her hair, —You can look.

She slid out from between his knees, extended her back and arms enough to slide across the clammy floor, caught hold of her blouse and dragged it over. There were no calls or messages. She tossed the phone away onto the heap of clothes and contracted back again, finding the wet warmth she'd left intact.

—Nice that I don't have to run away too soon.

—I wish you could stay longer, he said with the same unabashed affection as before, —I would like you to see the real Lagos, the one the Americans and Arabs are trying to erase. You could see Makoko, just south of the university. The houses are built on poles, and houseboats float on the creeks, and when you meet the water, there's the Makoko School floating in there! It's a pyramid all made of wood, and free, out on the water.

—A whole school?

—You can see through it, it's a lot of wooden beams!

—That sounds beautiful. I miss the ocean.

—But it's right here!

She turned her face up toward his. —Are there beaches in Lagos? He nodded and laughed at her. —I never thought about it while I was here. I saw the slums from the airplane, the trash at the water's edge, but nothing more.

—Your launch chief and his little friend don't go to the beaches?

—I never asked. I know, it's unbelievable.

—I'm only teasing. Well, one day you can come back again.

She stroked two fingers down his smooth forearm.

—Don't say that. I won't. I have to take care of my mother.

Iyiola breathed deeply and exhaled a sharp, quick gust of yeah. —Yeah, it'd be nice to see the beach without worrying about our mothers. If you love the sea so much, you should work for the ocean patrol.

—The coast guard? Then I could be dealing with rafts of refugees from Africa all day. And when I see them, I'll think of you too much.

—Ha! That's very sweet, isn't it. He peeled himself off of her, stood and activated his computer. She was afraid that he was offended, but then he took his place again at her side. Soon jazz flowed through the room, tapping thimbles against the walls, blowing hot air through horns, with a small, patient man singing sweetly in the middle of it. Zosime caught much and missed much of the English he was singing. The band would stand up and blow, then reduce its flame to reveal a piano and a bass guitar shuffling through church music that Zosime didn't know. He sang that some want all of the money, others want to conquer space. But without love, it's just a waste, and Zosime had the feeling that he was singing directly to her.

—This is very beautiful, she breathed at length, —and so strange.

—Did you hear it? He says there's nothing in the universe that attracts me more than you.

She grinned for herself. He was deliciously persistent.
—Is it American music?

—Yeah. He's called Allen Toussaint. He was a really respected musician from New Orleans. That's where American jazz comes from.

—He is wonderful.

—He was an amazing, educated, intelligent African man, like we all should be. He kept learning his whole life. When he died he knew everything about jazz music, black people's music, and could teach it to you piece by piece.

—It's sad he died. She turned toward him again, got her suffocating arm out from under her ribs, and the movements pulled them apart. —Do a lot of people listen to him here?

—No. I found him on the internet at the university. I want to always live in a house that has internet now, only for the music! I'm mad that the Americans want to tear down Ajegunle, but I couldn't live there again.

Zosime nodded and stroked his cheek.

—Was your family always poor?

—No. This city, this corrupt government, this economy that's driven by the greed of foreigners, all the trash from around the world, that makes us poor. When you go … I want you to stay as long as you like … when you go I'm gonna spend the money you gave me. I'd like to get a place for my mother and my sisters.

—What about your father?

—He's in prison.

Her mouth hung open in shock. —In prison?

—I know. A man his age, how could it be? Listen. Three years ago, here in the Mainland, there was a demonstration by the OPC when police started a fight. A lot of people got hurt. This has been going on forever, just like in Greece. It came to trial, and my father wanted to testify that he saw a policeman beat a woman and her son. They were fleeing, not attacking! And he beat them down. The court didn't want him to speak, so he published his testimony on the internet. They used the Act to Prohibit Frivolous Petitions against him, and he got two years for making allegations against the police. We're still waiting for him to come home.

—So you must also act for those who can't.

—Sorry?

—You said that to me when I told you about my brother. We're acting for those who can't. It's a surprise how much we are the same.

—Maybe not. A lot of people are in prison.

He rolled over onto his back and glared at the ceiling. Zosime was still in the dream of Allen Toussaint's music, but it wasn't working on the handsome young Nigerian.

—A lot of times it made me wonder if I should've even got my degree, instead of working a little for my mother.

—This is my whole problem, Zosime stroked his forearm again with a contemplative fingertip, —we have got to stop trying to do what is right because they tell us it's right. Do you understand what I mean? It was difficult for her to say so much in English. —Your mother wants you to be educated. When they take from us, like they took your father, and now your home ... we have to do something different.

His eye rolled toward her. —What? Ruining spacecraft, like you?

—Yes, or anything! When the people before us say that something is the right thing to do, it's because that thing was successful for them. But we can't ...

—We can't take it for granted?

—Yes! When we try to do that, in the meantime we're allowing them to take more from everyone. We have to do what makes things better, not what was right before.

—Life in this world is very complicated, Iyiola observed, —it's because we don't have strong traditions anymore, and we don't live together.

Zosime was quiet a while. Then she whispered I know.

—But even those men you work for, for them it's doing something different, too. Leaving Earth, changing the shape of the places where they do business. They think they're making the world better, too. So there's always conflict, even when we can all see the same problems.

—You're right. But I didn't mean that fighting back was the end, the solution. I mean that trying to make the world a better place, how you understand it, doesn't make you a good person automatically.

She shook her head. —Let's forget it. I'm thankful, you know, that we can talk honestly to each other. Since the pigs came, I've been thinking one thing and saying the opposite thing to my boss for a week. My head is hurting from it.

—That's how you know that you're working with bad men.

—They locked me in a box for animals. The story escaped her mouth, and she wished she could take it back. It was too late to discuss it.

—Why?

—I don't know. Perhaps it was an accident.

She took his face in both of her hands and kissed him, then sat up on the bed. —I should go and let you spend doctor Chesky's money. She dressed without looking at him. She wanted to ask if he'd write poems about her, but it was too sensitive. Not he, she was too sensitive. She wanted to cry.

—Are you alright?

—I've been so many places and stayed there so long. Of all these places, I made a friend like you here in Lagos. It's bad luck.

She tied her hair up in a pony tail, still-sweaty strands whose dampness aroused him, and looked at him for the last time. —I know you'll make your family proud.

—I hope so, Zosime. Let's hope that we set our families free. Thank you for this time together.

He watched her pass, grabbed her left hand with both of his, kissed her fingers once, and let her continue. She shut the door behind her. He rose, drew the curtains, and found rain falling hard but silent over the city, behind the music that walled his room off from the world.

Departing the bus stop, traffic was jammed completely by some obstacle up ahead on the Ikorodu Express Road, and the buses were moving only slightly faster than the rest of traffic. As the bus edged forward past the rainsoaked buildings and crowds of pedestrians beyond the road, an elderly man was standing at the front row enumerating reasons for the holdup to the bus driver. Zosime squeezed past the man. Being stuck on the bus would be better than stuck in the rain.

As soon as she found a seat, she felt her phone vibrate, for real this time. Her personal email was open, and she had a message from her father. He wanted to know where her mother was, and if she'd taken the job in Chile. News travels fast. She responded that she didn't know about her mother. Then it occurred to her after the fact, as it always does, to use the phone before replying, and try to contact her mother. If she were indeed in London, now they were on the same time. Zosime placed an unanswered call. The bus' tall windscreen wipers scooped sheets of water away to the side. A few minutes later her mother did respond with a message, saying she was staying in London for a day more until her back quieted down.

Zosime wrote a message back demanding the name of the hotel, did she have money, had she tried to call father, the minimal information. Her mother responded at length, just as the bus finally was gaining speed, with only the name of the Leonardo at Heathrow.

A telephone call interrupted her reading the brief message. What did doctor Chesky want on a Saturday?

—Hello, this is Zosime.

—Zosime! Chesky here. Everything all right?

—Yes, fine, thanks. What do you need?

—Are you at home? Are you out on the road?

—I just went out to do some shopping, she lied, —it's raining very hard.

—I know. Okay. I just … look, I don't wanna scare you, but there's a situation out on the express road. Some soldiers stationed in town just shot up two taxis from the same company. I don't know anything else. So just stay around your hotel, okay?

—I could use the bus.

—No, yeah, but please just go ahead and stay home so you'll be safe, okay? If you tell me where you are, I'll have the commander,

—I told you, I don't need protection and I don't want to see them.

—Please, Zosime. I'm kinda freaked about this. He was free about it? Briefed? She didn't understand.

—I'll be fine, chief.

—Okay, he changed the subject now as if it were unimportant, —doctor Glass could really use some help with her detail on the pigs tomorrow. Would you go in and help her? Yknow, it'd help make up for the lost productivity from yesterday.

She sighed. —Yes, I'll help.

—Great. Thanks, Zosime. I'll tell her to come get you from your hotel tomorrow.

A vehicle behind the bus was beating its horn and charging along the inside of the road, left of the fogline, and forcing cars in the left lane to veer into the right and cars in the right lane to climb over the concrete bumpers into the bus lane. Now the bus, and everything but the vehicle at far left, halted as it passed. It was a military vehicle, an armored truck. People started chattering.

—I have to go, chief, I'll talk to you Monday.

She turned her head around toward the voice of a man near the back row, who was waving his phone's glowing screen.

—The soldiers are shooting at taxis!

—I know why, a woman with a shaved head joined in, —it was that taxi company that kicked the drunk soldiers out. They take revenge on everyone no matter what the story is!

The first man raised his voice now. —These commanders are going up there to ask them politely stop please! These soldiers don't respect any authority!

The bus driver said everyone be calm, please, and they were silent. Zosime had almost forgotten to tell her father the news. She sent him the name of the hotel, no, she hadn't taken the job in Chile, she was going to fetch mother as soon as possible and come home.

As long as she was thinking about it, she looked up flights. She could leave Monday afternoon for Frankfurt-Main via Madrid, and from Germany either go home or to London depending on her reckless mother. She bought the ticket, put her phone down and looked ahead anxiously. She didn't see the small four-propeller toy drone that floated up from behind the bus and drifted away toward downtown.

♂

Sunday morning the rain had cleared up but left deep mud for the launch staff and mudsoiled water for the pigs. Zosime was a little shocked to find Clayton present as well. She still couldn't be comfortable around either of them. Martha suggested that they try to dry out the container before launch, and Zosime knew that there was a large space heater down in the silo. She would make Clayton install it, and stay away from the pig container herself.

—Do you have a code to go down the elevator, Martha?

—No, honey, Martha shrugged, —I just have the key to the gate.

—Clayton, she turned to the foreman who looked especially dumpy and soggy today, —I need your keys. You have a key to the elevator, don't you?

—I dunno, Clayton protested. He fished them out of his pockets and fingered them dumbly.

—Let me see, then, Zosime demanded. Clayton tossed them to her and turned away to Martha, who put him to work dragging the stacked cages out of the back of the box. —Zosime, bring the mop and plenty clean water in the bucket, too, please. Martha was in charge again, more sober and even-keeled today than before.

Zosime strode over to the elevator cone and tried Clayton's keys. None of them would go in. About to lose her patience, she stepped away into the clear and spotted the freight elevator's landing on the other side of the enclosure. She went over to it, found the keyslot shorter, just like the padlock-sized brass key on the ring, and with a snap had the angry freight elevator roaring up to the surface. —Why don't we load the box first, and then clean it inside the silo? she called to Martha.

—Is that okay to do?

—Clayton?

—I dunno!

—Let's just do it, Zosime said, —they deserve to be warm and dry one more night. Clayton, leave the cages in there, we'll take it all inside.

She rode the freight elevator down and brought the forklift back up to the surface, hoping it could haul the shipping container empty without sinking into the mud. It was indeed difficult to maneuver, and to keep the wandering pigs out of harm's way, but after a struggle she had the container hung on the machine's forks and drove it with her colleagues down into the silo, leaving the pigs to wallow on in the mud.

As fast as they could, they emptied the container, mopped it, and started in cleaning the cramped cages as best they could. Zosime kept Clayton in the container with her when she had to go in. While Martha and Clayton finished, Zosime took the one chance she likely had left. The lights weren't even on in the silo. A stain of natural rainy daylight splashed through the silo doors upon the upper stories of the shuttle stack, but down at the bottom it was almost the night of a tomb.

The frozen food and medical container was there, as she'd ordered, placed squarely on the yellow sensor-equipped square, ready to talk to the bridge crane. She thought of course Clayton literally couldn't lift a finger on Friday to have it loaded, mostly by automation. But then, maybe he couldn't because of the refrigeration. She saw the long umbilicus running out from the container around the silo toward the budget-stressed cooling system.

She followed it around the silo's rim, behind the space shuttle's engine cones and into the shadow of the huge rockets and the orange external tank. She tried Clayton's keys until she had the external fuel tank's governor once more at her fingertips. She put the tank down to minimum maintenance temperature again, and then let it down a little more.

It was impressive that so much cryogenic fuel had remained stable for a week as it was. If luck timed everything perfectly tomorrow, enough fuel would evaporate off by morning to render the tank useless and stall the launch a second time. The hydrogen could also overcome its venting system and blow the tank. But if the frozen fuel began to evaporate mid-launch, the slightest wobble in the tank's posture during launch, the slightest empty air pocket between the evaporating hydrogen, its oxidizer and the rocket intakes, could cause the rockets to take a gulp of fresh air and the whole shuttle stack would spend its last half-second of existence as a thermobaric bomb.

But she digressed. In the closet next to the cooling console she found the big, heavy, inefficient old heater, like something they'd intentionally bought in an antique store, and dragged it on its failing casters to the freight elevator on the other side of the drafty concrete hallway.

—Here's the heater.

—Great, said Martha, —set it up in there and see if it'll clear up what the mop left behind.

Now they had to deal with the pigs themselves.

—Okay, Martha exhaled, —best thing would be herdem into the freight elevator with the cages already in it, then puttem in the cages while they're in the elevator, so they can't run off down the hall. Is the cafeteria shut?

—Yes.

—Okay. How bout it?

Zosime nodded grimly, and she and Clayton hauled the cages back into the elevator. Martha opened the valise she'd been carrying and unrolled a set of syringes on top of a stack of cages.

Herding the pigs into the elevator wasn't hard, but then came the task of wiping them clean and sedating them. Martha had only a few rags, so Zosime had to keep refreshing the water in the mop bucket.

She and Clayton held each increasingly anxious hog, let it get its shot, and then awkwardly worked to back each of the fourteen animals into a cage. Each animal squealed weakly when it felt the prick of the syringe, except for two females who only grunted defiantly. They seemed not to have grown in a week, even lost weight, probably, but they groaned and kicked all the same as she and Clayton forced them into the cramped cages against their stubborn hind legs. Zosime did the whole thing with squinted eyes. She didn't want to see it at all, and she didn't want the tears simmering in her sinuses to overcook into her eyes.

The sedative worked fast enough to watch, and the hogs fell down into sleep as Zosime and Clayton hauled eight of the heavy, overfilled cages up to create the second row. In the pigs' caged faces the blue sky of their earthiness flickered in their corneas once again, and then extinguished.

Zosime convinced the others to leave the container's door open and the space heater running. They couldn't go get a coffee or endure the bombardment of their ears by Walter Cronkite and Robert Heinlein, so it was time to leave the darkened silo and get home ahead of the next rain.

—Thanks again for yer help, said Martha Glass. Zosime made sure that she saw her give Clayton his keys back, muttered that she almost forgot. —Go up. Martha and I will follow you.

Martha Glass watched Clayton stalk down to the elevator. Zosime looked sorry at her. Maybe she didn't order Clayton to shut her up in the cage. Maybe it was a mistake.

—Martha, I'm sorry for how I spoke to you at the restaurant. I don't know how bad it is to lose a baby. She hesitated, observed Martha's hard, exhausted face. —I still don't know if ... if he is on this launch. But I thought of something. Why don't you tell other people that his cells help with cancer?

—I don't know if they do! Martha's cry reverberated through the hall and ended in a choking sound in the back of her throat. Zosime wiped the outer edge of her right eye with a fingertip. Had this woman suffered any differently than her own mother, who abandoned her child in Iran? She felt ashamed. —That's just what they told me, Martha went on, —and then they paid me!

Martha's scorn washed away the shame, and Zosime was out of patience again. —I'll meet you up there. I will come up in a moment.

—What for?

As always, Zosime couldn't think clearly amidst a deception. —My ... I need to reset the clock in the box! So they know when to sedate the pigs on the space station.

—Oh, very good, Zosime, Martha nodded and waved a finger, all professional again. —we'll wait up for you. Twenty-four hours!

In the humid silo the shuttle stack hung there as ever it had, like a fossil, or a side of beef, as it appeared in this light. She punched her inventory code into the cold container's lock and it did nothing. She grasped the lid's handle and the hatch opened, never having been locked, spilling tendrils of refrigerated air to the floor.

The frozen food was packed tight into half of the container, as indicated in the work orders. She remembered the tone of voice with which Rodríguez had told her it was meat products, frozen potatoes, that kind of thing. And the company intended for businessmen to feast on these alongside barbecued pig, wheeling and dealing for space to grow giant low-gravity tobacco, cotton and cattle in a grassy-bottom plastic bubble on a Martian red-barn farm. They were all insane.

On the opposite curve beyond the hatch, however, hung a clear plastic box, long and only ten centimeters thick, with a red cross stamped on it. Her stomach rose against her liver. She unclipped the box from its cradle, took it out of the container and opened it. It was almost too cold to touch, but she balanced it on her raised knee. Inside were plastic sleeves vacuum-sealed flat. In each was a red splat, like a drop of blood, a handful of cells. Was this Martha's baby? How many clones of this thing were there? She shut the case again and reloaded it into its plastic cradle. Then she saw beneath it the cardboard box, about the size of a microwave oven, unequivocally labeled BIOFAB. An organ printer. There was no way to know.

The ever-recurring disgust and fear overcame her that meets curiosity when the adventure turns dangerous. She wanted to yank the cooling tubes out of the cylinder and go shut them off; if only she hadn't given Clayton his keys back! She slammed the container shut, tried to hold her face blank, and went up the elevator, finding her colleagues waiting impatiently for her.

♂

Monday morning came fast and would burn a void into the memories ahead of it, as important days often do. Somehow Zosime woke up as usual with a head full of dreams about Walter Cronkite and Robert Heinlein, this time telling her that her mother's spinal nerves had to be pinched in order to supply the power to launch her body to Mars. She ate breakfast while the monsoon rains pounded against the windows. Then she packed her suitcase, scoured her hotel room for any sign she'd been there, collected all her rhymes, ran Iyiola's remaining notes under the sink to the destroy them and tossed the wet wad into the trash. But she took the rhymes with her, just in case. She checked out of the hotel and caught the van to work.

The group of protesters at Olusosun, shrunken over the last few days, had manifested anew despite the driving rain, such that the van couldn't get in. Zosime and Clayton found themselves behind the bumper of a white limousine, doubtlessly full of astronauts. All around them closed the crowd of people, young and old, red and green and black, scavenger and student, waving signs and leaflets. They were no police, and no army. Perhaps they were running late. Perhaps they were running a their morning mile. The tumult was static, nonetheless, for everyone was too packed in to move.

Out of nowhere a gas can broke open and sprayed hot smoke up from the sodden ground. The crowd opened against the two vehicles' charges and the launch crew entered the landfill. People were still in Olusosun, children, adults, faces and noses down, rooting out their meager living as always. The landfill wasn't getting any smaller or shallower.

—I'm back, bitches! Gopman's voice sent the steady rush of last-minute preparations scattering in the launch center's stale air. Doctor Chesky looked up from his ten program windows. —You sound well, Craig.

—You ready to pound this bitch up into space, people? He wore a sparkly red shirt under a broad black rain slicker like a cape around his neck and shoulders. His beard was at precisely three and a half days, ageless, if age only went as far as forty. —I got eight hunnerd thousand pounds of fuckin thrust here too, baby! How's my systems doing?

Baldy and Long-ears went about their business with a dispassionate grunt. Gopman wiggled his fingers on his upraised palms like a magician and leaned over his desk. —We're lookin good, chief?

—We're runnin lean, but we're runnin.

—Swear! Headquarters set up everything for us?
—Pretty much. Did you gahead and read the press release from the boss?
—No.
—He wrote it himself. They've named this launch Operation Fourth of July.
—What the fuck?
—Cause of the barbecue meat and the pigs.
—Serious shit? Yeah, it's the start of a new country up there, that's fer sure, on Mars, baby!

Chesky kept things moving quickly for his tiny crew. Down in the silo the radio barked every three minutes demanding updates. Zosime and Baldy the payload engineer silently, blindly cooperated to load the frozen supply container, and then the pigs. Practice in the previous week had her well acquainted with the movements of the containers, how their mass swung and hung. She had the necessary chains organized and hung up where they'd be convenient, free of knots. She had both containers loaded in no time. By outward appearances she was still the model employee.

She took a breather to watch the old shuttle's payload bay doors swing shut when the radio chirped again.
—Zosime, pick up, over.
—Go ahead, chief, over.
—Ha ha! Chief, that's what you call me!
—Who is this?
—It's me, Gopman. You're takin the snacks to the shuttle crew, right?

The listed and then unlisted duty. —Yes.
—The lady says it's ready. Go get it, and there's a code in yer email for the elevator.
—Consider it done, over. She got the lucky chance to use that phrase she'd heard on television last night,

increasing her chances of remembering it longterm. Though if she never spoke English at a job again, it'd be too soon.

She walked down the huge empty hallway into the cafeteria. Martha was absent, maybe departed already. The adrenaline of impending escape was getting the better of her, and her sympathy for the woman was gone again. She cursed herself for not unplugging the refrigeration umbilicus from that stupid cold container. Now it was too late. The lady silently slid the plate of chopped vegetables, cheese and lunch meat across the polished aluminum counter. Then she placed three towering doses of cold white milk, like Pilsener glasses, on the tray and turned silently away.

The inventory analyst carefully cruised the tray over to the elevator, entered the chief's code and rose past the launch center to the green room on the ninth floor. It was decorated like a doctor's office waiting room, light blue paint, a set of shelves along one wall beneath a single print of a pastoral wheatfield and pond scene in knify acrylic, an overstuffed couch and two easy chairs around a coffee table, and against the silo wall the obligatory large-screen flat television. Near the gangway door sat their three bulky astronaut suits in a messy heap. No sooner did she step into the lounge than Lightyear, who'd gained weight, was on top of her. —Did you come to fix the TV? I'm sick of watchin the ethnic channel.

—I brought you this, she stammered, —where do I put it?

Morgan came out of the bathroom, doing vocal exercises of some kind and waving a safety razor around his creamed-up face. —Ah, thank you! Put it right on the coffee table, please! Lightyear, you better shave! You know it's a mess up in zero-G! Bum, bum, bum, bum …

Zosime bent halfway, set down the glasses of milk, and then bent all the way to put the tray down, with her body in profile to the observing astronauts, just like in a movie. But her mind was working.

—Can I see inside the shuttle?

—What for? Lightyear demanded. —Well, I've never seen inside one. I've been an orbital systems analyst, and I find it very interesting. Also, I could secure your payload if,

—Jonesy'll see to that.

—Besides, honey, Morgan put in, pausing his major scale, —it's not turned on. They don't turn it on until we go in, already suited up. Lightyear finally doffed his coat and threw it on top of the other astonauts' suit jackets, each of which had a little American flag pin stuck to the left lapel.

—Alright, Zosime said quietly and fled for the door. In an instant it occurred to her that she may be killing these men. —Have a good flight.

—Take care of Earth for us!

—I will.

She rejoined Clayton down in the silo. The new foreman had his left cheek blistered out and his grin jacked open by a bumper crop of bright green khat clenched between his ice-stunted teeth. She couldn't stand to look at it. She went to the locker room and finished the arduous and incomplete unlisted duty of organizing the timecards. At least she'd be paid like a model employee. She reinspected the blast door operation and the bulkhead. They were clean as a whistle, unobstructed, electrics working, door moving smoothly.

The radio squawked again. —Clayton, are you in your email, over?

Clayton whipped out his phone and frantically tried to log in with one hand while gripping the radio with the other. —Yah.

The chief sounded very impatient. —I'm still gettin messages about the temperature of the external tank. Will you deal with it, please?

—You got it, over.

Zosime reached her hand out, anxious to look. —I'll do it if you give me your keys.

—No, no. I can do it from my phone, doncha know. His doncha know was as deep as two grain elevators viewed from above. As she watched he worked at the screen of his phone, swore, and seemed to get it.

—Should be better, over.

—We've gotta shut the system down just before launch. I'm gonna rely on you for that. You got it, over?

—Sure thing. I'll be listenin, over.

Zosime's mind fired. That control must be in the folders within folders! —So, Clayton, didn't you bring Brittney to see the launch?

—No, he said away from her, —she's crazy.

His inventory analyst couldn't stop wondering how the girl's story had played out. —Aren't you getting on well?

—She took off last night, said she was goin to Paris.

Zosime laughed, covered her mouth with her hand.

—Really?

—Real funny, huh?

She went over to her laptop, turned its screen away from him, and turned it on. —We're ready. Why don't you go get a cup of coffee? I'll put away the cart and we can launch.

—Okay.

Overhead the astronauts' gangway lit up again like Christmas, a gay lineny tunnel for humanity's latest

237

wedding with outer space. She frantically withdrew the papers with the password rhymes on them from her pocket. The one for Clayton's password was the one about islands. She typed in the first letter of each word, then the two numbers, and was in. She scanned the left column, trying to find the right control.

Finally her rushed eye found the word cooling. She clicked, put his password dutifully in again, and had a digital illustration of the governor at her fingertips. Clayton had put the temperature up a little high. She drove it down to one notch below safe. As soon as the shuttle's engines turned on, the heat in the silo would multiply geometrically and they'd see what luck would bring.

—Zosime, can you pick up the phone please? The radio startled her. She logged out of Clayton's side of the interface once more, turned off her laptop and shoved the whole cart out into the hall beyond the bulkhead, where the telephone hung. —Zosime, pick up the phone, please, over.

—I will come talk to you at the elevator, doctor Chesky. She hung up.

Anxious as a thief she waited at the elevator. Finally he came down and stepped out, looked toward the silo and then right into her face.

—I am finished, doctor Chesky. Clayton is in the cafeteria.

His face was flushed. —I can't believe you.
—What,
—With the intern?

His eyes searched hers, but hers searched his back, perhaps even more fiercely. What did he know? About Saturday, about Iyiola's apartment? Or about Thursday? How could he know?

—I'm not talking to you about my personal life,

—But with the intern? After all I,

—Please stop. I met him at your Bushmeat restaurant and he was kind to me,

—We need to talk about what you two talked about.

She floated above all the technical details she'd learned, tried to play at someone she no longer was.

—There's nothing to talk about. I've loaded everything. Your shuttle is ready to launch. My mother is sick and flying across the world. I'm resigning today and going home to my family, and you will not have to suffer from working with me anymore. You can put my last check into the online account. Thank you for the chance to work here.

Her eyes were beyond him before she finished speaking. She'd called the elevator at some point, and before the words sunk into his ears, she was behind closed doors and gone.

The chief stomped into the launch center, and his voice was hard and imperative like his team had never heard. —We ready to go?

No one said anything, but kept their faces glued up close to their screens. —Craig, how's it look?

—Looks fine. I hope it's cool with the fuel temperature.

—You hope? That's nice.

Now Gopman looked over at him. —What's the problem, chief?

—Nothin. Go on.

Zosime peered around the elevator cone. There were no vehicles in the perimeter, no more box of pigs, just an overturned wading pool, drifts of trash, and the stuffed-up hole in the cyclone fence. She found the sun relative to the direction of the road and ran out beyond the razor wire.

She didn't even have an umbrella, and was unwilling to hold her suitcase over her head.

Soon she ran into two little kids no older than ten who were stacking sopping-wet cardboard and winding up lengths of wire. They saw the strange, light-skinned woman in the wealthy clothes before she saw them, and looked scared. —Don't be afraid, she said, —come with me, we have to get out of here. You'll get hurt. She ushered them with her hands. One of them had an umbrella, and she took it from the child, who almost turned despondent and cried before Zosime gained his trust. —Come with me! Are mom and dad here?

—No, the girl whined timidly.

—We have to go. Run with me! She doubled her pace, hid her head under the umbrella, and staggered as she carried the cold wet girl against her in one arm and the suitcase in the other. She knew her clothes and shoes were obviously not those of a scavenger, but the girl helped cover her.

They wound left and left again around two huge piles of trash, some of it decomposing in the rain and some of it durable. Off to the right Zosime started to see the protesters, so the gate was near. Then she saw the army truck on the road further right, and she made the children duck down with her behind the nearest shelf of cardboard and plastic debris. The rain damped down all the odors, but her eyes and nostrils told her that they were squatting next to something toxic.

She heard the truck's shocks rock against its weight as it braked, and then a soldier's voice barked out toward them. —Get outta here!

Zosime looked left, and a woman who had spotted her from behind was looking between her and the truck.

—Get outta here! One soldier leaned head and shoulder out of the vehicle and pointed toward the road. The woman started to trot away. Zosime choked down a breath that she'd been holding back, watched the truck pass and then dragged the children on.

Gopman called down the radio: —Okay Clayton, are all valuables stowed away down there? Clayton? Fuck. Where is he?

—He's in the cafeteria, Chesky said. —Go ahead and close up the silo.

Gopman clicked his mouse and then stood. He and Chesky went to the yellowed, once-burnt window and looked down into the silo, though they couldn't see much. At far right they eventually saw the main blast door slide shut, and then Chesky saw on his phone that the smaller blast door behind the shuttle had secured the utility closet and cooling and electrical controls.

—Looks like ya can't throw me down in the bottom of the silo now, chief.

—Stars of the show, Chesky said into his radio, ignoring him, —we all suited up, over?

—Almost, chief. Jonesy has a sticky temp regulator, on top of tryin in vain to pressurize that box of pigs, over.

—He already inspected the payload bay, over?

—Ten-four. Didn't give us much time to drink our milk this mornin!

—Sorry. You know the boss always calculates things should be done in about a third of the time it actually takes. He's a real disruptor of organizational time.

—Well, that's great for him.

—I'll wait to hear from you through the shuttle com, over.

—Roger that.

He switched channels. —Clayton, how's the coffee, over? ... Clayton. God dammit! Does he ever have the radio with him?

—Is the vet here, too?

—I dunno. I know Zosime won't be joinin us for the long launch lunch.

Gopman looked over again. —How?

—She just quit. Yeah, just now. Gonna work at the library with all the other ex-interns, I fuckin guess.

The analyst puffed scornfully. —That's gay. He reached around his neck for his kendama, but it wasn't there. Chesky caught him. —Pay attention, Craig.

Baldy approached Chesky's desk and gestured at the work that until recently required twenty-five professionals. —You sure you two have it?

—The last crew got the shuttle up and away with two people, the chief grinned at him cockily, —we're gonna do at least as well as them.

—We're going home, then, before it heats up in here. Oh! And the gangway. Don't wanna burn that up.

—Hold on. Everyone cozy in there, commander?

—Ten four.

—Okay, bring the gangway in.

The technicians cleared out the silo and prepared to leave. Chesky threw a switch and the silo's barred hatch clove in two and began to slide open. Immediately ropes of rain began pouring down on the shuttle's front window only six or so meters below.

—Silo shut down?

—Yep. Whenever they're ready.

Zosime led the children to the crowd of protesters. She picked one woman and told her very quietly that the spacecraft was going to blow out of the landfill soon, then started working her way through toward the gate. The woman shouted the warning, and soon it was echoing through Olususun. Soldiers, armed as ever, began to appear. —They're going to launch it! Get everyone out! The soldiers didn't carry the message, but rather their own message of stay calm and don't make any sudden movements. They would hold up the crowd trying to leave the landfill if they didn't get organized. Zosime ducked once more and hoped no soldiers saw her leave.

Chesky drummed his fingertips anxiously on his desk. His finger tapped the remote control for his drone. He was very sorry that he spied on Zosime, and felt a little like a monster for violating her privacy, but she'd forced him to. He was sorrier that he'd learned the worst: she didn't care for him because she'd already been enjoying Iyiola Godsend. Quietly he summoned Long-ears just before he went through the door.

—Yeah, chief?

—Do me a favor and gahead and go make sure everything's kosher downstairs. See if Zosime left anything lying around.

—Whatta ya talkin about? You think she left a task unfulfilled?

—Just go look, please. I'll meet you down there.

The intercom boomed from the walls now; it felt like they were launching for real. —Launch center, can you hear me?

—Loud and clear! Chesky replied to the room.

—How's the shuttle?

—System checks running.

Gopman's program displayed once again the little hourglasses, pie charts and colored bars like piston strokes that ran their courses, systems that checked each other, electrical circuits that ran their tracks, and percentages that calculated each other as the silo's brain drew up the shuttle's bill of health.

—Just like we said, Chesky ran through his list of provisos, —don't put your main engines in gear until you get out of the silo. Rockets heatin up okay?

Through the silo walls responded an enormous rumble like a massive race car revving.

—Pretty wet in here, chief, Morgan warned him,
—gonna have to get outta this hole fast. And I don't like how high the fuel tank's temp is.

—You'll only need a moment to get outta the hole.

Gopman threw his fists in the air and pumped them back and forth, swaying all the way down to his chest.

—You see this, chief? I got so much data crunching right now! We could launch inside a five minutes! We could fuckin tip the thing and my systems'd add up the correction!

—Good thing we can't tip a four million-pound piece of shit, Chesky replied. —Getcher laptop, we're gettin outta here. Jesus, why doesn't this window have blast shutters?

Zosime squeezed free of the rabble assembled at the front gate of the landfill, whose constituents were holding as many people up as they were pushing through. A blaze of shouting, soldiers barking, burned chaotically against the slapping rain, and no one could hear the message that the dump had to be evacuated. Down the road that bisected the landfill she wanted to sprint, but the mud was getting thick, so she stepped carefully as fast as she could.

Long-ears ran into Chesky and Gopman in the yawning darkened hallway.

—Everything's in order as far as I can tell, chief. But I found this paper on the inventory desk. I don't like the look of it.

—Lemme see. Where was it?

—Under a laptop.

Chesky took the light blue scrap of paper. Inscribed on it was a poem about an island:

> Tiny islands,
> Over ground again,
> Nine months at sea,
> Eight days of rest

—A poem? The chief flashed him agitated eyes. —I don't read poems. Get this outta here!

—I checked everyone's handwriting. It's the woman's. You don't think we should investigate?

Chesky tried to read it. —No. She didn't have access to anything important. Cmon, let's move on with the launch before the ISS moves. Get that outta here!

—Fuckin poems? Gopman laughed against the roar behind the blast door. —See, that's pre-tarded too! Swear!

—Stop it. Hurry and get up outta here before you get fried!

Chief Chesky, analyst Gopman and loading foreman Hieb huddled in the cafeteria, sealed off from the silo by two blast doors. They had their laptops set up and were scanning Gopman's interface for any sign of trouble.

—Can you hear me, commander? Chesky spoke into his ear-mounted microphone.

—Loud and clear, chief, the astronaut barked in his ear.

—You're good to go.

—I'm switching primary channel to mission control in Florida. Thanks for the hospitality.

—You got it, say hi to them for me. Let's make history!

Gopman looked up from his interface, a little anxiety on his own face. —Did you talk to the boss?

Chesky froze. —Shit. No.

Gopman stood and neglected his interface to go get himself a coffee. —So ... do you call him, or ... hey, what the fuck?

—What?

—The lady's not here! And there's barely nothin to eat! I don't want basic flapjacks!

—Well, we hadn't budgeted for two launch lunches.

—You didn't request it from the boss?

—No. I had enough to worry about.

—Fuck!

—Hey, Clayton broke his silence, —it's fine, now. We can smoke in here, right?

They calmed down for a moment. —Did Brittney express any interest in seeing the launch, Clayton? Chesky asked his screen.

—No, lowed Clayton, —we kinda broke up.

Both of his colleagues raised their brows. Gopman chuckled. —She liked black dick too much, uh? Hey, yer not alone, big buddy! I mean, chicks, yknow,

—Leavim alone, Craig, shit, Chesky bristled. Every mention of black dick was killing him. He'd see what was really afoot tonight. But he'd left his drone up in the launch center! Must not forget to grab it after the launch. —And bring us coffee, since you're up! I guess I should try to call the boss ...

Tables, floors, hanging televisions began to vibrate. The snore of the shuttle stack's rockets was now drowned out as the silo birthed a detonation. The three men braced themselves as the Doppler effect of the vibrations coalesced into a treble tune.

The volcanic roar of the rockets sent the last, bravest protesters out toward the edges of the landfill. A second sun rose on the horizon, farted smoke and fire and burnt everything near it as the shuttle stack rode it up into the sky.

A student from Unilag watched as two school-age children stumbled away from the noise and sunk into a recess of soft garbage like water into a sponge. Then garbage and children alike were consumed by the sulfurous tower of fire.

The student turned and ran rather than film the scene with his phone, and no one would hear how the children got fried nor care that it happened; not because the children were black, though now they were certainly nothing but black, but because they were poor. Smoldering ends of protest handbills followed the student out of the center of the landfill, and thousands of tons of the west's polystyrene computer waste melted down to ash where his footprints had been.

—Liftoff, we have liftoff.

Doctor Chesky's phone hung cradled in the palm of his hand, forgotten, as they riveted their attention on the launch data and the outside camera feed. He leaned over to see Gopman's screen.

—They're clear. You get the silo doors closed? It's gonna be a mess in there.

—Hold on ... yeah, we're good.

—Ventilation?

—Hold on! Yeah. Floor's opening ... fan's still good.

They nervously watched their screens, now free of control. They listened as the shuttle crew reported to Florida and each other.

—Climbing at eighty degrees, Jones' bum bum scales came faintly through the distortion, —downrange distance one kilometer. We'd like to start our roll with your ... what?

The word what drove the two young men's hearts and lungs down into their intestines.

—The fuel's too hot ... get me the reading ... mission control, repeat, the fuel's evaporating. No, now! Abort! Hit the main engines! Abort!

Zosime heard the explosion and looked behind her as she arrived panting at the bus stop. The shuttle stack grew like an enormous asparagus on its stem of fire and smoke, and the poisoned air that it blew out reached her face. The spacecraft turned over the dump, over her, and was out over the Atlantic Ocean before she knew it. She watched its arc, wondering what would happen.

Then it happened. The shuttle's huge orange external tank and rockets fell free and collapsed fast but slow, like drizzle, into the water. Operation Fourth of July exploded weakly, half-submerged, tossed sparkler sprites from the overcast waves. The coastal water was already so polluted that another catastrophe like this could hardly do the wildlife any worse.

The shuttle, trying to turn upside down as in a normal launch, now bent over into a painfully low arc against the horizon and began to right itself, cruising expertly in a wide circle and heading north toward a safe landing in Ibadan. The whole thing probably took a minute, and left an O written upon the sky like a sketch of the moon.

She grabbed a taxi, apologized for being soaked, and headed for the airport. Through the narrow space in the rolled-down window she smelled the cayenne and peanut of Lagos for the last time, and felt like she were leaving without a farewell. She found her phone and typed a short message into her private email: Look at the launch. Will you do one more thing for me?

Moments later, too soon to believe, Iyiola's reply came back: Anything.

The dim grim cafeteria was dead silent. Walter Cronkite, Robert Heinlein and Arthur C. Clarke were dead for good. Not even a coffee machine could be heard. The chief and the launch analyst listened as the shuttle crew reported their maneuvers and headed for the landing site, several days early. Gopman had slammed his laptop shut and had his arms crossed over it, head down like a recalcitrant high school student.

—I can't believe this, Chesky whimpered to himself, tore too big a painful piece out of his cuticle, then shouted at Clayton: —I thought you had that fuel tank temp!

—I did what you said to do! I don't know what happened! Clayton scratched at his black bristly neck.

—It was too low!

—Well you shoulda told me that the max was higher! I ain't a engineer!

—I know! And I don't know what the fuck I was thinking when I hired a moron like you! What the hell is that shit in your mouth?

—It's nothin.

Doctor Chesky threw his face up. Only now he noticed that overhead there was a small square skylight. Daylight fell down, down, down through it, unobstructed but by a few charred scraps of garbage that danced in the column of air somewhere between the surface and the windowpane.

—It mighta been the fact that we had it cooped up in the silo, Gopman put in, raising his elbows off his computer's lid, —the pressure in the silo was too much to keep it cool once they fired the rockets.

—Then what the fuck was last time? Chesky threw his face in his hands. —Good luck?

—Well, said Gopman, matter-of-fact, —I guess I'm takin my program elsewhere, uh boys? After this shit, I guess. He opened his laptop. —Oh shit, it's outta battery. He grinned innocently at Chesky. —Can I use yours, chief? Cool.

He waited for the computer to boot up and launch his interface, and kept chattering. —Well, you can chase your girlfriend wherever she goes, Clayton, I'm thinkin the boss is not gonna like this news. I mean, you don't know what a hard worker he is. He's fired people for small shit, yknow, not workin overtime. Least I got a whole launch's worth of … it's … where is it?

He squinted at the computer, opened the dialogue to open a file, but it wasn't there.

—What's wrong? Chesky moaned. The analyst searched the program's log. Seventy-five seconds ago there was stored a deletion. All algorithms had been reset. He lifted his designer-bearded, acne-scarred face and screamed against the forest of concrete. —What the fuckin motherfuck? No! NO!

After two hours the heavy blast doors opened and each young man silently waited blind for long stretches under splashing rain and the lurid glow of streetlamps, was dealt out by the van driver to his hotel, went his separate way. Between the streams of water on the van's windows they found the streets oddly deserted, as desolate as they themselves felt.

By the time doctor Chesky arrived in his suite and sat down at his phone, he already had an email from the boss's address. It was very polite, unusually, but down to business, expecting understanding. The launch center will be reconfigured according to new needs, launch chief and analyst will be folded into one job to reduce the chance of errors and assumptions, and he and Gopman and the two techs were suspended from their duties, welcome to stay in Lagos and wait.

At the bottom of the message he saw not the boss's name, but that of his seventeen year-old kid. He might go back into every mail he'd ever received and see how many were actually written by boss. There'd be plenty of time for that now.

At daybreak shafts of sunlight fell gently through the submarine cloudcover, shafts that struck the city at diagonal angles, giving definition to its moldy, sodden structures that barely stood against the gods of the tropics.

Doctor Chesky signed out of the massive online game when he noticed the sun was out. Between monitoring his drone's fruitless perch at the window outside Godsend's apartment and playing games, like the boss did whenever he wanted to celebrate a job well-done, the night had got away from him. He knew when the desiccating blue glow of his computer screen was falling away from the wall beside his long precipitous nose, away from the curtain hanging at the window. The screen's light was balancing now against the incandescent day burning behind the curtain.

He was tired of virtually crouching through designer wreckage and garbage anyway, tired of using exotic military weapons to blast simulations of poor people from the countries that supply the west with its raw materials. The boss only played these games when taking the first break in a week of nonstop innovation, except this week there was no innovation and nothing nonstop. There was one thing. His empty feeling was nonstop.

He rose, crossed his suite to the minibar, found it empty, peered at the mister Biggs wrapper on the table, found it empty, and poured himself a glass of water. He was ruined. And what was that note that Zosime left behind in the silo, anyway? Some love letter from her to Godsend? He felt just like he was back at Bushmeat, with everyone laughing at him, then back at Stanford, with all the women judging him as he self-castigated, then back in every instance of nerd trauma since he was ten. He couldn't take the pain anymore.

There was a message in his phone from Gopman. It said syonara chief. Another email from the human resources department, which mentioned as if in passing that his two failed launches had rendered the livestock operation financially infeasible, and then asked if he had decided whether to remain on standby. He didn't reply.

Stuck in his head was the line from Arthur C. Clarke, that he'd heard so many times and not taken seriously until now. He said yknow, I think, Bob, we science fiction writers've brainwashed the engineers, so they may be doing things now, copying our stories, which is why it looks familiar. But they may not be doing it the right way. We may have given them the wrong directions, and there may be better ways of doing some things than we've said!

He just wondered. Besides that, all he had left of the silo was his white scientist's lab coat. He put it on and descended. He didn't check out of the hotel; he wanted someone to notice he was missing.

He got on the bus that he knew went toward Bushmeat. There was one transfer involved. On the bus he wondered if, or rather how fast, Gopman would find a buyer or client for his program. Maybe a logistics company, UPS or Walmart. It was nice for him that he had that one product, which in California was more valuable than all the things Chesky had learned, all his expertise that counted for nothing if it weren't proven to cut costs and make money immediately.

A handful of people had this vision about how companies should be run, how innovators should offer themselves up to be bought out by capital, and now it's an entire country's set of values, an entire culture's mode of communication, for which its youth are being prepared and all its resources are being funneled. But is there any humanity, or creativity, to be found in that movement upon subtraction of pre-programmed innovation? When the fear of not fitting into a business plan disguised as a dream, that maybe no one really ever had, goes away? Chesky didn't recall in that moment the admonition by Robert Heinlein that there've been too many young people in this country with a defeatist attitude toward things.

Doctor Chesky got off the bus in a foreign, dirty district two kilometers north of the Agege train station and the stadium. He needed no more time to think, and luckily the train didn't give him much. It had left the station just now and was picking up speed. Leaving his bitten and bloody cuticles and fingertips to hang by his side, he lingered against a signal pole until the right moment. The glimmering shafts of daylight streamed through his eyes and illuminated his white lab coat, or maybe it was the train's dim headlamps. He stepped onto the tracks.

♂

Zosime was watching the headlamps of airplanes materialize from above the thick woolen rainclouds that permanently blanketed London's garish, desperately decadent skyline. She was back in polished, manicured, orderly Europe, and it was so different than where she'd been. The pebbles on the sidewalk had a different hue, the weeds that grew along the railroad tracks were shaped oddly, but there were trees of heaven infesting the roadsides here, just as in Ecuador. The land was low and rolling, not steep and rocky like in Quito, not oversaturated and eroding like in Lagos, the packaged snacks were somehow plain and unchallenging. It was just plain Europe, and beyond it lay her beloved, extraordinary Kérkyra, her poor abandoned father, and the inevitable future.

Her mother finally appeared, walking on her own two feet in flight from the security gate, and she rose from her seat and ran to her. —Mamá!

Her mother made her daughter hug gently, guiding her left hand to well above her aching hip.

—I said I am from a pre-Islamic religion, but they made me go through the machine anyway, her mother drawled in cranky Farsi. —I don't think they understood.

—Are you alright, Mamá?

—I'm fine. I should've spoken more Greek with you while we were away. I don't know if I'm ready.

—Just think of all the beautiful things Baba told you when you were young.

—Oh! her mother laughed, —you're killing me!

They sat down on the seats again, her mother made herself comfortable but was careful about it, unwilling to show her age or her condition. —Don't worry, I feel better since this morning.

—Have you nothing but your purse?

—I checked my bag. All the things we bought in Quito,

Zosime nodded patiently. —I know you had to leave them when you left.

—I had them shipped to Baba.

They both laughed, knowing that Zosime's father would find it all a clutter and a bother.

—Especially the clothes. It was extremely expensive! Her mother withdrew a copy of the Financial Times from her purse and unrolled it. —Your spaceship in Nigeria made it into the paper, her mother pointed at the second page. —Lucky no one died.

—I'm happy for that.

The mother whispered: —Did you make the rocket blow up?

—They were so unskilled and incompetent, the daughter stalled, not wanting to sound like a lunatic, —I just took advantage of them.

—Well, stupid men are easy to take advantage of. I don't recommend making a habit of it.

Zosime and Iyiola had agreed that what they were doing were efforts to make their families proud. Could her mother and she trust their father and her half-brother with this story? Would they, or even her mother, be proud of what she did?

—I made the decision for myself. I know it won't stop them, but it will be someone else who has the blame of helping them. You see, Mamá, I learned when to rebel.

Her mother looked a long time at her, at the endless universe in her left pupil, and then laughed. —Is that what this was all about? Why do you look upset?

—You told me that I should learn when to rebel. When I told you that I couldn't tolerate my job!

—I've had a lot of pain, dlakam, I don't always know what I said.

—And I also did it for Behrouz. I want to show him that I stood up against the rich innovators once in my life.

—That will be amusing to watch. You may be disappointed in what a freedom fighter he is. Did you tell Baba that you landed? Her mother chased a strand of hair from her temple. —He told me that he started a vegetable garden for you. I hope he still will see me, after all the time I've been away.

—Don't you think he will?

—I don't expect he waited for me, nothing like that.

—Well, I don't either ... Zosime watched her, looked for answers in her own girlhood, found none. —He agreed to help Behrouz, so he can't be too upset at you.

—I convinced him to do it, her mother sighed, squinting away tears, —I intended to make the obligation as short for him as I could.

The mother and her daughter turned their heartshaped faces up toward the airplanes in the hard, dark sky, each dreaming of the lifetime to come. Perhaps it would be simpler, easier to find the bond with the land that they both needed so badly. Perhaps it would be the same as in Utrecht and Ecuador, only in familiar lands.

Zosime was just happy not to have her heart torn in two, not to be in conflict with her environment. Their achievement would be achieving only balance and happiness, their success would be succeeding at nothing, their great, strange universe would be home and a changing family, complex enough, and beneath the same stars as Mars. They wouldn't have to displace or erase anyone to do it, nor build any impossible dreams in the sky. In the bosom of blue Earth there were enough new lives to live, enough places to go.

San José, December 2015

About Eugenio Negro

Author of diverse comics, fanzines, articles and stories, Negro lives in central California where he enjoys chewing and burrowing.

Inquiries may be directed to negrocomics@gmail.com.